CARNAL KNOWLEDGE

THE ADORATION OF A DANGEROUS WOMAN
AND THE DEATH OF A DREAM

LEXI MOHNEY

For everyone that enjoyed this wild and crazy journey along with me. You're truly a blessing.

To those that helped inspire this work, an author's duty is to bring just as much life to the villains, even if they come disguised.

When someone allows you into their inner circle of
life, the unspoken agreement is that you don't abuse
the proximity.

— DAUVOIRE

FOREWORD

Emotionally, pain inflicted intentionally on another being is about control. A powerplay of such malice usually ends unfavorably for those closest to the control-seeker with intent to render their victims harmless. Whether accidentally employed or not.

By no means is this method of life-play recommended in the instance of retaining friends. There's always the option of collecting weaknesses in a similar way that Da Vinci drew bodies, by dissecting them in the same way I pick through someone's head. But for anyone who walks the more sadistic road, I can say that it's almost bound to come around and bite you at some point.

CONTENTS

PROLOGUE

A BEGINNING OF SORTS

*L*ife sneaks up on you...most of the time.

Many people exist, unperturbed by the passage of life, and even fewer live to play it or thrive in the game they choose. Before encountering the greatest game to challenge my own, I was unaware of actually participating in playing life, and the pain is the only thing I remember with certainty.

There's a lot more to the name of her game, though.

Evan's lesson number one: Stay where I put you.

"I thought you were nothing," she stated as obtuse as a closed door.

I'd heard this story before, the one about the first time Evan and I met, but I always loved knowing I'd deceived her at least once in the four years of us knowing each other. Her blue-green eyes grew distant at the memory. She pulled her left knee into her chest and hugged it in protection from me: the one that got around her defenses.

I admired her vulnerability from my place on our old,

sunken, brown leather couch we'd inherited from the apartment's previous tenants. The way her feet curved were unintentionally elegant as she sat blank-faced in a disintegrating swivel chair that lived halfway between our kitchen and living room as a poor college student addition to our three-bedroom apartment. We meant for it to be a breakfast chair, but the convenience of being able to roll it all over our living area meant that we usually always ate around the coffee table instead.

Though small, her feet had the curve of someone far more agile than Evan. I knew she'd never been a dancer like I had, so it seemed an unlikely trait for her to carry. Did I ever envy those feet, though. They were gross, as feet are, but their lines pleased my artist eye to the point that I'd memorize her sitting curled like that just to retain the image of her feet.

At only five-foot-six, heavier set, and about as open and affectionate as an ostrich with its head stuck in the sand, Evan Adams wasn't anything remarkable. Her hair, when not greasy from days of unwash, was a golden-yellow/ochre color cut to the tops of her shoulders. Though now, it looked more like what I could assume as day three without a shower.

Kodi, our third roommate, could claim being that kind of filthy influence on Evan, though.

At least, I could count on Evan to still brush her teeth.

Her face, round and pleasant in happiness, held a series of threats behind her eyes towards whoever crossed her. Those threats, as I recall, being far more dangerous than the colorful string that rolled from her mouth with the practiced ease of a seasoned sailor. It always reminded me to never say anything useable against me in a court of law; advice from Evan given before I even knew what it meant.

When she laughed, o-ho, it was magic! Her pinkish-pale skin would alight with a life and vitality that tasted like fresh snow and melted into fresh basil at the back of my tongue. Her eyes would crinkle into happy crescent slits, scrunching up the bridge of her cute, upturned pig nose.

"Yeah, but what changed your mind?" I asked, already aware of the answer but attempting to oust the deadness that sat too well on her features. If left too long, she'd withdrawal even further, and I was already in far deeper than the kind of damage control I'd become accustomed to handling with her. I'd owe her even more if not.

She released her knee and propped her elbows on her thighs in thought. "It was that one day in Kayla and Kodi's dorm. You'd followed Kayla home, we were there, and as soon as you leaned against the doorframe, flicked your hand in that nonchalant wave of greeting, and settled back, my entire opinion of you changed from 'no one' to 'dangerous.'"

We laughed knowing how wrong she'd been, and the tension eased from both Evan's body and the room. She remained the only person to ever think of me as someone dangerous, though.

I liked it.

The laughs died down, and Evan got up and walked a few steps before turning back. "Now, you're just a stupid art major," she commented with an intent to put herself back in control of her emotions, and mine. Then she continued the last few steps to the hall bathroom.

At least she was showering.

PART I

FRESHMAN

1

NEW FRIENDS

*D*rawing 101 sat atop a pedestal as one of my least favorite classes if only for the fact that it was basically everything I'd learned in a life drawing class I'd taken in high school, and was now forced to relearn it once more as a serious misapplication of my time and personal capacity to forward my art skills. I'd only been there a couple weeks, and I thought of myself as the only person a little turned off by the whole thing.

Thankfully, Kayla had the class with me.

She'd been the only one to invite me anywhere of all the new people I'd met at college. We'd pull the old metal stools together at the beginning of class, testing a few of them to be sure we didn't get the ones with missing pegs that teetered while you were trying to draw something with intense detail. They'd rock with the slightest shift in balance and would mess your drawing up if you weren't careful.

Our drawing professor, Natalie, had the most rigid personality that I knew of in the art building on campus. Though, she'd be sweet and demure in any instance where you found yourself in a face to face conversation with her.

Natalie had classical training from one of the many prestigious art schools on the East Coast, and she brought those skills and expectations to her students at Western. I couldn't say how she'd ended up in the mountains of Colorado, but she seemed to enjoy her job as an instructor and took the subject she taught far more seriously than every one of her students did.

Despite the strictness within her classroom, Natalie was kind and young; less than a decade older than us freshmen at most.

I knew some of the people in our class were only attending at that point because they thought Natalie was beautiful and were just there to ogle her as she made her rounds. Whether they ended up learning anything from her at the end of the day was a whole different ballgame.

Part of me agreed with the oglers.

Kayla swooned over her often and would tell me all about it in hushed tones from the corner of our studio-style classroom while Natalie moved around the gray linoleum on the other side of the room.

Natalie had the sunniest yellow hair—even under the draining fluorescent lights—that she kept out of her face in either a half pony or by pulling it all back at the base of her neck. She stood a touch over five feet tall, which was short by anyone's standards, and made it difficult to keep track of her as she made her rounds on the class and easier for her to sneak up on you if you weren't paying attention. She had dark blue, keen eyes that assisted her in spotting a distressed student faster than the kid might even know they were struggling, and her sharp features accented the narrowness of her face.

Natalie's soft, optimistic voice carried wistfully throughout the small studio classroom directing us on our next in-class assignment. "Alright everyone, today we'll be studying the features of the face and doing a partner drawing. Each of you grab your drawing boards and pair off, please."

Kayla peered at me hopefully, and I glanced at her knowing I didn't have anyone else to go to in the first place. I knew names of my classmates from the few weeks we'd been there, but comfort levels dictate social order, and people usually stick with someone they at least consider a friend.

The class moved their screeching stools across the linoleum, and we settled so that Kayla and I could face each other without our drawing boards knocking while we drew.

"So, what are we supposed to be doing?" she asked cracking her neck to each side, then her shoulders and fingers, before popping each elbow sharply. The motion more than the sound always made me cringe. Per usual, Kayla never paid attention to much of anything that went on around her, relying on others to catch her up on things.

I settled with my drawing board across my lap studying her for a minute, and I watched her fidget a few times under my steady gaze before answering, "We're drawing each other's portraits."

"Oh. You wanna draw first?" Kayla nudged at me hedging for my consent. She lacked the confidence required for going first or putting herself out there in any way, so I'd been expecting her to ask.

Might as well.

I had everything ready, anyway.

Kayla was a curiosity to me. Since she'd opted for modeling, I considered her snub nose and pouty lips as they twitched uncomfortably under my study like she'd never had anyone actually look at her face before, but it may have been the intensity of my study, too.

To be fair, she sat in uncertainty as often as a chihuahua shakes, but she had no reason to around me. I only cared about the integrity of the drawing itself, which wasn't going to be any good if she kept moving her face.

There's a definite bonus to her uneasiness, though. The power I held over Kayla in that moment, the power she unintentionally gave to me with every squirm and twitch, gave me quite the superiority complex.

Who knew the discomfort of others could erase the insecurities in me?

It's all a part of my game, though. I am brave because others feel scared. I am kindest when people are indecent. I am most human when people seek perfection. I try balancing whatever my environment shows me at the moment.

Like a personality chameleon.

Because of her insecurities, Kayla made me feel strong and superior more often than not. I imagine she kept me around to bodyguard for her since she clearly lacked whatever it took to be more than a quivering, anxiety-stricken mess. She had so many self-doubts that they sat with her in every fiber of her being and uncertainty clung to every sentence she spoke, and every word gave anyone the option to refute her if they chose without her fighting back.

It could have stemmed from her lack of a mother, as well, but that was merely speculation on my part.

Once she'd realized that I wasn't going to start pointing out her flaws, she settled. I sketched in the basic rectangle shape of her head, the slope of her downturned eyes hidden behind rectangular, black-rimmed glasses, and the touch of shade beneath her button nose. She'd always styled her hair in dark, bouncy curls that hung an inch or so below her ears and that she'd usually always ruined at the ends because she played with them whenever she felt the least bit uncomfortable.

"Alright everyone, it's time to switch partners," Natalie's sweet, airy call floated in around us and I grimaced at my drawing. I'd only managed to draw the basics of Kayla's features. There weren't even any freckles, yet.

Even if it wasn't my favorite, art classes never did last long enough for my taste.

I turned to Kayla who'd already settled with her board on her lap and swept a quick glance over my face before she started drawing.

Amateur.

Because she hadn't taken much time to study before drawing, Natalie came swooping in like a moth to a flame. I wondered how long she'd been watching Kayla for her to come around so quickly. Natalie must not have much faith in Kayla's drawing abilities if she'd stepped in almost as soon as the first lines were on the paper.

"Kayla," she prompted in the gentlest way she could, feeding into Kayla's anxiety, "how's it going over here?"

Kayla jumped, her breaths quickening making her chest rise and fall in rapid succession. I watched her eyes dart about in search of a safe hole or corner she could hide herself in as she turned into a cornered rabbit right before my eyes at the slightest hint of her possible wrongdoing. After all, why else would Natalie have singled her out?

"I don't know, this is hard!" she whined, and I stifled the urge to roll my eyes at her.

Some people's kids.

"Oh, no! This is simple, and you have a great model to start with," she said pulling her own stool next to Kayla's and taking the drawing board from her. Natalie propped it at a better angle for drawing and truly looked at me. Her gaze followed every line and curve of my face as she went, too.

"Desi has great facial features," she explained sketching out the basics. "She has a nice oval face making it easy to divide when you start to draw the features more clearly. Her eyes have more of an almond shape than what you have here, and because they're lighter in color, we'll accentuate them with more shading in the lashes since her eyes aren't deeply set."

Kayla nodded along allowing Natalie to continue drawing for her, though I'm not sure if she did it in under-standing or to avoid picking up the pencil again. "How do you draw the nose? That's the hardest part to draw, I think."

Natalie, happy to oblige in teaching Kayla what she could, continued imparting her knowledge onto the pair of us as she drew me. "Noses, without proper lighting, blend right into the face and look flat. The trick is in the shading, though. Too often we get caught up in drawing lines where there aren't any.

"Desi has a nice straight nose that doesn't stick out too far from her face but has these nice angles that make for good shadows. When you lay the mouth out beneath, just make these a bit fuller, like this," she said showing Kayla where she'd needed to enhance my features more.

"Then you'll just have to add those long brown curls, and you'll have a solid base for starting her actual portrait. Good start, though!" she said before getting up to check on the rest of the class.

Kayla tried for all that she could after Natalie handed her drawing back, but I watched her fake drawing for a while before Natalie called class to close for the day. Kayla never ended up studying me the way Natalie had, even after she picked up her pencil again. The result was an abysmal drawing of someone that looked something like a cross between Kayla and me. Artists that don't study their subjects end up drawing people that look like the person they're most familiar with, themselves.

"Are you coming over tonight?" Kayla asked as we packed to leave for another of our classes upstairs.

"Yeah, I'll be there. Anything special happening?" I asked hoping we'd be doing something like all the other hall rule-breaking activities Kayla told me happened; though, I never seemed to get an invitation to them.

"Probably just hanging out."

"Alright," I agreed knowing I'd be there no matter what we ended up doing, even though I continued to hope for something better all the same.

2

LACKING IMPRESSIONS

"Simon's installing the Adobe programs on my computer tonight. Wanna come over?" Kayla asked dubiously as we packed up another art class.

"Sure," I agreed, having little else to do without any homework to occupy the time and wanting nothing more than to hang out with Simon, my mutual friend from Kayla, since he'd started growing on me over our time together.

"Dinner at six, then?"

"Yeah," I said sliding my sketchbook into my bag before slinging it over my shoulder to leave.

I can't say why Kayla and I became friends. She played life strangely in the sense that she got people to be friends and do things with her through her insecurities and their own guilt that she couldn't fend for herself.

I'd done it for lack of other options.

Kayla had a knack for gaining friends and then stuffing all of them into a small, round booth in the cafeteria on the second floor of the student center. We'd usually end up pulling spare chairs over to get as many of us around the table as possible, and the meal we'd enjoyed that evening had been another large gathering of all the people Kayla seemed keen on collecting. Meals with a crowd happened so frequently, I wondered if Kayla could dine any other way.

Once we'd finished dinner, Kayla and I said our good-byes, and we meandered up to her dorm complex. She lived on the north side of campus in Crystal Hall which sat on the opposite side of campus from the complex I lived in called Mears. Many of the residents in Mears and I didn't get along well. I didn't much care for any of them because the walls were thin, and the parties usually raged well into the morning.

My own struggles with making friends were, in part, due to where I lived on campus, as well. The party noise got so bad that I'd taken to sleeping with earplugs each night as noisy neighbors tend to ruin all hope of forming bonds if you keep opposite hours to them. I'd already been planning on moving to another complex to get away.

I'm sure none of my neighbors attended any of their classes at all, either, and everything was a chore to walk to on most days because all the buildings on campus had been constructed onto the side of a mountain and uphill from my dorm.

With me coming in from a flat part of the country, most of the beginning weeks of school had me struggling to get around all while acclimating to the drastic elevation change and attempting to breathe everywhere I went.

"I need to grab my stuff from my room if you're okay with heading up there first," she told me as we neared the heavy, rust-colored door and she pulled out her keys to unlock it. The smell of laundry came wafting from the room beyond, and I admired that their laundry room wasn't in a dungeon of a basement like the one in Mears.

We climbed two flights of metal stairs to the top floor

where Kayla lived, and they banged underfoot as we trudged up them. I felt the further strain on my lungs and muscles as they worked against gravity, mountains, and thin air.

The hall had been painted a bright white that looked yellowish under the lights. The floor felt like someone had put thin gray-speckled carpeting over some concrete, which probably saved the school money in the long run and didn't prevent students from loitering in the hall in the least. A bulletin board hung near the end that'd been decorated with fun facts about the area and each of the lightly stained wooden doors had some kind of decoration taped to them.

As we made our way down the hall to her room, a busy-looking blonde person came rushing from a door down the hall towards us. The door she'd left banged shut and rattled on its latch in her wake.

"Oh, Evan!"

The Evan?

Kayla caught her attention briefly, though she seemed to sigh in a silent prayer for patience as she didn't look happy to see Kayla at all the way Kayla seemed happy to see her.

"Hey," she greeted quickly, still rushing.

I watched her as she made her way down the hall to us walking as quickly as she dared in her approach. She wore jeans, a navy-colored t-shirt with yellow NJROTC written on it (whatever that means), and old, dirty sneakers that'd definitely seen a better day. Her hair held a shiny yellow that grew slightly past her shoulders that she'd tucked back behind both ears in her haste. She wore no makeup, as far as I could tell, which made her plain and unassuming as a person.

Evan stopped before us looking impatiently at Kayla and

attempted to mask it with a quizzical arch to her right eyebrow.

Kayla looked nonplussed by the way Evan was rushing as she stopped her to chat. "So, this is Desi. Desi, this is Evan, the one I always tell you about," Kayla explained chuckling embarrassingly at the realization that she did talk about Evan a lot more than she'd initially realized.

I could attest to her realization. Kayla spoke almost non-stop about the people she'd befriended in her hall. Evan, of all of them, being the one person Kayla wouldn't stop talking about.

It was only fitting that I should start to meet the people in her hall, though. Meeting Kayla's hallmates was at the top of my priority list, particularly the person standing before me then. I'd hoped to be invited to their hall gatherings sometime, and Kayla and I spent so much time together, too, that I couldn't even explain how I hadn't met any of them, yet.

"Hi?" I said with uncertainty. She didn't seem like the legendary figure Kayla had portrayed to me throughout every one of our class days together, but the last thing I wanted was to mess up our first meeting.

Evan's look of determination and concentration struck me the most as she was, no doubt, a woman on a mission who didn't have any desire to be stopped in the hall to speak with us. Or, maybe, she just didn't think being introduced to me was as important as me meeting her.

I watched as she gave me a disdainful once-over glance before throwing a "Hey," over her shoulder and continuing on to wherever she'd been rushing off to in the first place. Clearly, it had been more important than the two of us.

"Well, ok...that was Evan," Kayla said disgruntled, frowning after Evan's fleeting form as she threw open another door and vanished into the evening. But it didn't matter much to me. The jealous little monster feeding me bad notions about Kayla and the fun times I hadn't been invited to were quelled for a mini instant that passed through my day just as quickly as Evan had. She'd been quite disenchanting.

At least I knew what I had to compete with, now.

Turning to continue our journey, we made our way down the hall to Kayla's dorm. Her hall had mostly men living on it with five rooms set aside for the ladies so that they could balance out the testosterone. Their RA made them door tags with playing cards, and there was one with Kayla's name scrawled in neat letters and another that said Dakota and a third with Kodi written on it.

"Who's Dakota?" I asked as I looked at the rest of the stickers on their door that ranged from a large circular dry-erase decal and markers taped to strings so that people could use them, and they wouldn't get lost, to other stickers with Kayla's name on them. Kayla's neighbors had been using the markers to draw out a cartoon war on the decal.

"Oh, that's Kodi's real name. Our RA was cool enough to make her a new one when she found out she didn't like or go by her real name. I did ask Kodi to pick some of her shit up, so sorry if it's still a little messy. She hardly ever listens to me about keeping things clean," she explained as she unlocked her door.

"You took your bunk beds down," I commented glancing over the new layout of her room as she opened the door.

As far as I knew, each of the dorms in her complex had an alcove to one side and a window across from the door. The alcove on the right wall that used to house their bunk beds now held only Kodi's twin bed with a slew of blankets strewn about it like she'd thrown them off in a rush to get somewhere; though, I couldn't ever recall seeing Kodi's bed made. All the "shit" I assumed Kayla had asked her to pick up also looked as if she'd thrown it there and she'd take care of it (maybe) at a later date or time.

Kayla's bed now sat under the window next to the pair of desks she and Kodi decided to put there for lack of anywhere else to put them.

While they had all the same furniture that I had in my room, theirs seemed a bit harder to fit into the space that they'd filled even further with a mini-fridge, posters over every conceivable wall space, two wardrobes to the right of the door, and tapestries and string lights draped across the ceiling with push pins to hold them in place.

Kayla and I had discussed her strong dislike of her roommate. She thought Kodi was unhygienic and filthy, and to be fair, she was correct. According to Kayla, she never helped clean their dorm or did her laundry, so it was left to pile and overflow the hamper in the corner. I'd get to hear all about it from Kayla during class, lunch, and dinner, so I knew quite a bit about the situation, and I didn't envy her in the least.

The fact that Kodi would sleep all the time and through any situation bothered Kayla most about her, though. Kodi worked nights at the Walmart off campus, and the exhaustion left her little motivation to do much of anything else around her classes. That meant that tensions ran high between them since Kayla wanted to be in the room during the day, but Kodi would be sleeping and make it nearly impossible to hang around.

On top of being gone on anthro field trips a lot, Kodi didn't have much room left in her schedule for things like helping Kayla clean, showering, or brushing her teeth. The opposite of everything that Kayla enjoyed doing.

Kodi happened to be gone as we entered the room. The skies were darkening already, and the dim lighting from the tapestry-covered ceiling light didn't help in illuminating the room much more than the sky outside did.

I saw Kayla heave a quick sigh of relief in not having to deal with Kodi as she flipped through the covers on her own bed to find her laptop. Then she rushed out the door taking us swiftly down a flight of stairs to Simon's.

I preferred being at his place, anyway.

3

EXES PAST

Another weekend, another chance to hang around Simon's dorm with my new friends and Kayla. She'd gotten Simon and me to confess to her that we liked each other earlier in the week, which goes to show how nosy Kayla is, but she'd done her job in passing the information on to the two of us. Unfortunately for all, I still had my high school sweetheart waiting for me back home that I'd carried into college with good intentions.

I admitted to liking men and women after turning sixteen, shortly before he and I had started dating.

I considered all the times he and I had discussed the various aspects of our relationship. Our dynamics had skewed a bit since I lacked a lot from our partnership, being polyamorous and bisexual at the same time, while he'd told me time and again that he wanted nothing but me *forever*. While we dated, I agreed to try being monogamous for him, but I'd come to realize that, too often, people fall in love and out of it just as easily, or the best is that you fall for many people all at once and have to fight with society's perception of polyamory. It's finding people that fulfill different needs that one person can't cover alone.

Our relationship came down to that difference in sexuality, though. I'd left him back home to pursue my college dreams in a place thousands of miles away without hope of engaging other people in fulfilling my needs, and I hadn't been able to cut the ties before I'd gone.

First real loves and all.

We'd crumbled to the point where we weren't even talking all the time like we had after we'd parted ways and I began my university adventure. I'd been having fun with my new friends and my new life and falling for people who were physically present to receive my love and to love me in return. The inevitable breakup loomed over my head longer than I cared to admit, but I couldn't bring myself to end it, yet, either. I couldn't crush his faith in me until I knew it'd come down to crushing his monogamous mindset if I didn't.

Curse sexual differences if love is involved.

I picked up my phone and scrolled to find his contact, toying with the keyboard while I debated my next move. It'd been over a week since we'd last spoken to each other and for someone who believes you're his soulmate, that's a helluva long time not talking to them.

Hey, we should talk. I texted him while I was putting my stuff together to head over to Simon's in Crystal Hall.

He texted me back immediately, **Hey! What's up?**

I swallowed my conscience for what I was about to do next. *It's not a huge thing. I've moved on,* I reminded myself as I gained the nerve I needed to break things off.

I don't think we should date anymore. It's too hard to keep this up. I typed, and half waited for a response.

I couldn't be sure what he'd think, but I knew I'd definitely be late if I didn't leave soon and I didn't really want to face the aftermath of everything. The excitement of seeing Simon again since finding out we had an interest in each other became a little too much to bear as the week passed, and I appreciated punctuality. I could always continue the conversation until I got to his dorm, anyway.

I picked up a few things to take with me to Simon's and closed my door behind me walking a little quicker than normal out of excitement.

Can we talk about this? Can I call you?

I pursed my lips and frowned at the phone as I paused halfway down the breezeway connecting each of the buildings in the complex. Despite the nagging feeling that I should at least sit down and talk with him about it, I told myself that I'd be able to talk about it with him come Monday after I knew where Simon and I stood with each other. I couldn't talk about such private matters in the breezeway where anyone could walk by and hear me, though. **Sorry, I'm busy. Can we talk about it later?**

Ok.

I read it, and it felt like the most pitiful "Ok" I'd ever laid my eyes upon. The guilt crept into my throat and lodged there like a massive cotton ball for my misdeed, and I had to shove it down forcibly with thoughts of the potential fun the weekend would bring. He'd been the first serious relationship I'd ever had which carried quite a bit of weight in my world, and he'd been the first in *a lot* of other ways, too. It wasn't the best way to pull the plug, but I did everything I could not to burst into horrible wracking sobs of my own on the spot.

That is, I put a locking lid on it and prayed that it'd stay closed until I could properly deal with it.

I arrived in Crystal Hall as an official single lady for the first time in almost two years. I amused myself with how trivial the time was that I'd be that way before Simon and I started dating.

A laughably small amount of time, to be sure.

Simon lived on the all-boys floor below Kayla's, and she'd actually been the reason I'd met him in the first place. They'd had a pipe burst in their laundry room that'd caused the lower level to flood and the building to be evacuated. If not for the two of them basically being neighbors, our differing majors and lack of almost everything in common would likely have never had our paths crossing.

For Simon, being the quintessential nerd had its perks. He'd disregarded the threats from ResLife towards the people that ruined the walls of the rooms with large nails and screws and hung a massive projector screen on the right wall as you entered his room. He'd hung a few posters and his personal Wi-Fi router. There were computers and laptops all over the floor in various stages of fixing, and many had been carefully disassembled to do so.

"Hey!" Simon called as Kayla opened the door for me.

When I'd entered the room, Simon sat fixing his projector as he uploaded some new programs onto Kayla's computer. He'd been there waiting for me as Kayla sat rocking in one of the wooden chairs with the faded green upholstery by his desk. Ben, with his mushed mousy hair in his typical gray t-shirt and jeans, lay on the top bunk that Simon had opted to keep in his room for the sake of space.

Like me, Simon decided to live without a roommate, which I couldn't blame him for since it was hell for all my friends that found themselves living with strangers they weren't getting along with.

I'd wondered a few times if he knew that Kayla had been using him for his technological know-how, but I never pushed the subject on him. I figured he could handle it himself if he had any real problem with it. *Maybe he liked the female company?*

I smiled at the room as they greeted me and sat on the bottom bunk to watch Simon work. His black hair usually held a slight sheen of grease, but he seemed to have showered it away for the evening. He wore black, thick-rimmed glasses that sat on his hooked nose which made his eyes look bigger, and he looked as if he hadn't seen the sun (in Colorado of all places) in all his life.

I'm a sucker for intelligence.

His nasally nerd-voice over-ruled a little of his inner Texan which came out in a subtle drawl. Many of the native Coloradans didn't like the Texan about him at all.

I'd learned in my weeks at school that Coloradans didn't like Texans because Texans came off as more entitled and only came into the state to clog up the slopes as the worst kind of tourist. Anyone stopped in the middle of the slope causing traffic gained no sympathy or respect from the true mountain folk.

At least, that's what they told me was the reason.

Simon usually wore jeans and too-big t-shirts that held some sort of theme around technology. Today's model was a black shirt with the Apple logo on the front.

Simon loved Apple.

I saw where he came off as stuck up since he usually felt he knew more than most everyone in his computer science classes and there was no hiding his Texan. I couldn't say whether the two were actually correlated, but I imagined that his pretentiousness came from winning an app lottery that made him richer than he knew what to do with. So, he drove his money around in a black Audi A5 that I wasn't sure would make for a decent winter vehicle.

It being the mountains of Colorado and all.

Throughout that first month of school, Kayla, Simon and I would hang out at least once a week with the occasional Ben thrown in here and there. She used him in any way she could. Dating him hadn't been of interest to her, but the friendship afforded us many occasions where we'd take trips to Walmart or decide to drive around town for no real reason in a way that I imagined was him trying to impress us. The three of us would cram into his Audi, that barely had a backseat, and take off, and it became more of a chore to fit all of us in the Audi when Ben came along, too.

Simon and Ben got along famously that first month. Ben lived down the hall from Kayla on the third floor and they'd only gotten to know each other after hanging around Simon. Ben rarely said much of anything to anyone, though. He squinted ruefully at anyone who disturbed him in any way, and he sat around playing video and computer games most of the times I'd seen him.

That's all I really knew about him.

That, and the fact that he always had mushed mousy hair, gray shirts, and jeans. *Always.*

None of them knowing what'd just transpired between my ex-lover and me, Simon chatted with me about his day, and we made plans for how we were going to spend the evening.

We opted for a movie after he'd shown me pictures from a crayfish fry he and his family had over the summer that made me nauseous with the way their black beady eyes seemed to stare out helplessly as they were lowered into the boiling water.

Being so tech-savvy, Simon had a plethora of movies and games to choose from, but one stood out as being nostalgic for me, and it won the vote.

Ferris Bueller's Day Off rolled onto the projector screen, and Simon hopped onto the bed next to me where we cuddled from the first "Chk-a chk-a" until the movie credits played on the screen.

I missed being cuddled and adored so much.

Kayla claimed homework to do and left sometime after that but shot me a knowing look before the door closed on her.

Ben stayed to play video games with Simon while I watched. With autumn creeping in and the darkness of the night bleeding into the darkness of the room, Simon and I always seemed to find ourselves touching one another in some way, whether holding hands or having the outsides of our legs and arms resting against each other.

Simon asked me to stay that night after Ben left and I slept on the top bunk. We parted for mere hours the following Saturday so that we could both shower and change into better clothes and then reconvened that afternoon for more Audi adventures and movies on his projector screen.

"Would you wanna stay the night, again?" Simon asked in his nasally semi-accent. He seemed a little shy when he asked, but I couldn't say why. I beamed happily at him.

"Sure!" I agreed. "Do you want me up on the top bunk again?"

He blushed glancing shyly away from me. "No," he refuted.

I staunched a giggle by holding my lips together as I smiled.

"Okay."

Exhaustion took over after a while, and I climbed onto the bottom bunk with Simon climbing in next to me. As every other bed in the dorms, his twin mattress left something to be desired now that the two of us were on it. It made for some amazing cuddling between us, though.

Simon hadn't done much besides a quick peck on the lips or little goodnight kisses that he'd given me the night before. I got the impression he felt apprehensive about the whole thing since he knew I had more relationship experience than him. I accepted everything he offered, though. Virgins sometimes needed far more encouragement than what was normally required.

We'd discussed a lot of things since becoming friends. One of the most tragic things I'd learned about him since we'd started getting to know each other happened to be that his girlfriend he had before coming to Colorado had been drugged at a party to the point that she'd overdosed and died, and Simon had still been dealing with the emotions from that.

I could tell he wasn't quite over her since he'd informed me that they'd been pretty serious. I could tell by the way he spoke about her, so I didn't push him into anything he didn't feel ready for, yet.

Man, did I miss it, though.

As we snuggled in and relaxed further, I began to prod, searching for my boundaries. "What do you think of having sex early in a relationship?"

"If it's right, I don't think it matters much," he said holding me against him.

I sighed in thought slightly relieved by that. "Have you ever done anything sexual before that wasn't sex?" I asked.

He considered for a moment. "Does masturbating count?"

I laughed. "You know what I mean, but I guess something is better than nothing."

He laughed with me. "Yeah, definitely nothing. Abby

and I spoke a lot about it, but we never really got to that point."

I frowned in the dark. I had my work cut out for me.

We sat in silence for a little while where I'd plant kisses on his face and chest every now and then to let him know I was still awake. Then the idea struck me.

"Would you be offended if I took off my clothes?" I asked. "I usually sleep naked, anyway."

He grew a little tense under me as we held each other, then he slowly relaxed, and all I could feel was his head nod against mine before he moved and took off his shirt.

Excitedly, I stripped naked in the dark in front of him, still not expecting us to do anything more, but leaving the option open for him if he wanted it. We slept like that in his bed with me pinned between the wall and his body while he'd stripped down to nothing but boxers.

I awoke too early the next morning wondering why I couldn't get myself to sleep in, but I'd expected as much since I usually get excited by the morning and being in bed with other people.

Early bird problems.

I'd ended up facing the wall in the night and tried not to move in case I woke him. I felt small movements from him beside me and questioned if he'd been awake, too. I looked carefully over my shoulder to find him sleeping deeply with a prominent boner that he thrust ever so slightly into the air as he lay there on his back.

I chuckled a bit. *Nothing to bat an eye at,* I thought examining all that I had to work with in the future. Definitely not something I could let go to waste if I could help it.

Wanting to wake him as gently as possible, I rolled to face him and started kissing him slowly in different places around his face and chest. I had to give him credit, the man could sleep like a rock, but I eventually succeeded in my task, and he blinked slowly awake and cringed at the light of the morning.

"What were you dreaming about?" I inquired curiously.

"I wasn't," he grumbled rubbing his eyes.

I hate when dreams *and boners* go away so quickly.

Damn.

I lay there lazily next to him while he woke up a little more. He wouldn't touch me in my current state of undress out of respect, but I could always be enticing for future situations.

"May I touch him?" I asked when I thought Simon was awake enough.

He hesitated before agreeing, and he fidgeted a bit and seemed to consider what to do with his hands while it happened.

I started rubbing him back to life through his blue boxers which seemed to do the trick. I released him from the cloth and kissed him tentatively.

Simon groaned a bit, having never experienced that kind of foreign contact before, and I took the opportunity to lick him and then take him into my mouth for a minute before letting him rest once more.

Simon seemed to enjoy it, but as much as I desired sex, he still wasn't ready for it, yet. I always had time, though. I respected him as he'd respected me and let him have all the time he needed for it.

I left him that morning to get my own stuff done that I'd been neglecting in favor of being with him, and things were fine for me once the week started.

4

THIRD WHEEL SYNDROME

Though there were many attractive people all over campus and the ratio of six males to one female skewed mainly in a woman's favor, the men of campus still found the time to be picky. That included the art majors, which seemed weird to me as fun-loving and free as we are.

I can say that the ones that did want to date usually never found themselves without a girlfriend, though. Kayla jealously coveted a few of our classmates, but none quite as much as James Wilde. He had the most tattoos and piercings of all the people in the art department. He had snake bites, and his septum pierced, several tattoos all over his body that I couldn't even count out, and one notably huge tarantula over his shoulder that he told me he'd gotten as a reminder to face his fears.

I'm all for tattoo meaning, absolutely, but not with a *giant* spider tattoo. *There's a line.*

James had a sort of skater fashion sense. He wore hats and beanies all the time and had quite a bit of brownish hair not only on his head but also his face when he let his ginger-colored beard grow out. I personally liked when he wore his purple shirts with his skinny jeans that truly showed off his thin frame. His fashion sense was drowning himself in too-big black hoodies that he'd always leave unzipped that gave off a punky vibe to me.

As the weeks wore on and bonds formed among us and our classmates, Kayla made a point to be as close to James as she physically could get. By proxy, he ended up becoming close to me, as well.

"Wazzup?" he rasped mockingly as he sat at our table in our 2D class.

I watched Kayla smile flirtatiously at him before answering, "Same ol' stuff, ya know?"

"Oh, yeah. I know," he replied bringing his voice back to its normal smoothness. "Do you guys wanna come over later?"

Kayla jumped at the opportunity to hang out with James outside of class. Anything that brought her that much closer to him. I think he just believed that she and I never did anything separately, so I'd been invited by proxy. I didn't mind, though. It gave me something to do, and I kind of had a thing for James, too. That's what happens after hearing so much about someone's attractive features for so long, you start to see what they're talking about.

As far as Kayla's attraction went, though, sometimes I wondered if she actually saw anything under all of James' decorations. James was kind and not nearly as hard as his facade alluded to. At least, that's what he let me see.

After class, we packed our bags and made our way down the hall where we paused at the door for a minute before leaving. I'd checked my phone for the millionth time to find that the question I'd asked Simon a few hours back had not been responded to, yet, and I felt more and more dejected by the second.

A dreaded silence fell over our text conversations the week following my blissful weekend with him. I'd send him something and never hear back from him. An absolute sign of disinterest, but I couldn't understand why.

I sighed, and Kayla saw me look at my phone and then put it back in my pocket again.

"What's up?" she asked me with her hand on the metal door latch ready to push it open.

"Nothing, just Simon hasn't been talking to me really since the weekend, and I don't know why," I explained crossing my arms uncomfortably.

"Really? That doesn't seem like him. Was everything alright when you saw him last?"

"Yeah. I am just feeling a little down about it is all," I told them, and James quirked the corner of his mouth concerned.

"Do you want a hug?" he asked moving away from the door he'd been about to walk through to get closer to me.

I nodded sadly, and he came in to give me a soft, sympathetic hug. Kayla mimicked him giving me a hug as well before pushing open the door and walking outside with James. I followed feeling slightly better.

James lived in Mears like I had before I moved, but it seemed to suit his lifestyle and attitude a bit more. I imagined he had more luck with living there than I did.

"Kinda sucks being single again," James mentioned as we walked.

Don't I know that, buddy.

Last I knew, James had a girlfriend that he brought in from home. That bit of news lit Kayla's ears up like a Christmas tree.

"You're single?"

"What happened?" I asked over her to seem more concerned for his well-being than excited about the news. Kayla could take a hint.

He shrugged, "So, I had my girlfriend, right, but I found out from a friend that she cheated on me. I fucked her sister, who's a neighbor of mine in Mears, and we ended it."

My steps faltered with that rollercoaster of a story. What kind of a sibling relationship causes someone to do that to their sister? Maybe she felt the same way I did in hearing all about James' virtues and couldn't help it?

Not my circus, and definitely not my monkeys.

I did feel bad that James had been hurt by his ex, though. He'd taken the news way better than I would have, but I suppose that the retribution of revenge sex would make anyone's day a little brighter.

You win some, you lose even more.

After hearing that news, Kayla jabbered even more enthusiastically than usual as we walked. James made conversation when he could get a word in, and I hung back and listened to her make a fool of herself for the sake of attraction. Not that I hadn't been guilty of it on occasion in my life.

He opened his gray-painted metal door for us, and we entered a similar room to the one I'd had on the other side of the complex except James kept his room dark with a blackout curtain they'd pinned to the wall. All Mears dorms were different from the ones Kayla (and now I) lived in. Every two rooms in Mears were paired with one bathroom that they had to clean and share. The four large bathrooms per floor of Crystal had two shower stalls each and were cleaned by a professional crew.

I did not miss having to clean and it looked a lot like James and his roommates hadn't cleaned anything at all.

James pulled one of the angular rocking chairs out for me, and he and Kayla jumped up on his elevated bed to sit together.

Hello, third wheel syndrome.

"We had this crazy hall party the other day that was blacklight, and everyone wore white and drew on each other with highlighters," James mentioned as we sat together, and I watched Kayla inch closer and closer to him.

"That's so cool," Kayla said batting her eyes at him. "Where was your RA?"

"Oh, he's cool. He's almost always out, so we never have to worry. That or he ignores us and lets us do our thing."

I rolled my eyes. *Wasn't that the truth?* RAs were never around in Mears. I don't even think a single one actually lived in the rooms designated to them.

As soon as my eyes focused again, Kayla had pounced and started leaving little kisses in various places on James' body. He took pause in her forwardness for a moment before he seemed to melt into it. Not needing to stick around for that, I grabbed my stuff and rushed towards the door. I glanced back a moment and found James lying on his back and Kayla fighting with the fasten of his pants.

Okay, that's enough for me, thanks!

I left them and didn't look back till I was well on my way up the mountain to the library for my last class of the day. I didn't mind being nearly an hour early, I could kill some of it if Evan were working the IT desk upstairs.

I pushed through the doors and found her hunched over some paper with a pen waving around between her fingers as she read it. She flipped back to the laptop open next to her, and her fingers flew quickly over the keyboard as she typed. I couldn't tell if homework occupied her time or if she had some sort of freelance project she had a deadline for that she'd been trying to crank out, but I didn't mind interrupting her for a moment.

"So, I've been having trouble with my computer. Can you help me?" I asked making my voice sound high and nasally.

She looked up from her work and quirked an eyebrow at me. "Your problem is the fact that you have a Mac and nothing more," she told me, being a tried and true Apple hater. She smiled at me all the same.

"So, Kayla and James are hooking up right now," I mentioned as I pulled up a chair and dropped my backpack next to the help desk.

Evan scowled. "'Bout time for that, honestly. She's been pining a little *too* hard for him recently."

"You've been hearing about him, too, huh? What do you think about it since you two are apparently dating?"

"She's allowed to do whatever she wants. We aren't exclusive," she said casually, and my heart gave a little leap in response. I'd have to look into that later.

"Well, I have a bit of time to kill before my next class, do you mind if I chill here with you?" I asked to be sure that I hadn't interrupted anything crucial. She shook her blonde head at me.

"Evan, what don't I know about you?" I asked settling in.

She quirked an eyebrow at me, "There's a lot right now, but what are you asking about specifically?"

"Whatever you wanna tell me about. Nothing extreme."

She pursed her lips decidedly. "Have I ever told you," she began, "I was born on an airplane a month early when my parents were on their way to visit my family in Ireland?"

Shaking my head in the negative, I prompted her further.

"It was pretty chaotic as I've been told, and they had to turn the plane around as I couldn't make it to Ireland without gaining Irish citizenship then. We landed in New York where the doctors asked my parents if they wanted to give me my records and they said they'd rather wait until we made it back to Colorado, so we did.

"By the time we got back it was already the next day, so what should have been October 18th printed on my birth certificate, is, in fact, October 19th, which is the day everyone celebrates as my birthday."

"Hmm," I mused wondering if hospitals couldn't actually change information in their systems to reflect a baby's actual birthday.

Looking up from her work, she caught my eye before I could think too hard about it. "Wanna see this cool new set of cuts I got that I'm hoping will turn into a scar?"

"When'd you get cut?" I asked quirking an eyebrow at her.

"Oh, when I went home this past weekend. Not a big deal since it could have been *way* worse but look! Now, it looks like the clown from *IT* tried to grab my leg!" she cheered pulling up her jeans to show me three thin slices across her ankle as if Wolverine had attempted to cut her foot off.

"Worse? What were you doing?" I asked, my brow creasing in worry.

Evan paused staring at me. Thoughts flittered across her mind in time with a slew of emotions that played in her eyes from shock and conspiracy to consideration and resolve. "It was just a training. Maybe we can talk about it later," she concluded, letting me know that whatever additional questions I had about it would have to be put on hold until she brought the subject up again.

Deciding not to push it, I went back to my homework and wasting time before class.

5

CHILDISH THINGS

Whenever people find out I'm bi it always becomes a question of 'why *both*?'

My answer: The same way you like whatever gender you prefer. I consider it liking and falling in love with *people*.

It's worked well for me, so far. I've fallen for some pretty amazing humans and had some pretty amazing humans fall for me, too. Sometimes, those humans that fall for me aren't all that great, though.

Delphinium fell *hard* for me, and I couldn't give her the same courtesy. She had this abrasive personality and the over-animated way she moved her hands when she spoke made her seem like a puppet with an untrained marionettist practicing with her throughout her daily life. She'd lost her sense of self being the oldest child of eight and she'd always been terrified of becoming her mother, which eventually ruled and became her life.

We'd started meeting each other regularly between classes and chatting about all kinds of things going on in our lives and with her boyfriend she'd left back home on the Front Range. Eventually, we decided to make a date of it and started printing out coloring pages from the library to give us something to do while we solved each other's problems.

Delphinium and I had about fifty pages of Disney-themed possibilities. I enjoyed the therapy it provided. Delphinium enjoyed spending time with me. A win for both of us as our friendship grew.

She listened intently to my woes as I coped with building my new life at school, agreed with me on several things that had to do with our group of friends and the people that lived on her hall, and made a point to tell me all about the things going on with Eddie, who'd become a little clingy and possessive since she'd gone off to college.

Delphinium never did well with being herself and having a significant other at the same time. She'd decided to stay with Eddie though they'd be a few hundred miles apart and spent every moment she could talking to him about life and their days and telling him repeatedly that she missed him *so veowy much.*

Her devotion went a little extreme even for my taste.

"Eddie insists we have phone sex at least thwee times a week," Delphinium explained in her R-less drawl that reminded me of one *wabbit*-crazed cartoon character. I'd gotten used to it enough that it no longer bothered me while she explained their latest phone call. "It's hawd to keep up with sometimes now that I have pwojects all the time."

"That's a lot of time he's asking from you," I mused grabbing the yellow crayon for Pooh Bear's body.

She shrugged. "It's not a *big* deal. At least I get off."

That piqued my interest since I knew she hadn't ever actually had intercourse with anyone before.

"How many times have you cum in a row?" I asked curiously.

She considered a moment before answering me. "The

most I've done is sixteen, but that's on special occasions and when I have time."

Holy shit!

I'd been expecting her to say two, maybe. I'd planned on bragging about the 5-ish times I'd managed. I needed to step up my game!

"That's crazy," I admitted finishing my drawing and grabbing a new page.

"Yeah, I know," she stated casually and continued with her own coloring.

My phone buzzed on the bed between Delphinium and me.

Come over.

Kayla had signaled the end of our solo play date in favor of a bigger gathering. I could only imagine her hall must have been up to something.

"Kayla wants us," I said placing my crayons back in their box and stretching. "Wanna go over there?"

"Suah!"

She mimicked me in stretching before putting her pages into a pile and cleaning up her crayons, too.

We wandered our way from my room, down the stairs, and through the breezeway to Crystal. We'd both donned our comfiest clothes for our coloring date and opted not to change out of them as we made our way to Kayla's.

Upon opening the door from the stairs to the hall, we were struck by a group of Delphinium's hallmates gathered on the floor in front of the girls' dorms. Kayla with her dark, curly hair and glasses, Rachael, Evan's roommate, tucked innocently into a ball near her, Evan on Kayla's other side with her beat up sticker-covered laptop in her lap typing away.

Across from them sat Ben with mushed hair in his usual

gray shirt and jeans, one of the neighbor girls with her dark hair that looked like she was trying to dreadlock the bottom of it all together, and some stoner from the hall who sat dazedly staring around higher than a kite flies.

"Hey!" Kayla greeted moving barely enough to flick her hand in a wave.

Several of the others looked up at us as we joined them sitting in the hall. I plopped down next to Ben and Delphinium curled up next to me barely touching my side as she did.

As the days had passed, it became clear that Delphinium's *thing* for me had been growing more than I could manage. It would be handled, eventually, and I did my best to move away from her without trying to hurt her feelings.

She scooted closer again, and I gave up on everything and let her lean against me.

"Hey, Ben, how's it going?" I asked him trying not to let Delphinium's weight push me into him.

He sighed. "First, you lost The Game."

A chorus of groans sprang up from our little group. It'd always be that way with Ben. Never any peace from The Game when it came to him.

"Second," he continued, "it was fine. Simon apologized to me for the other day and we're on good terms again."

At the mention of Simon, I became a little melancholy. He hadn't said anything to me since last month.

"Ew, Simon," Evan cringed across from us.

We both looked up at her as she spoke.

"Hey, it's not my fault you dated him. No one in my class even likes him except this one exchange student."

I ignored her stab at my choice in men. Still too fresh for me to start making jokes about him.

Ben seemed to ignore her stab, too, since he also considered Simon a friend.

"How's that guy you've been talking to?" Rachael squeaked from beside Kayla.

Kayla turned beaming. "Brian? He's good. He took me out the other night and we had sex!"

"Great, another Brian," Evan jeered knowing we already knew a few others including "Little Penis" Brian and Big Bee.

I chuckled. "Yeah, you say you hate your name so much! What if *that* was your name?"

Everyone paused glancing at Evan whose nostrils flared in agitation for being put on the spot. It disappeared quickly remembering our mixed company, though. "I've never met another girl with my name! Sure, Brian would suck if that were my name, too, but it's not my fault my parents gave me a boy's name anyway! I have this friend Remi back home that has that same cute E sound to his name like you have. He rubs my face in it every time I see him until I threaten to cut his dick off. Then he shuts up and things are okay."

Laughs went up from the people that normally didn't hang around us and I followed Evan's lead when she joined them. It didn't matter that I already knew that she was absolutely capable of something so violent, we couldn't let anyone else know that.

Once we'd settled again, Evan turned her attention back to Kayla. "Didn't you just meet him?" she asked.

"Is that the one with a kid?" Kat asked over her, glad to return to what was clearly the more important topic in her mind.

"Not just..." she glanced away embarrassed, "and yes. He's with him tonight."

"How was the sex?" Delphinium asked curiously, and we all leaned in a bit to hear of her sexcapades.

She blushed a little but shook it off promptly. "I don't know what it is, but he has the biggest penis I've ever seen."

We all had varying stunned and puzzled expressions on our faces begging her to elaborate further.

"Well," she began, "we went to Sherpa Café and he had a motel room booked for some reason, and we went back there, and we did it on the sink in the bathroom and the faucet stabbed into my back. It left the craziest bruise and hurt really bad but definitely not as bad as it hurts fucking him. He makes me feel like a virgin again!"

"That sounds terrible," I said clenching my legs together at the thought of experiencing that pain again.

"Yeah, it's pretty bad, but I'm going to see him this weekend, I think."

Kayla started twisting the curls she could reach around her fingers in thought, and I glanced around at the other women in the group to see their reactions.

Evan scowled a bit, and Kat seemed a little horrified, but beyond that, no one else could really weigh in as Rachael and Delphinium hadn't had sex with anyone, yet.

"You know what we should do?" Kayla asked changing the subject from that of her sex life. "We should build a fort."

We all glanced around at one another considering whether there would be any repercussions to sharing such an innocent experience with one another.

We enjoyed each other, why not?

We sprang into motion then. Evan and Rachael moved into their room to gather blankets and Kayla grabbed the rest of us to come in and help her steal some of Kodi's blankets and sheets while she was away on another anthro field trip.

As we'd spent every other occasion together, Kayla and Kodi's room became the hub of activity. Emmett and Kat managed to slip away around then, deciding not to take part in our fun, and Ben and I helped Kayla and Delphinium start pinning sheets to the ceiling with pushpins.

Bbrraaappp.

"Yellow!" Kayla cried after she'd burped and we all looked confusedly at her.

"Green?" I asked wondering if we were supposed to follow with more colors.

"You've never played the color game?" she asked us shocked that more colors weren't being called.

We all shook our heads in the negative, and she sighed indignantly.

"Well, anytime someone burps, you say a color without repeating someone else's color. If you repeat, you lose, and you have to make a sex sound. If you're the last person to say a color then you have to make a sex sound," she explained and then promptly burped again before shouting, "Green!"

"Yellow!" I said quickly.

"Oh, uh, pahple!" Delphinium said.

"You all lost The Game," Ben sighed.

"What the hell, Ben?" Evan complained pushing open the door followed closely by Rachael with arms full of blankets.

"You really say that during sex?" I asked Ben though I knew he did it just to be difficult.

"If you must know, yes," he chided.

Evan frowned at the four of us. "I feel like we missed something."

Kayla sighed and quickly explained the color game again as we worked.

Leaving enough space for the door to swing inward, we managed to encase their dorm in sheets, leaving the blankets as a cushion for the floor where we all piled inside to admire our handy work and go to sleep.

I couldn't sleep, though.

I'd been pinned near the door between Evan, who'd gotten near the middle of our little cuddle puddle, and Ben who was on the outermost edge by the door. Thoughts of Simon and how Ben had seen him and knew something about him swirled and eddied around my head, and I found myself turning to Ben several times once we'd settled down to ask him questions.

"Ben," I prodded, "did Simon seem okay?"

Ben grumbled inaudibly into his pillow before turning his face to look grumpily at me.

"Never better," he intoned before turning back again.

"What happened then? Why'd it really fall apart?" I asked him without giving him a chance to get comfortable enough for sleep.

"Shut up!" Evan growled from beside me though I kept my attention on Ben.

Another Evan lesson: You can only be awake while I'm awake. No disruptions otherwise.

He turned frustrated to me. "You know what happened. I saw it coming, too."

"Really?"

Ben sighed at the night before kicking off the blankets around him and motioning me to follow him.

We made our way out of the fort and Kayla's room barely disturbing anyone. He took me a few doors down the hall to the student lounge where there were a few TV chairs and a sofa, all with hideous fabric prints on them. Ben took two if the armchairs and pushed them side by side and sat in the one on the right waiting for me to join him.

I'd learned over the time I'd known him that Ben loved being enigmatic. He'd only give information he felt would placate and nothing more. I knew the reason he played The Game was a control tactic played off as a memory device he'd associated with himself, too. There was more to him than met the eye, and he tried to squash all possibilities of you figuring it out by being as unassuming as possible. He was definitely the person I needed to talk with about this.

"I don't know why you insist on clinging to Simon, but he's no good for you. Let him go," Ben insisted as I sat, and he had my full attention. I searched his face as that'd been the longest sentence I'd ever heard him say.

He was being a well-meaning friend, but it still stung me.

"I know, I just need to know why!" I admitted. "The fact that there's no explanation haunts me."

After Simon had ghosted me, I went searching for an explanation. Granted, in my quest for answers, I may have turned into a psycho with the intensity of my quest, which definitely made things worse, but I came out with quite a few lessons learned.

1. Don't break up in any way that may force karma to act upon you.

2. Don't do anything that may irritate your current interest's exes.

3. And never underestimate the reasons a ghost may come back from the grave.

Abby, Simon's dead ex, came back to haunt him as soon as we'd parted ways for the week, and to make matters even worse, she came back to tell his dream-self that she didn't like me and that he shouldn't hang around me anymore.

Perfect.

Not only that but I'd been left single, as well.

Thanks, Karma, you're great!

Ben sighed again not truly enjoying the topic of our conversation. "He was terrified after she showed up in his dream. I tried to warn him about it, too, but he wouldn't listen to me until after it happened and by then it was too late.

"He couldn't face you after that. Every time you came around it'd remind him of Abby and he'd be forced into a confrontation with something he hasn't made peace with, yet. He was so afraid that he even tried to push me away and spat in my face for it."

"Gross! He really did that?" I asked as my lip curled disgusted.

"Yeah. It was partially a control tactic, too, but I wasn't going to stick around for it. We only started talking again this week because he said sorry," Ben confessed.

"How did you know that was going to happen?" I questioned knowing that not everyone can see something that specific coming.

Ben shrugged again. "You get a knack for it and just kind of see the signs. You weren't meant to be together. I'm sure even Kayla understood that but who can help attraction?"

"What else can you see?" I wondered hoping to gain more insights from him.

He considered this a moment before answering me.

"I don't believe we'll be able to maintain the group of friends that we have. I'm pretty sure we'll disband soon."

"When?" I demanded, suddenly terrified in living a life without Ben. I hadn't realized how much he meant to me now that he'd been helping me get over Simon, but it felt like a great deal more than I'd let on even to myself.

"Soon. Anyway, I've tried to have friends in groups of five because that's ideal for balance, but it always falls down to four people and then everything falls apart. I believe you're one of the people that will help me keep this together, though," he concluded holding my rapt attention.

"Who are the others?" I asked twisting myself so that I could look into his deep green eyes in the dim light of the room on occasion that he wouldn't avoid eye contact while our chairs were still side by side.

"I can't tell you that or it'll ruin the whole thing," he said giving me a look like I obviously should have figured that out already. It could never be easy with him.

"If I guessed, would you tell me?"

"I guess," he sighed considering my proposition.

I thought about all the people Ben kept company with. "Is it Kodi?"

Ben paused at that and heaved another sigh, "Yes."

"So, what does she know about keeping things together?" I queried.

"I told you that I can't tell you that," he deadpanned, and I took a moment to think around his statement and come up with new questions that'd yield the most information for me.

Ben wanted nothing of the new questions, though. He avoided information with riddles and made it difficult for me to pin him down with anything. Eventually, he pulled himself so far out of our conversation that he told me to wait in the lounge so that he could grab his computer and show me something.

He came back with a blanket and laptop in hand and

handed the large blue comforter to me before he began setting things up.

"What are we watching?" I asked snuggling in and realizing how cold I'd been without it.

"*Red Versus Blue*," he told me before logging in and getting everything ready to press play.

He'd been so good at distracting me with it that we ended up watching the entire first season of RVB until the arrival of dawn told us we should get some amount of sleep and headed back for bed.

I struggled wondering what I might do to keep my group of friends.

6

BARE CONCRETE

*E*van took Ben and me to Auntie Betsy's in her powder blue Mustang to climb the incline. Kodi couldn't come because of an anthro field trip, and Delphinium didn't want to leave her new boyfriend Todd since we were getting so close to the end of the school year. Her time with Eddie became too stressful after he'd started pressuring her to have physical intercourse with her before she was ready, so she'd moved on to someone new.

Panting, sweating profusely, wanting only to sit on the rock next to me for as long as I possibly could so that I could catch my breath and not even think about the climb back down the mountain to the car, I groaned and looked angrily down at the mountain trail we'd climbed so far. I'd taken the rail tie steps in increments of fifty about halfway up to remind myself to breathe and get in way better shape than I'd started climbing with. I'd be content in never doing that climb again if I could help it.

Damn the fat rolls, sometimes.

Ben, Evan, and I sat on that rock for a while watching

more and more people make it to the top, and some immediately make their way back down it again.

Those people were nuts, and in *way* better shape
than me.

I asked her whose brilliant idea it'd been for us to climb
the incline about a quarter of the way up as the drastic
elevation change crept up on me. Now, I could definitely be
proud of myself if not absolutely breathless and exhausted
for making it to the top.

"So, we have two options. We can go back down the way
we came, or we can go down the path over there that's a
little more forestry and winding," Evan said flicking her
hand limply towards the small dirt trail we'd been watching
several other people wander down once they'd recovered
from their trek up.

"I vote the trail," I wheezed immediately not wanting to
think about potential vertigo that might happen if I walked
down the incline with nothing but the vast Colorado
Springs area beyond.

"Trail," seconded Ben though his scrawny self hadn't felt
much of anything compared to his more voluptuous
climbing partners.

"Let's go, then," Evan urged looking at the time on her
cracked phone screen. "We still need to grab dinner, and I
wanna do that before it gets dark."

I had to agree with her. I didn't want to be on the incline
in the dark, either.

We made our way down after I'd found my bearings and
my legs had stopped being so wobbly. It felt much nicer
going down than it had been coming up, and I couldn't help
being grateful for the easiness and the burrito waiting for
me at Chipotle on our drive back.

We returned to Auntie Betsy's and were greeted by

Evan's aunts and more alcohol than the three of us knew what to do with. The handle of Svedka, the tall bottle of Jäger, and the pack of Smirnoff Ice were usually enough to intoxicate all of us plus our friends in Crystal, but Auntie Betsy wanted to be sure her favorite niece and her friends would have everything they'd need to get wasted.

I couldn't say why Auntie Betsy loved Evan most of all her nieces and nephews. They definitely looked something alike, but I supposed besides the blonde hair and wide pig nose, Evan did look a little like her mom with the roundness of her features. The connection being that Auntie Betsy and Mrs. Adams were sisters.

Sandy, Auntie Betsy's roommate and lesbian lover, had blonde hair, which made me laugh with the irony of it, and nice wide hips. I imagined they came with the birth of Sandy's now teenaged son, but I couldn't be certain. I'd learned that Sandy and Betsy had met through their work at the correctional facility.

They had all the power and toughness to intimidate me, easily.

"You wanna play Asshole?" Evan asked as Auntie Betsy handed each of us a bottle of green apple Ice from her fridge.

"Sure," I said thanking them for the alcohol and sitting at their little breakfast table against the wall.

Ben joined me silently, and Evan happily wandered over with the bottle of Svedka that she placed in the center of the table. We'd be drinking that soon enough.

"Well, you kids have fun with that. We're heading to bed," Auntie Betsy bellowed as she and Sandy moved around the corner to their room.

"Night!" Evan chirped in their direction before picking up the pack of cards and handing them to me to shuffle. She liked to watch me since I could make the butterfly and the bridge with the cards.

After the best game of Asshole I'd ever played in which I ended up being President more often than not and had a running set of rules including: touching the bottle of slowly draining vodka in the center of the table, knocking on the table and sticking out our tongues, the green man, and touching our noses and the odd man out on all of them had to drink, we were all pretty trashed since we would enact those rules at any time we chose. One time it even took Evan several minutes to notice she had to drink for being the last one to touch the table with her thumbs.

With the draining of the bottle of Jäger and the last of the Smirnoff gone, we were laughing hysterically at the recapping of how we were now playing the rules without the cards to see who'd be forced to drink again.

"Shhh," Evan slurred between giggles. "We'll wake everyone up!"

Ben and I giggled, too, but not quite as loud as we had been.

"C'mon, let's go to the basement," she told us motioning to the stairs that provided a little buffer between us and the back hall where Betsy and Sandy were sleeping.

I staggered to my feet and moved with Ben towards the stairs and down into the sparsely furnished concrete area where they had a card table, a plaid couch, and a ping-pong table.

"Let's play!" Ben said scurrying over to the table and grabbing up the paddles and a ball.

I looked skeptically at him knowing my hand-eye coordination didn't add up to par on a normal day, but I took the paddle from him and made to await his serve.

He hit the ball to me and I managed to hit it back

though it caught on the net. Ben picked it up and called a point for himself. *At least I'd hit the ball.*

Clack.

The serve sounded again, and I hit it up into the wooden rafters on the ceiling.

"Oops," I said after the ball got stuck.

Ben scoffed at me and I scowled.

"Here, hold this," he said handing me his paddle and making to get up on the table.

I looked at him uneasily. "Are you sure you should do that?"

"Yes. It's fine," he said hoisting himself up and standing on the table. He swayed a bit before grabbing the rafter and peering up to find the ball. He climbed back down unharmed and I considered him lucky more than anything else. I knew how much each of us drank upstairs and ping-pong tables never seemed all that sturdy to me.

Being done with ping-pong, I headed over to the plaid couch and plopped down in time for Evan to come down and join us.

"Hey, sorry, I was just putting some stuff back in the fridge," she explained and came to sit down next to me.

Ben walked over to us and stood in front of us feeling energetic. "Fabulous!" he lisped popping his hip and flipping his hand expertly.

Evan looked at me and we both burst out laughing at how perfectly he'd done that impression. "What the hell!"

"That was too perfect, Ben," I told him still giggling.

"Yeah...I practice," he joked, and we laughed harder.

Evan looked at me and smiled. "Would you mind if I kissed you?"

My eyebrows rose a little surprised. "Of course."

She smiled harder and leaned in to give me a quick kiss on my lips before Ben sat next to us.

"Ben!" she cheered turning and kissing him on the mouth as well. His eyebrows rose in shock like mine had.

Satisfied, Evan got up from the couch and moved over to the table. It left Ben and I looking at each other uncertainly.

"Can I kiss you?" I asked him since he hadn't been opposed to Evan's kiss.

He shrugged but didn't move from his place next to me, so I leaned over and kissed him sweetly.

"Come sit down. I have something I want to tell you," Evan called to us from the small card table near the stairs.

My eyes maintained their half-lidded state as I staggered to my feet and steadied myself on the back of the couch and Ben's shoulder. He looked at me with slight concern before wandering over to the table where Evan sat and waited for me to stumble over, too.

I felt the drunkest I'd ever been in my life, but I felt no worse for wear than any other time we'd drank together. I sat heavily, and both Ben and I looked expectantly at Evan.

She gulped and fidgeted for a moment or two while we watched her. Apparently, whatever she'd planned to say had died in her throat and she had to war with herself to bring it back up again.

"If it's too much, you don't have to tell us," I reassured knowing it must be something much bigger than anything she'd told either of us before, which said something since she'd already told us all about her childhood and the Sloths.

"No, no...I want to tell you guys. You should know," she told us and breathed heavily to steel herself to her own resolve. "So, uh, I have cancer. I've had it for years."

Ben's eyes bugged at her confession and I couldn't breathe.

Evan lesson: Never get too comfortable.

"How bad is it?" I asked concernedly.

"It's pretty much all over at this point," she admitted sadly leaning against the tabletop for support. "I've been in and out of a hospital since I was little. It sucks."

Ben let his face collapse in his hands to hide the tears that'd started falling down his cheeks.

"Is there nothing they can do?" I begged, refusing to let my own tears fall. I would not give up if she decided to keep fighting.

"We've done pretty much everything we can. I've been told I'm running out of options," Evan explained sadly, and I could tell she seemed angry at that prognosis, too. I would have been if I were her.

Worry marred my features as I watched her think through her life for a minute. It was all so overwhelming that I had to put my head down on the table to collect myself. I'd started swimming in deeper waters than I'd ever been before, and I couldn't handle it with the kind of alcohol in my system.

Ben mumbled something that I couldn't understand as my world spun with the sudden change in my orientation and the urge to gag threatened the back of my throat. I forced it down once, but it came back with more. Too much.

Oh, no.

A liquid rush of semi-transparent fluid (mostly vodka) and undigested corn kernels from the burrito I'd eaten after our climb poured from my mouth and nose onto the concrete floor, my socks, Ben's socks, and everything within a three-foot radius of us. It burned horribly and made my eyes water fiercely, though I'm sure the tears I'd been holding back added into it.

"Oh my god, I'm so sorry," I said horrified that I'd thrown up on the floor of Evan's aunt's basement.

Ben picked his feet up and quickly removed his socks so that he wouldn't track my vomit all over the house as he helped Evan clean things up.

Evan, like a seasoned pro, moved swiftly to my side to pick me up from the chair carefully so that I wouldn't stumble or step in it.

"Are you okay? Do you need me to get you a bucket? Do you feel like you need to throw up again?" she asked holding my arm to steady me, and I breathed deeply to clear more of the fog from my head.

"No, shower. I can make it. Just move slow," I told her as she walked me up the stairs and into the bathroom at the top. "I'm so sorry."

Evan turned on the shower and felt the temperature before she let me get in so that I wouldn't be drunkenly trying to fight with an optimal water warmth.

"It's okay as long as you're okay," she told me helping me take my vomit-laden clothes off and held me steady as I stepped over the bathtub ledge.

"Thanks," I told her as she closed the curtain on me.

I stood in the shower swaying under the water before my brain caught up and told me that standing was way too dangerous for me. I carefully plopped down on the bathtub floor and let the water run over my back while my eyes were closed. It felt so good that I did nothing but sit cross-legged letting the shower rinse away the throw up for who knows how long.

"Desi? Are you alive in there?" Evan called from the other side of the curtain.

"Hmm," I acknowledged not wanting to move at all.

The curtain pulled back a bit, and the water stopped falling on me. "Time to get out, okay?"

I grumbled unhappily at the sudden chill of the air outside of my little shower cocoon and the fact that Evan started pulling on my wet arm to get me up and out of the tub.

Ben stood behind Evan to help her if she needed it and I had to give him credit for being as cool as she'd been. The mild realization that neither of them had seen me completely naked before that moment floated blissfully around my head then flew away, and I took to enjoying the care and concern instead.

"Here," Ben said handing Evan my towel.

She took it from him and wrapped me in it. "Which clothes do you sleep in?"

"Maroon shirt, black sweats," I mumbled slowly rubbing myself dry as she moved away and left Ben to watch me in case I stumbled or needed help.

Evan returned moments later with my clothes. "Alright, put these on and let's get to bed, okay?"

I licked at the roof of my mouth and grumbled at the taste, "Toothbrush."

She sighed but conceded that no one would want to go to bed with lingering vomit in their mouth. She loaded my toothbrush with toothpaste and handed it to me. It felt sloppy like I'd missed a few spots, I knew from my jerky movements, but mint tastes way better than acidic vodka and burrito.

After I'd dressed, Ben took one of my elbows and Evan held the other and they walked me to the long suede couch in the middle of Auntie Betsy's living room. I laid down on my back and nearly passed out on the spot until Evan nudged me.

"Desi, hun, you can't sleep on your back, turn over."

I grumbled indignantly at her for disturbing me, but I turned my head to the side to placate her.

It seemed to do the trick because I slipped into blissful sleep right after that.

The light and movement around the kitchen made me scrunch my eyes tighter together as if they'd be able to block out the need to get up. I stretched unhappily, moving the muscles I hadn't budged throughout the night and blinked slowly to life.

Ben had been doing the same, but he seemed a little angrier about it on his little loveseat to the right of my couch. Evan hadn't been on her couch at all.

"The sleeping beauties are up," Sandy snickered walking from the back hall into the kitchen.

Evan's blonde head poked around the corner of the stairs with a scowl on her face to see Ben and I grumbling at the earliness of the morning. "I didn't sleep at all last night, you know. All because of you. I kept thinking you were gonna throw up again and choke on your own vomit and die and it haunted me!"

I looked sheepishly at her. "Sorry."

"Oh, good. You know the basement smells like throw up now? We may never be able to go down there again," Auntie Betsy joked heartily as her own dark head poked around the corner and then vanished.

My cheeks flushed. "Sorry," I said again wishing I could melt into the sofa I'd been laying on.

"Anyway," she said coming in around the corner with three plates full of scrambled eggs and toast followed closely by Sandy holding three boxes containing large chocolate bunnies. "Happy Easter. I hope you had a fun night besides that."

I smiled at them gratefully and took the plate being offered to me. "Thank you!"

Evan, Ben, and I ate quickly as we had to hit the road and beat as much of the holiday traffic we could. Plus, we heard it was supposed to snow on Monarch, and that'd never do for the Mustang.

But man, I had so much fun besides throwing up.

Hanging out with them. Getting drunk with them and knowing I'd be kissed. In love and adored. That's all I wanted.

It certainly became a weekend of destiny for the three of us.

7

RANGER MISTAKES & EXTREME MARATHONING

"Do you wanna go camping this weekend as a last celebration?" Evan asked us as we all sat in the lounge facing the TV having finished the *Prisoner of Azkaban* and working towards starting *Goblet of Fire*.

"Sure, you wanna go to Blue Mesa again?" Kodi asked thinking about the other times we'd been there that semester, and all the times it'd snowed on us because we were camping in March or April in the mountains.

I couldn't help but think of that, too. We'd go camping with a thirty percent chance of snow and it seemed to snow on us without fail every time. Even Delphinium's birthday had snow in the forecast, but we still set up our tent and cuddled for warmth that night.

"Nah, I was thinking somewhere close like Hartman's or something," she said hoping for a quick getaway with minimal effort.

"Wanna invite Delphinium?" I asked thinking of our fifth friend who'd escaped us in the middle of the movie to go be with Todd.

"Yes, how many more times are we gonna get the chance

to hang out with her if she manages to keep making plans with him like this?" Evan asked frustrated and clearly unhappy that Delphinium hadn't also been spending her time with us and balancing her relationships.

"I'm sure she wouldn't deny a camping trip with us if her birthday was anything to go by. She was drunk enough, at least," Kodi added thinking about St. Patrick's Day and our little fire we'd made in the pavilion grill on the shore of Blue Mesa.

"Oh, god, Delphinium and alcohol. That night was crazy and will hopefully never happen again," Evan said, and I imagined the mess that Delphinium had been and how she'd tried hitting on me as we were huddled for warmth in the snowfall that happened that night, too.

"Camping it is," I said believing that a getaway from town would be exactly what we needed as a last hurrah with each other before our freshman year ended.

With Delphinium in tow, we made our way to the outskirts of town up into the recreation park to find a nice place to set up camp.

"Oh, what about that one?" Kodi said pointing to a nice flat clearing that had a large blue port-o-potty standing to the side of it.

"I wondah why that's theah?" Delphinium mused pointing out the outhouse as the five of us clamored out and stretched from being crammed into Evan's Mustang together.

"I bet they had a race or something this morning," Evan said popping her trunk and unloading the box with the tent and the bundles of firewood that she handed to Kodi to start getting the fire going. Ben and I helped her put the tent together and Delphinium dug into the beverages we'd brought along to help give her a head start above all of us.

Not that she needed it.

I considered how far she'd come from the girl I had to convince to start drinking if I'd started drinking, too. I thought about how she'd been so right about how she knew she'd turn into an alcoholic like her mother in that she couldn't stop drinking once she'd started. How she only knew her boundaries with alcohol if we told her what they were and that she'd still drink beyond them.

I sighed knowing it'd be another night of us babysitting her, but I don't think any of us truly minded. She'd proved to be tons of fun up to a certain point, after all.

Once the tent went up and the blankets were down inside, we closed everything up and made for the alcohol and the freshly made fire that Kodi and Delphinium were already huddling around.

"Seems weird that we're already here," Evan mused thinking about everything we'd done over our first year in college.

"Don't say that! I can't even bear to think that it's practically over. What am I gonna do all summer without you guys?" I asked earnestly, and each of them nodded their heads in agreement. It definitely wouldn't be the same after I left the state even if only for a summer.

"Do you remember that blanket fort we made that pretty much sealed us in as our group? I don't think any other freshman has done the stupid stuff we did," Evan chuckled thoughtfully holding her hands up to the fire to warm them a little more.

Ben laughed. "Pretty dumb. And that motel in Salida."

Evan and I laughed at that. Only we could have enjoyed

such uncontrollable hysterical laughter for no reason at all in a motel.

"And what about Kodi's bahfday?" Delphinium added, and we all laughed at that remembering how drunk Kodi had been.

"I haven't thought about Anderson in a long time," Evan mentioned, and we all nodded. "I wonder how many more of our friends won't be back next year?"

We sat quietly hoping the answer would be none, but already knowing that Ben had been talking about not returning for sophomore year.

I sighed, "Here's to good friends."

Everyone else held out their glasses over the small fire and clinked them against mine before we all drank.

"Did you ever start talking to Simon again?" Kodi asked me taking a second swig from her bottle.

"No, he's got a fiancée now, I think," I admitted pursing my lips at the mention of him.

"Ew! Who would ever want to marry Simon?" Evan asked as an ugly contemptuous snarl marred her features and we sat around the fire.

"Good question," I stated coolly as Delphinium laid her head on my shoulder. "I barely even dated him."

"Your stupidity," she mocked, but I ignored her as I had the past year of her throwing that choice in my face.

I'd learned a lot about Evan and the rest of our group of friends throughout the year. We were all misfits in some way, and that only cemented us together more.

Kodi would always follow Evan, especially after the two of them dated for the few weeks they did, and she always looked for opportunities to take care of her. Despite the fact that she sometimes tried to undermine me in little ways out of jealousy since I was clearly closer to Evan, I didn't mind her attempts at mothering.

Delphinium attached herself to me as one of the few people in her life that actually cared and wanted her around as a friend. I wished she'd pick better men to date, but I didn't think Todd would be around for very long. He was way older and on a totally different life path from us. He wouldn't be sticking around.

Evan, Ben, and I were the core of the group, though. After our trip over Easter, I wouldn't have been surprised if we ended up buying a house in the future and living together and inviting the others to come along. It became a dream of mine as I got to know them all. We complimented each other well.

Darkness fell on our camp on the mountain. We were between rounds when a pair of headlights came over the hill towards us.

"Shit," Evan growled grabbing our empties and stashing them on the side of the tent. "Delphinium, don't say anything!"

Since I'd been sitting next to her, I put my hand on her knee in support since I knew she'd need it if the newcomers stopped and were anyone questioning our alcohol.

A ranger in a deep green truck pulled up into our little clearing and got out of the driver's seat. I couldn't see him very well in the dimness, but he seemed friendly.

"Hi, I just wanted to check in here before we head off the mountain. What are you guys up to out here?" he asked with a small backwoods accent to his authoritative voice.

"Hi! We're just out celebrating our last week of school," Evan told him, and I glanced at Ben staring blankly into the fire across from us thinking that this truly might be his last week in school ever.

My stomach clenched at the thought and I stuffed it down before it made me feel ill.

"Oh, you're Western students? I wondered if you were high school kids. It's prom tonight and all," he chuckled thinking he'd be catching a bunch of kids skipping out on their prom to get drunk.

We all chuckled in various intensities thinking that so long as he left, we'd be fine to continue underaged drinking ourselves.

"Nope, definitely college kids. Weird to think that it's already their prom, though," Evan agreed, batting her eyes and smiling in the sweetest way she knew how. It looked unnatural on her face.

I admired her ability to speak to authority as she did, though. I would have panicked already.

"Well, you have a good night. I hear it's supposed to snow tonight so be careful," he said glancing at the dark sky before hopping back into his truck and taking off.

"Fuck, that was close," Kodi sighed.

I held similar sentiments.

"Well, that's not gonna stop us. Who needs another beer?" Evan asked digging into the packs we'd stashed in the car.

We continued drinking heavily and paying no attention to the weather that, with our luck, would definitely start snowing on us in the beginning of May.

We only had a week left of freshman year, though, and things were closing far too quickly for my liking.

What if we came back after the summer and things had changed so much for us that we weren't friends anymore? What if we couldn't regain what we'd gotten out of this amazing year in any year to come?

WE'D TAKEN to watching marathons to savor more of our time together especially while Evan worked in the library in the evenings.

I wandered my way from Colorado Hall down the short patch of sidewalk in the gradually dimming evening air to the tall gray building of the library.

The building felt as home to me as my dorm did. It's gray brick and stacks of books held more and more people as finals descended on Western and the students started panicking for last minute grades.

Thankfully, none of us were those kinds of students.

Ben had already been tossing around the idea of not coming back, which hurt all of us more than we cared to let on. Evan had already been devising a plan to get him to stay.

Kodi knew all that she needed for her exams and couldn't be bothered by anything else at that point.

Most of Evan's exams were built around programming which meant projects more than anything else, and I had art to focus on with drawings and PowerPoints ready to present for my exams. A bonus about art classes was that exam days usually consisted of food and parties.

I saw Kodi standing by the IT helpdesk talking with Evan sitting behind it on a tall swivel stool. Evan's observant eyes turned and brightened when they focused on me. Kodi, too, greeted me happily as I saddled up to the counter as we waited for Ben to come in and join us.

"So, now that we've finished *Harry Potter*, what do you wanna watch next? Kodi's been giving me stupid suggestions," Evan told me glowering halfheartedly at Kodi.

"Well, do we have any choices?" I asked thinking about all the amazing things we'd seen together already. They ranged from *HP* to *Saiyuki* and everything in between. I could honestly say that pretty much anything we picked at that moment would definitely be worth our time if we started watching it together.

"Well, nothing where the dog dies, obviously," Evan grumbled shooting Kodi a dirty look that let me know she'd already made that suggestion.

"What? How was I supposed to know you didn't watch movies like that?" she mumbled defensively.

Evan shot her another look before turning to me conspiratorially to explain. "So, remember how I told you about how I formed the Sloths, right?" she whispered just inches from my face as she leaned in close. "Well, they gifted me a puppy before kidnapping me."

Evan glowered at the desk remembering the moment and started picking fuzzies off her sleeve.

"When they had me," she continued, "they had no need for the puppy anymore. They killed it right in front of me, and my life changed forever after that. It's the whole reason I refuse to watch movies where the dog dies."

I searched her face for any kind of emotion and found a small frown as the only indication that she felt anything for it.

"What was that puppy's name?" I asked wishing to kill those people that hurt her myself.

She pursed her lips frowning further. "I will never speak its name again."

I nodded knowing the name alone probably brought up horrible memories for her, so I dropped it in favor of thinking of the next series for us to watch.

"What about *Avatar*?" Evan suggested after some moments in thought.

"Blue monkeys or *Last Airbender*?" Kodi asked frowning.

"*Last Airbender*," Evan clarified, and I was all for that idea.

"Ben!" Kodi chirped, greeting him as he settled on the counter next to me.

"You lost The Game," he sighed in his own humdrum way we'd become accustomed to.

"Ben, what do you think about watching *Avatar: The Last Airbender* with us?" Evan asked him since she'd already gotten confirmations from Kodi and me.

"Yes, definitely," he said quietly, though his immediate confirmation let us know he'd been excited about it.

"Cool, you guys wanna grab one of those study rooms? I'll be in in a sec," Evan said handing us the keyboard for the TV and letting us wander off into the next room while she put someone else on the desk in her place with a request that she come in and help if it started getting busy.

"Are we sure we're gonna be able to finish this in a week?" I asked thinking about how many episodes we'd have to fit in around classes and sleep and packing.

"Who needs sleep?" Kodi scoffed, though the irony of that made me laugh. If anyone in the group loved sleep, Kodi did.

"We'll figure it out," Evan confirmed starting the first episode. "I mean, it's our last week to spend time together before classes end."

She made a valid point. The idea of spending my time in any other way seemed ridiculous to me, honestly. I needed to savor what I could, and time sped up because of that.

Much as we had in every other series we'd watched together, we'd picked up the funniest quotes, disturbed the masses of responsible students cramming last minute knowledge into their overloaded brains, and laughed until our cheeks ached from smiling so hard. It had been everything I'd dreamt of and more and the exhaustion I felt only added to the hilarity of it all.

Because of Evan's most valid point in that we only had a week left with each other, I answered every summons to come over that had been texted to my phone. I packed early in the day after or between exams if I had enough time and managed to shove all my collection of things into a small, closet-sized storage unit with Delphinium's stuff for the summer.

Though Delphinium had been invited to our marathoning, she panicked with the fact that she also wouldn't be seeing Todd over the summer, either, and tried desperately to arrange as much time with him as she could. I couldn't blame her. If I loved anyone else similarly or more than Evan, Kodi, and Ben, I'd have spent my final days with them, too.

Evan hated it, but we still managed. Even with a lack of sleep, which had been our lives basically that entire last week of school, we managed.

I glanced at each of my friends that I hadn't imagined gaining at all when I on-a-whim decided to attend a school thousands of miles from my home. I loved them and would be damned to see us part ways at all.

I made a mental note before leaving to weather any storm that came between us if only to keep them all in my life. *Always.*

PART II

SOPHOMORE

8

A GRILL, TWINS & AN APOCALYPSE DREAM

odi's and Delphinium's apartment became the hub of activity for our little group within the first few weeks of starting our sophomore year at Western. Their apartment faced one of the largest quads on campus that sat surrounded by the gym, Shavano, the student center, and a small building that used to be the old dining hall before the student center had been constructed. They were lucky for the view since the alternative for their building was the parking lot.

Evan, Kodi, and I happened to catch Delphinium at a time that Todd was busy with something. I knew she loathed her time away from him since she was so *in love*, but I held a firm belief that some time apart is good for relationships no matter how attached you are.

Delphinium's hair was a bit lighter than Evan's from her time in the sun over the summer, and their blonde was way lighter than Kodi's on any day. It hung a touch shorter than my rapidly growing locks, too, but her hair was much curlier than mine.

She had the kind of blue eyes that always seemed to

want to twinkle but never quite got there and a set of crooked teeth that made her Rhotacism worse since they got in the way of her tongue as she spoke. On top of that, her voice carried an ever-present whiny sound which made it difficult for her to make any friends.

Why she started pushing all of us away linked directly to Delphinium's boyfriend, Todd, and that made Evan angrier by the day because her purposefully placed control over her friends, that we mostly ignored, dwindled in Delphinium by the second.

Taking advantage of the little time we had with her, we decided to use the metal barbecues set up outside the building for a small cookout. Evan and Kodi enjoyed grilling, and as far as I'd seen, Evan never cooked anything unless it went on a grill.

They got to work preparing the steaks and what Evan considered the greatest things you could actually make on a grill: aluminum foil banana s'mores.

Kodi doused the charcoal in the grill with liquid fire starter and packed a few more pieces of paper between the grates like she was making the fire for Delphinium's birthday last year. She had a propensity to go way overboard when fire-building or cooking was involved, and here we'd gained more than a motherload from her.

"Jesus, Kodi! This isn't Delphinium's birthday! We actually have to cook stuff on this," Evan chided causing Kodi to stop stuffing the poor grill and sit back a little dejected as her short hair flopped over her forehead.

I sniggered at her kicked puppy pout that she wore a little too well. Kodi could never do anything right in Evan's eyes, but I knew this time she had actually failed.

That didn't stop her from trying harder, of course.

"Well, we'll just have to burn it off now," Evan sighed

inspecting the damage and realizing nothing could be done to save it at that point. She lit a match and dropped it into the little grill. "Here's to hoping things don't taste like fire fuel."

The tinder in the grill lit quickly with a loud *whoosh*, and all the tinder in the grill burned hot and fast. Delphinium and I stepped back slightly looking uneasily at the flames that continued to lick too high out of the metal bucket before Evan walked over to speak with us.

"Kodi!" she exclaimed exasperated glancing back once. Kodi, before the grill was even hot enough, whipped out the steaks and threw them onto the grate while Evan had her back turned as she spoke to the two of us.

"What? It'll be fine!" Kodi explained nonchalantly sticking another one on where it gave more of a fizzle of torture than a sizzle which definitely told all of us exactly how impatient she was while she'd been trying to prove to Evan that she could actually do something. On top of that, Kodi tended to be a little too stupid to stop herself sometimes.

Evan barely contained the facepalm that we all were feeling as Kodi placed another cut on the grill.

Fizzle...Death.

She heaved a sigh, "Good fucking thing stupidity isn't contagious. At least she won't ruin the chocolate-banana goodness of the s'mores. They're made individually so you can do it yourself."

Delphinium and I nodded as we watched Kodi continue to poke at the steaks on the grate in a way that I imagined she thought tested their doneness. *Poor, stupid Kodi.*

"Damnit, can you not do anything by yourself?" Evan cried walking back to Kodi's side to elbow her out of the way so that she'd leave the meat alone while it cooked. It'd be a slow process at the rate we were going which Kodi made even slower with her incessant pestering.

Once the meat seemed to be done, at least according to Kodi, we each got a cut on our paper plates that sagged beneath the weight of the meat and sat around the picnic table the school had placed near the grills.

It may have been the grill deceiving me, but the steak smelled a lot like fire starter as it sat limp and unappealing on my plate.

I cut a bite and coughed. *Definitely not the grill.*

The steaks had been ruined by the unnecessary fire-building materials in the pit that Evan had been trying to burn off before we'd started cooking.

Evan took a bite and immediately spit it back out coughing and growling. "What the *fuck*?"

"It's not that bad," Kodi said attempting to cover her own tracks while she chewed the piece in her mouth with a painful grimace on her face.

"*Not that bad*? Really? Too stupid to cook even a steak. There goes that perfectly good meal! All that money, wasted," Evan growled pushing her plate away as if it personally offended her.

Kodi continued looking dejected as Delphinium and I pushed our plates away, as well. I don't think a master chef could have saved that meat.

"Now that that's been *ruined*, let's eat something that actually tastes good," Evan sneered at the unpalatable steaks on the table and Kodi.

She pulled out her s'more ingredients from a bag and got to explaining how to make her treat. Cutting us all pieces of foil, she laid hers out on the picnic table. Evan took a banana and sliced it long-ways down the middle. Setting it on the foil, she ripped open the bag of marshmallows and a

Hershey's chocolate bar and began stuffing a whole manner of sweetness around the banana before enclosing the entire thing with the foil it sat on.

Figuring that anything would taste better than the steak Kodi ruined, we follow suit and started sprinkling mini marshmallows and chocolate around our bananas and then wrapping the foil up around the concoction. Sticking them all onto the grill that was now properly warmed up, we waited only moments for everything to melt and warm before taking it off and digging in.

The horrible sweetness of it bit at my teeth, and I felt a few of my taste buds die off right then.

Must not be my day for flavor.

I sighed and picked around the bad stuff to at least enjoy the banana.

"You know, I had a dream about us last night," Evan mentioned as she happily ate her banana boat ignoring Kodi as she discarded her own steak in favor of the banana boat ingredients. "It started right here at this window, actually."

Delphinium seemed to be fine with her treat while nibbling away and Kodi sulked, but Evan certainly had our attention.

I continued to pick at my banana while avoiding the rest and looked up at the brick building in front of me. It blocked out the sun from the west, and I admired the beauty of the day as I sat and listened.

"It was us and Ben," she explained motioning to our little group of friends. "We were hanging out here and we needed to go to Iceland, but all of us couldn't go for some reason and because we didn't go to Iceland the world ended."

"Really? Why Iceland?" I asked playing around with my marshmallows and chocolate before it hardened.

"The economy is bad, obviously, and we could have saved them if we'd gone, but because we didn't, they collapsed, and the rest of the world went with them."

"Huh," I shrugged not knowing much about the world economy.

"Anyway, it started with Delphinium being shot through your apartment window which signaled the apocalypse."

"Wait, I died?" Delphinium asked incredulously. Her eyes got really big when she said it and it seemed that hadn't been the news she'd been hoping for.

Evan looked sheepish, "I can't control what happens in my dreams!"

"I get that, I guess," she said frowning a little.

"So, Kodi, Ben, Desi, and me all clamor through the window and there are zombies coming towards us, and we're thrust into the fray. People are fighting everywhere, lots of them were dying and years passed of the world being like this and we were all so badass.

"We all looked like we'd been fighting a war, too. Ben was fucking crazy muscular, Kodi looked even more like a boy than she does now, and Desi had this scar that ran across her face that was the coolest battle scar I'd ever seen. Seriously, it looked awesome on you. Fucking gorgeous."

"Wait, where was the scar?" I asked feeling empowered by her story and driven to be more beautiful if only for her.

Evan lifted her finger to my face touching a point above my left eyebrow and tracing lightly across my eye over the bridge of my nose to a point in the middle of my jaw on the right side. She left a tingling trail where her finger had been, and I kept my eyes closed relishing the feeling as it lingered and faded away.

I must have that scar, I thought wondering if it might exist on a Desi in another universe. I imagined it being as clean and beautiful as the one on Evan's left arm.

"Anyway, I woke up after that, but to prevent the apocalypse from happening, what would you think of making a trip to Iceland?"

If Ben wanted to, we were all game for Iceland, too.

Delphinium left us to be with Todd shortly after that and darkness fell over the mountains. The three of us felt a little disappointed in our dwindling group as Ben had dropped out of school and moved back to his parents on the Front Range and Todd gained further control over Delphinium as the days passed.

I thought about how the group had been before we'd left each other last year. How Delphinium had cried uncontrollably about missing us for her summer away. That each of us would be keeping in touch though I wouldn't be able to see any of them face to face until I came back to school again. Now that we were here, it wasn't what it had been, and all of us knew it.

We cleaned up the picnic area we'd been using, having to scrap pretty much everything we'd attempted to cook and decided on a walk around the buildings since it was still a beautiful summer night in the mountains.

"I have something to tell you, but for their sake, you can't tell anyone," Evan told me as we walked together with Kodi trailing behind as Evan's scolded puppy.

Kodi's ears perked at her words and interjected, "Are you sure you wanna say that?"

We slowed to a crawl in our walk as Evan and I both looked at Kodi. Evan seemed to consider her for the barest moment before a frown creased her brow. I wished desperately for Kodi to back the fuck off and let her tell me whatever it was she needed to say.

Secrets were my jam. I collected them like I breathed. Plus, Kodi couldn't know more about Evan than me.

"Are you sure?" she prodded again.

Shut up, Kodi! I'm trying to learn things.

I willed her into silence at the same moment Evan opened her mouth. "Yes, I'm fucking sure! Don't pretend like you know anything," she snapped, and Kodi shrank back at her words. She knew as well as I not to dig a deeper hole than the one you'd gotten into when it came to Evan.

I turned to her expectantly though trying not to seem overeager.

She looked down once more and made a decided nod.

"I have twins," she told me as we stopped our walk completely.

I frowned at her taken slightly aback.

"Well, they aren't mine in the sense that I didn't give birth to them, but they're seven and mine and Hatsu's," she explained further.

Still I felt confused by the news and waited for her to elaborate. She'd told us about her group of friends/allies back home and how Hatsu seemed to be the closest to her after all that they'd been through that I knew about, but there had never been any mention of twins.

She looked away from me and put her hand up to rub the back of her neck in thought. "So, their parents were a part of the Sloths and got into a bad car accident a while back and both were killed. It was horrible, and I cried forever, but it was lucky the boys didn't die. Hatsu and I are their godparents and now we have custody of them."

"How's that working with you being here at school?" I asked wondering how she felt about being thrust into any form of motherhood. I'd have panicked, and I knew to some degree that she didn't actually want any children of her own.

"Hatsu and the Sloths have them," she explained. "They're staying with my parents right now and will probably move around amongst the houses throughout the year as they have since we became their guardians."

I shrugged. It didn't seem like a stable environment for two newly orphaned boys, but I wasn't going to tell her that. I'm sure she did the best she could for them at any rate. "What are their names?"

Evan raised her eyebrows at me. *Was she shocked I'd ask?* "Hatsu and I changed their names when we got them because their parents gave them stupid names at birth. Hatsu picked Kel and I picked Kyo. Kel's a little mellower and Kyo is a hot head. I named him after the character in *Fruits Basket*."

I nodded knowing she'd gained many of her name choices from that series including Hatsu's. "Thanks for telling me."

"Yeah," she nodded feeling more secure in her choice to tell me about them. I wouldn't judge her for it, she knew that.

Kodi's worry over Evan telling me about them puzzled me, though. I considered putting more distance between the two of us if she felt that mistrustful of me. Not like she offered me much of anything, anyway, as far as it concerns our friendship, at least. It seemed like I'd need to be more careful of her attempting to undermine me in favor of Evan.

We continued our walk as I plotted out how to gain more leverage on Kodi that she'd be unable to stop me in the future if more information came up like this.

9

RESLIFE RELATIONS

If rules seem ludicrous, I have the propensity to break them. The most difficult thing about going in and working for Residence Life on campus had to be that I'd already been breaking the rules I'd been set to enforce for the incoming students.

I worked alongside my RA, the very same James Wilde I'd been crushing on in our freshman art classes, as a Peer Advisor. I lived in the dorms, the very same Crystal Hall I'd spent almost all of my waking hours in as a freshman, and much as I had all of freshman year, I broke the rules.

- Letting residents party on campus
- Drinking on campus
- Smoking on campus
- Partying with residents
- Partying with residents *on campus*
- Getting involved with residents and colleagues

There are plenty of others, I'm sure, but those are the big six.

Ah, the beautiful things that can happen while putting well-being over authority.

The greatest thing about having James as my RA happened to be the wonderful fact that Kayla worked for ResLife, too, and lived all the way across campus. All the feelings I'd harbored for him out of sheer jealousy for what Kayla got to do with him now fell into my lap. Who knew?

I like to call sophomore year the year that my dreams came true for me.

Our residents were a bunch of partiers and troublemakers. Of course, the snow-junkies usually were. None of that mattered, though, because they were ours and the hall had been set up almost the same as Evan and Kayla's hall the first year. One little corner of girls to a hall full of boys.

James barely came out of his room for anything besides classes, and I didn't blame him. He preferred leaving his door open and allowing people to come in and see him if they needed him. I followed suit, but I usually enticed people to stop by with a bowl of candy that didn't last very long when it went out.

Since James and I also had classes together, we spent almost all our time together. I took it a step further and visited him in his room a few doors down the hall from mine.

Knocking on his lightly stained wooden door, I waited patiently while I heard him rustle around before coming to open it.

"Hey!" he greeted opening the door wider and walking back inside expecting me to follow in after him. His snake bites had been changed into black rings with balls in the middle of each one. He'd shaved recently, too, and let his face get kind of scruffy as it grew back.

My favorite.

I followed him in and heard the door click shut behind me. "How's it goin'?" I asked glancing around his room.

"Oh, it's goin'," he smirked in his typical fashion.

He moved into the open area of his private room that I'd coveted a little since it had twice as much space as mine and every other room on the floor. He sat in the black circular hammock chair he'd placed between his bed and his decent-sized TV. He had more space than he knew what to do with in his room. I'd only ever seen him utilize the space around his bed and the entry. That, of course, didn't mean he couldn't decorate his walls.

He had a blacklight Marley poster, several Grateful Dead tapestries, American, German and Nazi flags, and a Sublime tapestry. I knew of his German descent from the various conversations we'd had where he'd informed me that his two Scotties were trained solely with German commands. He loved them more than anything in the world except his grandma who he spoke fondly of as she'd been dying of cancer.

I understood pride in heritage, but I had to question the Nazi flag on more than one occasion. While he didn't claim White Supremacy for himself, he'd told me that he'd hung it to remind himself to learn from the history that no one should erase. I'd accepted the answer since I knew he kept reminders like that all over and even tattooed a spider on his body for a similar reason.

I'd worn my slippers to his room and kicked them off as I laid on his bed to watch the latest episode of whatever series he'd happened to be watching. The growl of car engines sounded on the screen and Jeremy, James May and Hammond popped up on the screen driving RVs.

Top Gear.

"I was about to flip over to *Assassin's Creed*. Almost got all the puzzles collected and completed," he told me as we worked through finishing the episode before we switched over.

Netflix and video games were James' jam, and I'd helped him solve a few of the puzzles he'd been trying to unlock, so I let him pick his preferred entertainment so long as he continued including me in the choice.

"Get stuck on any of them since I last saw you?" I asked.

"Nothing that I couldn't YouTube through," he admitted as the ending credits rolled and he flipped the Xbox over to the game already in the console.

"That's cheating," I scoffed at him.

"Hey! It's just for the badges. Doesn't mean anything."

I rolled my eyes at him and watched him log into the game and play. We'd spent hours in his space learning and growing from each other. I'd grown to like him again and thoroughly enjoyed his company. Sometimes, I thought he liked me in the same way, but I couldn't be sure with some of the things he did around me.

One of my most recent efforts in displaying my affection to him had been in the form of tracing patterns over his shoulders while he played. I'd reach out my hand and move my fingers lightly over his shirt covered back, arms, chest, and head; anywhere that didn't ruin his concentration. He'd remove his hat more often than not so that I could play with his hair as he grew it out and he'd let me run my fingers through his reddish beard. He'd even ask for massages sometimes which I happily gave him if it meant he'd come sit on the bed and let me sit against his back while I rubbed his shoulders.

"Tell me something I don't know about you," I requested stretching for a moment before continuing to trace patterns across his arm.

"What do you want to know?" he asked as he watched his character jump across a large gap in the buildings and make it safely across.

"I don't know. Whatever you wanna share, I guess."

He considered that for a moment before answering me, "So, I belong to a gang that's actually not as horrible as you might think, but it's helped me through some stuff and I'm glad I joined."

I paused staring at the side of his head. *What is it with Coloradans and gangs?*

"Can you tell me which one?" I asked him curiously knowing that the likelihood of him having anything to do with the gang Evan *ran* was pretty slim but needing to know anyway.

"Sure," he said pausing the game to grab his phone. He pulled up some pictures of the Southside logo, and I watched him as he flipped through each one.

Switching gears, I turned to him thoughtfully again. "James, you're free to tell me no if you want, but I've been wondering what your deepest darkest secret is," I told him as I ran one painted nail in a squiggle down his bicep while he started the game again and moved his character over the rooftops of the buildings.

"No, I don't mind," he said pausing the game for a moment to turn and face me. "You'd be the only one I've ever told this to, but I have a son. I'm surprised more people don't ask that question, actually."

He said it so casually that my eyebrows shot up into my hairline. "Where does he live? How often do you see him?" I asked.

James shrugged. "I don't normally. She went ahead with it knowing I wasn't really into the whole dad thing. Still not, really. I've met him a bunch of times, but he refers to me as 'Uncle James,' and I don't mind it."

"How could you not want to be a part of your son's life? How do you know he's yours?" I asked incredulously.

"Oh, he looks just like me. It's unmistakable. I'm just way too young to be a dad and I really never wanted kids. It's just easier this way."

I knew his dad hadn't been super great to his older brother, either, but it by no means meant that he had to follow the trend. Plus, I felt bad for her.

I considered that news for a moment in silence. I searched his face for any sign of remorse or curiosity for a person he'd helped create, but nothing showed up. He'd made his peace with it.

"What about you? What's your big secret?" he asked me as he turned back to the screen and picked up running over the rooftops where he'd left off.

I knew he'd ask, but I couldn't say which of my deepest and darkest secrets I could share with him. Since he'd honored me in answering truthfully, and it'd been something that I, as an outsider, had been privileged enough to learn, it couldn't just be any secret. He deserved something of equal value in return, at least. I could give him something.

"Mine's similar to yours," I confessed at last.

"You have a kid?" he nearly shouted at me in shock before he reeled himself back in and paused the game again.

"No," I told him, and he relaxed back into his chair. "I've been pregnant before."

He frowned at me, "Did you abort it?"

"Miscarried," I admitted a little sadly. Weird since I actually didn't want kids, either.

"Oh, I'm sorry about that. What made you want to keep it?" he asked.

I pursed my lips before answering, "It didn't feel right to do anything else."

He nodded as if he understood that personal dilemma. Heck, maybe he'd encountered it with his baby mama for all I could guess. He understood enough not to judge the decision, though. I smiled gratefully at him for it.

We chatted about other things that evening, too. He'd been telling me more and more about the things that he liked both in and out of the bedroom. He loved cars and the color purple but not as much as metallic cherry red. He'd even been designing things for airbrush and asked me for ideas for his logo.

He showed me his trip pants and told me about how he'd been a rave dancer and knew how to do all the moves that the people in the YouTube videos he showed me knew how to do, though he'd never actually show me the moves himself out of embarrassment.

Most importantly, he started telling me about his kinks, and boy, that kid had some interesting ones.

He'd slowly introduced me to his collection of porn. It started tame at first, nothing I hadn't seen in passing before. Then, he upgraded me to men cumming with prostate massages, which still weren't anything I was unfamiliar with. Once he knew none of that scared me off, we got into the truly raunchy stuff.

He sent me a text with a link to a porn he really liked. Despite sketchy porn sites and all, I waited until I'd made it back to my room before I'd opened it.

Horse Porn.

I had no judgments for James and the things that turned

him on, but some people are ridiculous, and I had to wonder how he'd gotten into that in the first place.

When I didn't run away from that, he upgraded me *again* to the darkest parts of the porn-sphere that I'd only ever encountered as an innocent 15-year-old in high school being exposed to *The Pain Olympics* for the first time. I'm not even sure I'd started watching actual porn by then, honestly.

James sent me a link to these transvestites with boobs and penises that were so large that they couldn't be anything but fake, and the whole video had been cumshots strung together like they were practically popping champagne for the ejaculation scenes. He'd sent me an entire video to show me what truly, amazingly turned him on, and it took a montage of all the other videos to be sure that an attraction to trannies and having things in your butt were his thing.

What we do for the people, dare I say it...we love?

I'd walked over to his room almost directly after that to ask him about it, and he pulled more up on his TV screen to show me as if he were offhandedly turning on the weather. Whatever tickles your fancy, I suppose. I certainly didn't have the dick he seemed to be searching for.

This moment of being in his room watching him play Assassin's Creed and hanging out as we'd done for months of being neighbors gave me a chance to contemplate all of it. They were huge pieces of information he'd entrusted me with and I only yearned for more moments with more people that would yield me so many other intimate details. People could be so *fascinating* as James continued proving to me.

"Wanna know something else?" he asked turning off the game and flipping back to Netflix. "I've had this...*craving* to get a blowjob while I'm sleeping."

I frowned at him, "Doesn't that defeat the enjoyment of a blowjob?"

"No! Can you imagine how intense that dream would be?" he groaned in longing for that particular scenario and I questioned why he'd told me. As far as I knew, despite my own speculations, he didn't like me like that.

"Hmm," I mused, "are you asking me to do that for you?"

"Would you?" he asked without missing a beat. He didn't seem turned off by it in the least.

"If you asked me then yeah."

He hopped up on the bed next to me and turned off the TV before lying back on the right side of the two twin beds he'd pushed together, flipping off the lights, undoing his belt, and laying down to sleep.

"That's hardly asking," I mumbled waiting a few minutes and several heartbeats to see if he'd pop back up again and admit he'd only been joking with me and that my face had been *so* priceless for it.

Instead, he lay motionless and no amount of poking at him or softly calling his name seemed to rouse him.

Seems alright to proceed, I thought touching the front of his pants gently before I started undoing the button and zipper there. My heart beat frantically like the wings of a bird against the bars of its cage. The terror in waking him sat heavily on my mind if only for the fact that it'd be exceptionally embarrassing getting caught in the middle of any of this. I couldn't help imagining several rape scenarios for a minute that I had to breathe through since he'd been the one to ask for it in the first place.

Consent is important. I know, and I had it. Stop freaking out!

James didn't stir in the slightest, though. I managed to get the pants undone without incident, but he lay as limply as a fresh-cooked noodle. The flaw in his plans came all the way down to being absolutely unable to sync his dreams with his reality, but we'd gotten all the way to catching him with his pants down, so I had to try something.

I glanced over his plaid boxers and realized they didn't have a button over the hole in the front. As delicately as I could, I felt around and managed to pull him out where he remained quite flaccid even while being moved around.

I considered James' limp dick for a moment before leaning down and placing a kiss on him. James didn't wake up and the dick didn't move in the least.

I held him and licked up the front of him. It got a little more of a response, but barely enough to consider doing anything else with it.

I took the whole of James' penis into my mouth and started sucking. That seemed to do a little more for me. He even got hard for the barest of seconds, but as soon as I pulled away, he went limp once more.

What the hell, James? Do you want it or don't you?

I tried again to make him hard, but I couldn't get him to stay alert while the rest of him lay relaxed on the bed. Seemed he'd stay as dead to the world as James while he slept. *I give up.*

Tucking him back into his boxers, I made sure James hadn't ended up in any awkward positions before I left him. I paused taking in how adorable James looked while he slept. His lips parted slightly and his hair, though not so long, splayed around his head, and his chest rose and fell with each calm breath.

He'll never know, I thought.

I leaned down again and lightly pecked him on the mouth with a kiss. Then, I left deciding not to stick around and see if he ever happened to wake up again that evening.

Did you do it? He texted about an hour after I'd left him. *Apparently, he'd woken up.*

Yeah. I responded. I wondered if he'd asked because it hadn't provided the effect he'd been desiring.

Did I cum? He asked.

I thought a moment. I didn't really want to disappoint him.

Yes. I lied.

I waited a while wondering if he'd respond or *how* he'd respond.

Would you come back and do it again? He asked me, and I couldn't believe he did.

In your sleep?

No, awake. He responded, and my eyebrows raised slowly up on my forehead in surprise.

I thought for another moment.

I think we should talk about what this is. I told him hoping to see where we might go from there.

He had to pause, then. **Yeah, I guess.**

Considering that I did not want to go back over to his place, I left it at that and knew I'd be seeing him the next day.

That topic of conversation never came up for me the next day, though.

"Hey! Can I come in?" James asked breathlessly. He grinned cheekily. I wondered if he'd run from somewhere.

"Sure. What's up?" I prodded thinking I'd finally get the answers I'd desired from him.

"I met a girl!" he told me excitedly, and my heart did a freefall for a brief second before I could pull it together again.

A girl? I didn't even know he was courting anyone!

"We've been eating together for the past few days and I

think I'm gonna ask her out," he explained not bothering to move more than a few feet into the space of my room.

I placed a firm fake smile on my face before answering him. I know that my own want for his happiness felt genuine, but the fact that I hadn't been chosen to provide that happiness myself made the fire burn in my belly and I couldn't show him that kind of fury as one of his best friends.

"That's great," I lied paying close attention to the muscles around my eyes as to not give more away than necessary. "Tell me about her."

"I will, but she's coming over tonight, so later," he admitted before he moved to exit my space. "Her name is Jordan, though, and I think you'd like her."

I considered the name and the girl and James as he left knowing that I wouldn't be hanging out in his room that evening. Probably best since I'd only be sulking that night, anyway.

10

THE WRONG PEOPLE

"So, I convinced a friend from high school to come up for school. She's an honorary Sloth, and she's been told to report on anything that threatens the organization, so it'd be cool if you didn't talk about any of that around her unless I bring it up," Evan pleaded with us as we sat waiting for her friend to arrive.

Patilda Perez didn't seem like much of a gangster to me, though. If honorary only meant that you gained protection and owed them favors, then I could maybe see it, but she and Evan were nothing alike.

Evan had always been a little edgy and dangerous. She let us know things about her life when we needed to know them or when she felt she could trust us enough to let us in a little bit more. Maybe to slowly pull us into the fold, too, but I couldn't be sure.

Perez came off as sweet and insecure about herself. She'd speak softly if she had to and usually always stayed silent if she could help it. I didn't think there was a dangerous bone in her body.

I knew enough about the Sloths to never want their wrath upon me, though, so I complied with Evan's request.

Some people weren't that bright.

As Evan had introduced her to us, Perez and I hit it off pretty quickly. She'd come into our little band of misfits and slowly took the place of Delphinium, since she never came around to hang out with us anymore, and that seemed fine for all of us at the end of the day as Todd continued to morph her into an entirely different person from the one we'd made friends with.

I couldn't help remembering that Ben predicted we'd struggle to maintain the group of five. We'd been sitting in the lounge for the hundredth time of us spending the night on the little armchairs talking, and he'd come out and told me point blank that he found the prospect of a group of five an ideal number of people, but that he'd never been able to maintain it.

I'd told him that wouldn't happen to us, but I found the group struggling shortly after that when Delphinium met Todd.

I hate when he's right.

Perez and I took to hanging out regularly with one another as I had with Delphinium in the beginning. She bonded to me in a similar fashion to the way Delphinium and I became friends, actual human contact, which contrasted to Evan and the fact that she sometimes gained a bit of a God complex and opted out of pleasant encounters when she felt superior to us.

I knew a lot of it had to do with me working for ResLife and having to enforce at least a few of the rules on campus, but I would not let any ridiculous rules stop me from enjoying time with my friends.

Perez unconsciously paraded her quirkiness everywhere she walked. She accentuated her shortness by making herself as small as she could manage in every situation. If she came up to hug you, she'd bend her shoulders and come in to grab around your middle. If you were eating with her, she had the daintiest movements where she'd poke at food quickly with a fork or grab things with her barest fingertips and nibble lightly at it.

Even while walking, she seemed to develop a sort of creeping along as she went as if she were trying to go unnoticed by the others around her.

It worked perfectly for her since she was so keen on living her life in the background, but it drove me a little nuts.

Make a noise or something! Do I need to put a bell on you?

Her silence astounded me, too. You'd think someone as apple-shaped as Perez would lumber even a little bit, even her head lacked the chin and neck structure to differentiate her face from her chest, but I imagined that she used it to make up for her lack of outward femininity. She struggled with that more than she let on.

She did have one thing going for her, though. She won people over with kindness, and that made her vastly different and more favorable compared to Evan or many of the other Sloths as far as I could imagine.

Perez and I had decided to spend dinner at the little café on the lower level of the student center. It had better hours of operation compared to the cafeteria upstairs and some freaking fantastic chicken tenders and curly fries that you couldn't get anywhere else. We both enjoyed the break from the greasier food we'd normally be eating in the dining hall.

In irony, we happened to run into Delphinium and Todd

as we were leaving, and they were coming in to play pool with some of Todd's friends.

Todd was about a decade older than we were and looked it. He hung around campus before even dating Delphinium and in the entire time I'd known him, he hadn't been taking any classes. He came to campus for fun which came off as creepy to all of us after some time.

He looked as apple-shaped as Perez, though I imagined his gut came more from the amount of beer he drank than anything else. He wore a backwards baseball cap with a pair of aerodynamic sunglasses perched on his head that I'd seen him remove only once in the handful of times we'd encountered each other. He'd been using it to hide his thinning hair. On top of that, he had the accent of an uneducated person that's been cooped up in some small mountain town for too long.

He did make Delphinium happy, though, so I couldn't complain too much about him.

Happiness is all that matters, right?

For all she'd been worth, Delphinium's new gaudy stud stuck boldly from the right side of her nose in a space that seemed way too small for such a shiny piece of jewelry. She by no means had a petite nose, but that bad boy sparkled so distractingly that it made you forget that the poor girl had no eyebrows at all.

To my knowledge, Perez hadn't met Delphinium, yet, and she most certainly hadn't met Todd. The three extended pleasantries before Todd turned to me.

"So, uh, wha'd'you think about this gang business Evan's been sellin'?" he queried not even bothering to disguise his voice in the least.

I glanced at Perez and did my best not to look like the cornered rabbit I felt I'd turned into.

Delphinium chuckled uneasily to mirror my feelings, but Todd pressed on.

"Yeah, she's been tellin' Delph all this stuff about some gang bullshit and that she's a boss and I just don' believe it. It's kinda crazy, don'cha think?"

Delphinium and I both chuckled uneasily at that and exchanged a look. He'd walked onto some dangerous ground and he had no idea he'd stepped on it in *gang affiliated* company. I don't even think either of them knew that Perez belonged to the Sloths either.

Perez, though a little stiff, passed it off as nonsense to all of us. She seemed to be shocked by what Todd had said and spoke little more about it. It took Delphinium pulling Todd away for the conversation to end. I don't believe he would have let us leave otherwise.

The rest of the evening went by without incident and everything seemed fine in my world.

Things weren't fine for Todd and Delphinium, though.

She and I met for our weekly study date after her math class and she filled me in on what started happening to them after we'd last seen each other.

Apparently, she and Todd found themselves in the center of a ring of threats and blackmails that came at them from several sides that only ended after a week of the anonymous parties being sure the message was made clear: *Shut up or die.*

Talking out like that about the gang would not be tolerated by anyone, and their lives and the lives of the people they loved depended on their silence.

"If only Todd had kept his stupid mouth shut we wouldn't be in this mess!" she whined as she flipped her blonde hair in agitation. "I love him but come on!"

I sympathized with her, honestly. Some people were too stupid to know anything about time and place.

"What's been happening?" I asked as she turned a few pages of her textbook without reading it. Clearly she felt unsettled.

"We've been getting notes all week. Lettahs thweatening us and our families. And they show up wandomly, too. We can't get away," she told me, and I frowned thinking about it.

Her chomping at the piece of blue gum in her mouth didn't help thinking much, and I went back to floating around in my head for a minute. Puzzling indeed, but I could definitely be glad I wasn't the one in their place.

Hell, I felt uneasy being that close to her right then.

We did our homework together and parted ways shortly after where Delphinium left towards the parking lot behind the math building since Todd said he'd pick her up there after we finished.

Knowing Evan would be finishing her class soon, I wandered down the hall to see her when she got out.

"How was class?" I asked as she joined me.

"Fine. The same," she shrugged as we walked.

"I learned something interesting. Do you have a minute?" I asked as she moved us towards an empty classroom she'd been tasked to fix the projector in.

She got to work but nodded at me to indicate she was listening while she did.

"So, I have a friend that I found out is also in a gang and I wondered if you would tell me if that gang had something to do with yours or not."

Evan paused looking at me considering my proposition before continuing her work, "If you have a name, I'll tell you."

I sighed, "He says he belongs to a gang called Southside."

"That's for sure an enemy. You should not be hanging around whoever your friend is," she confirmed, and the pit of my stomach dropped out in a free fall.

Stop hanging out with James?

"That or cut me out, honestly, because that's serious," she finished glancing at me with death in her eyes.

"Hmm," I mused knowing that I didn't want to lose her, either. *Maybe they just wouldn't need to know about my continued friendships and it'd all work out?* I decided to change the subject instead. "I also saw Delphinium today. She said they've been having...trouble."

Evan glanced at me as her eyes grew cold and calculating and mulled the thought around in her head wondering how to address it to me. "Todd's an idiot, first, but Perez did what she was told to do if ever anything came up in front of her that wasn't sparked by me. She reported it, and they're acting in the best wishes of the Sloths. They should be afraid, though. I could have them killed for spouting off like that in front of everyone."

Killed?

I swallowed hard taking my time thinking that over and knowing that the course of action, though logically flawed and a little overboard, made some sort of sense. They were right in protecting their own and I couldn't argue with that. Though I didn't really want to if it meant my life could be on the line, too.

"When are they really gonna let up?" I asked her knowing she had some sway over what happened to Delphinium even if she still seemed angry at her for choosing Todd over her friends.

"Sometime. I'm not really sure, but that's of little consequence in the grand scheme."

I heaved a sigh and continued on our walk back to the dorms. I wouldn't get anything more from her at the rate we were going, but I'd learned never to say anything about any of them around Perez. As unassuming as she was, that girl didn't mess around when it came to her honorary post.

11

GUMMY BEARS & JELLO-O

"I'm so excited for Ben to get here. What time did he think he'd arrive?" I asked impatiently sitting around waiting for him in the living room of Kodi and Delphinium's campus apartment.

"Soon-ish. Who knows with him. You know he doesn't tell anyone anything," Evan intoned flatly since she felt equally as annoyed by Ben not communicating with us as I was with being forced to wait.

"What do we have to drink?" Kodi asked hoping to kill our time with alcohol.

"Getting an early start?" I asked not all that surprised.

"It's better than waiting around sober," she shrugged slowly standing from the black gaming chair in the middle of the space and opening the fridge. "Hey, do you wanna make the Jell-O shots and gummies now?"

My ears perked, and I considered how much of a time killer it'd be. "Might as well."

Kodi started pulling alcohols out of the fridge and then moved to her cupboards to grab the Jell-O mix. The bag of chewy gummy deliciousness sat on the counter already.

Bbraaaaapp.

"Blue! What flavor?" she asked.

"Yellow!" I cried.

"Dammit!" Evan said before tilting her head back and moaning loudly.

I considered the flavor choices looking at the mix of different colored Jell-O flavor boxes scattered on the counter. Considering that Jell-O shots were a new alcohol experiment of ours and the last ones turned out pretty well, I flipped open my phone to consult Almighty Google and figure out what we could make with the ingredients we had.

"It says there's a Jell-O shot called Pornstar. It's two colors, too."

Kodi leaned over my shoulder to see what I'd found online. "Ooo, let's do that!"

"It's going to take more time because of the layered colors," I explained as she started on doing her dishes so that we'd have some to actually make the shots in.

"Yeah, yeah, but look how cool they look!" she exclaimed tilting her head back towards the screen and the blue and pink Jell-O concoction.

"Fine. You're right," I conceded.

Evan, not paying us much mind, pulled out her laptop and started on some programming work she had for her computer science class.

Pornstar required a blue Jell-O and a red/pink one which meant there were at least two alcohols in it, but knowing that Kodi was involved (and me, too, honestly) we'd probably end up combining as many as we could so long as it tasted fine.

Thankfully, Kodi would be more than willing to do the taste testing for us, too.

We started with the blue first. Kodi had the blue raspberry, which is possibly my favorite flavor of blue-colored anything and after the Jell-O packet dissolved, I killed the burner and added in the cold mixture that'd help the layer set.

"What'd you put in this?" I asked looking skeptically at the pitcher since I hadn't watched her select an alcohol but taking it from her and pouring it in anyway.

"Svedka," she chirped taking the pitcher back and rinsing it for the next batch.

The impressed look on my face must have been enough as she smiled at me sheepishly. "I can control myself sometimes."

Evan snorted from the couch. "Right."

We chuckled a little before pulling out a baking sheet and pouring the Jell-O mixture in.

"Since it's such a thin layer, it shouldn't take very long to harden," I explained as we placed it carefully into Kodi's fridge on top of the myriad of other things that looked like Kodi and Delphinium had been tossing things into the fridge without looking or caring if something else tipped over.

"So, what do we do till then?"

I shrugged and pulled a Smirnoff Ice green apple flavor from the fridge before I closed the door. "We could put the gummy bears in to soak, too."

"Yes!" Kodi exclaimed pulling a plastic Tupperware from her cabinet and handing it to me. We dumped the bag of gummies in and then poured vodka in over them.

"I sure hope these taste good," I considered as the color of the vodka changed slightly pinkish with the contact from the gummies.

"It'll be fine!" Kodi assured though she'd also never made alcoholic gummies before. "What's next?"

Evan closed her laptop and moved it onto the crowded coffee table. "Kodi should finish her dishes since it's disgusting," she stated making Kodi grumble and gripe though she still moved to clear the rest of her sink out. The last time she'd let it get so bad her sink had started growing fruit flies.

To be fair, even after Kodi had washed the few we needed for the Jell-O shot project, the sink still overflowed with dishes to the point that you couldn't even really use the faucet anymore. Definitely a necessary thing that only Evan could get her to work on.

"Have you started watching *Naruto*, yet?" she asked turning to me as I plopped down on the green couch.

I looked away from her sheepishly. She'd been trying to get me to watch it since last year and even though she considered it her favorite, I struggled with finding the time or the will to get into it.

"C'mon! Fine. What would you say to starting it right now while we wait?"

I shrugged. "It's something to do."

Accepting the answer, she grabbed her laptop and started her search for the first episode of *Naruto*.

"So, don't worry about how annoying the characters are right now because they're going to get better in the future. Like way better. If you hate it, *please don't hate it,* we can stop."

I smiled at her concern that I wouldn't like something that I knew she and her whole family were into. The bonus about anime over regular cartoons is that anime actually had a storyline and depth to it and the art was usually way better. I trusted her. I probably wouldn't hate it.

The first episode started, and I got nothing more than "Naruto, the number one hyperactive ninja; I'm going to be Hokage!"

"You're right, he is kind of annoying."

"Yeah, but it definitely gets better. You haven't even seen him become anything, yet," she explained pressing play for the next episode.

Kodi, knowing that she'd be left out and that she'd have to finish the dishes if she wanted to take part at all, did a rush job on the dishes that remained to be able to sit down and watch with us.

Several episodes in, it got better, but we still had the second layer of Pornstar to make, so I asked Evan to put them on hold so that we could at least get things together, and before we'd even finished a knock rang at the apartment door.

We all exchanged quick glances questioning whether it might be an RA since we had alcohol in Kodi's on-campus apartment and we all were underaged, and I did actually work with the RAs and could get in huge trouble if we were caught. Evan got up and peeped through the spyhole in the door.

"Ben!" she cried flinging open the door and dragging him inside.

"Ben!" Kodi and I chorused finishing up the strawberry layer of Jell-O that Kodi had added more vodka and peach schnapps to.

"Hey..." he greeted with an edge of uncertainty as he tended to do whenever he was faced with meeting all of us again.

"How was the drive?" Evan asked moving back to the couch and closing her laptop since none of us were going to want to waste the precious time we had with Ben doing anything besides conversing and making out, hopefully.

"Eh," he shrugged, "pretty normal."

I smiled hearing his quiet voice and slight lisp. Same ol' non-committal Ben I knew and loved.

"We made Jell-O shots!" Kodi told him as he settled into the apartment looking around at everything.

"Are they done?" he inquired, and Kodi made a face of contempt.

"No, maybe another hour. We just finished," I explained handing Ben a Smirnoff Ice of his own and joining him and Evan on the couch.

"Oh, by the way, you all lost The Game."

"Ben!"

"Damn! You ruined my streak!"

"Leave it to Ben to ruin the moment," Evan chided as we laughed.

Just like that, we were back to the way we'd been as if several months hadn't passed since the last time the four of us had seen each other.

I reveled in the familiarity.

"Where's Delphinium?" Ben asked looking around the apartment again and pointedly back at each of us as if we were responsible for the whole of our group being together and one of us had forgotten to pass the memo.

Kodi and Evan looked away sneering.

"Todd," I explained. "She said she'd be able to hang out later this weekend, though."

The hope in my voice lifted our moods minutely, but we'd practically given up on Delphinium completely at that point. With the little bit we'd seen of her since the semester started, it'd become clear to all of us where her priorities lay.

"I still hate him," Evan said as she pulled another swig from the bottle she'd had Kodi grab for her earlier.

We nodded our agreement but couldn't let that ruin our moods.

"What are we having for dinner?" I asked offering a new, more important topic.

"Chinese?" Kodi asked. "They deliver."

God bless college towns.

Evan got on the phone and called up the Double Dragon. "Hi, can I place an order for delivery?"

Chinese food is one of those things that you get a favorite and stick with that favorite. None of us needed to look at a menu as we'd already found our Chinese food of choice. Double Dragon did well with everything on their menu, but it wouldn't change the order in the least.

"Sweet and sour chicken."

"Potstickers, beef and vegetables."

"Shrimp fried rice."

Evan shot us all an annoyed glance.

"Yeah, can I get wonton soup, two orders of potsticker, shrimp fried rice, beef and vegetables, sweet and sour chicken, and orange chicken?" she asked looking down at the coffee table in concentration.

"Hold on," she said pulling the phone from her ear. "White rice, right?"

"Yeah," we all chimed.

"Yes, white rice," she said returning to the phone. She told them our address and that she'd pay with a credit card and hung up the phone.

"Should be here in, like, thirty minutes."

"Cool," I said before settling further into the sofa.

We chatted amicably until the food arrived and around that time the Jell-O shots had set as well.

Granted, they weren't actually shots, and we were probably just going to scoop spoonfuls out of the tray, but none of it mattered now that Ben had made it.

With full bellies and a nice buzz, the real fun began.

"We should play a game!" Kodi said after scooping herself another colorful spoonful of Pornstar.

"I lost The Game," Evan chuckled.

We all groaned having lost, too.

"What do you want to play?" I asked taking another swig from my bottle and playing around the rim with my tongue.

Definitely intoxicated.

"I just got all those glow in the dark makeup crayons. We should paint our faces!" Evan cheerfully suggested as we mulled more ideas around.

"Yes!" Kodi agreed getting out of the gaming chair and wandering to her room down the hall. She brought back a bag and handed it to Evan.

"Yay!" Evan exclaimed pulling her packet of goodies out and tearing it open to hand each of us a crayon.

Slowly, we began to draw not only on ourselves but also on the various surfaces of the apartment. Ben got the worst of it since he complained and resisted very little, and we were soon basking in the lights before killing them and viewing our creation.

Evan had taken to marking up her hands and grabbing Ben's chest so that it looked like his non-existent boobs had been groped. Kodi started drawing patterns on her face in the mirror. I, being the least inclined to want crayon on my skin, started drawing on the various objects on the coffee table including the empty schnapps bottle.

"Hey, we should play spin the bottle!" I said holding up the one I'd been decorating.

"Yes!" Kodi agreed excitedly.

Evan soaked the bottle in light for a minute before setting it on the ground and killing the lights. You couldn't see it very well, but we'd figure it out.

"Who goes first?"

"Ben," Evan volunteered which seemed perfectly fine for all of us girls since we all, in some way or another, desired kissing Ben and had yet to have the luxury of doing so even with all the fun we'd had freshman year. I'm pretty sure I was the only one privileged enough to have kissed him besides Evan by that point.

I imagined Ben shooting Evan a dirty look in the dark before taking the faintly glowing bottle and spinning it.

It landed on Kodi.

Had it been light in the room, I imagine Evan and I would have exchanged a look right then, but darkness prevailed, and we couldn't sympathize with each other without speaking and giving away our thoughts to everyone present.

"Kodi's turn," I said stopping the makeout session going on next to me.

Ben sat back and Kodi spun.

It landed on Evan.

Jealousy, the green-eyed monster, crept his way to the forefront of my mind with each passing spin in which my friends were getting to make out with my other friends and I wasn't.

Nearing the end, it came down to one obvious point: The spins were rigged and Kodi and Ben had ended up spinning each other more times than Evan and I had even been graced with spins.

Damn.

By that point, we were all fully intoxicated and the making out became a more in-depth approach to the exploration of each other's mouths. We all tasted somewhat like the fruity Jell-O, but the distinctness of Kodi tasting something like Cap'n Crunch stuck out. She'd concluded that the combination of Cheetos and Jell-O did the trick.

Evan kissed the best, in my opinion. We understood each other more than I can explain in words and I relished each moment of tongue-play.

Finished with the game, Evan flicked on a side table lamp sitting next to the couch and lounged across it to relax a while. "We should tell stories."

Knowing that none of us had stories to compare to Evan's, we all looked at her expectantly. She suggested it after all.

"I want to hear your life story," I implored when she didn't respond to our looks.

Lying fully on the couch with her legs propped up on the armrest, she tilted her head to look over at me. "It's not that interesting," she stated trying to deflect my interest.

I scoffed at her, "Right. Not that interesting. Sure."

"I wouldn't even be able to do it justice in my current state of drunkenness," she tried to explain, but they were all measly excuses. I didn't think she actually wanted to talk her way out with how wishy-washy they seemed.

I thought about it for a moment. "Fine, tell us what you can tonight, and we can pick it up at later times. You could even write a memo to yourself so that you don't forget in the future."

She sighed unwilling to argue the point further. "Alright, give me your phone."

I smiled and handed her my old sliding keyboard phone. She opened it and started typing a note to herself before handing it back to me.

I promise Desi that I will

tell her my life story in full

detail and without skipping

over anything important.

-TeiLuce

Kodi peeked at it over my shoulder and looked to Evan concerned. "Are you sure you wanna do that?"

Again with the information blocking. What the Fuck, Kodi?

"Yes, I'm sure!" Evan snarled drunk and unhappy. She seemed as angry with Kodi for questioning her judgment as I was with her trying to kill my knowledge hoarding. "Okay, where to begin?"

Evan lay across the couch dramatically as if she were on a therapist's lounger and she'd planned on telling us the many woes of her life.

We had nothing but the deep yellow lighting of a tall corner lamp for company as Kodi, Ben, and I gathered near her to listen to a story the three of us had been dying to hear since bits and pieces of it had leapt from her mouth at various, inopportune moments where she couldn't delve any further into them. I found myself in the black gaming chair across from the couch. Kodi sat on my right leaning against the beat up black coffee table that surprisingly held her weight. Ben found a spare wooden chair with faded green upholstery and perched himself on it near the end of the green couch looking intently at Evan as she played with the hem of her too-big blue t-shirt.

"You want me to start from the very beginning?" she asked me hesitantly.

I nodded. "Please."

"You already know a lot of the start," she told me confirming to me that she felt scared to tell us this story. I probably would have been, too, if I'd lived the life she had.

"It's okay," I told her, "tell us what needs to be said."

"Hmm...Have I ever told you about the Bernards?" Evan asked getting a round of no's and head-shaking from the three of us.

"Okay, well, I started planning the escape from Roger

who was the ringleader of the whole organization, right? So, shortly after that," she paused looking pointedly at each of us as if confirming something, "I shot Roger dead. Then, we had to rebuild. A lot of the kids Roger had didn't have anything or anyone to go back to, and the power vacuum left behind after that was too large to leave open for others to step into it, so we started the Sloths.

"The crazy thing about it is that there are a lot of perks to being a gang of kids. We'd gotten into trouble at the beginning and had the cops on us and the guy was so concerned that we were kids that he let me sit down and tell him my plight and what we were doing, and instead of taking me in and putting a stop to the whole thing, he offered to help us. I have no idea why since it's kind of his job to stop us, but he was the start to the Bernards. He was the original Officer Bernard, actually, and the whole reason we gained more of them, too.

"I remember this one time we were in a car chase trying to escape these rivals, and the original Officer Bernard got involved with a rookie who freaked out the whole time about it, but eventually became my favorite of the Bernards which says a lot since I hate cops."

I thought about her story. How Roger had the cops in his back pocket while he was alive, and one had taken a young Evan and raped her without Roger knowing. The cop had been murdered for that, but it didn't stop the damage from being done to her. How horrible to be taught to respect authority when you're young and associate that with safety and have it turn around and hurt you.

Evan sighed. "I still had touch with my family since I could go back and grab things sometimes, but my parents couldn't do anything to keep me around for their own safety, so I would pop in, let them know I was still alive, and leave again. They don't like to talk about that time or the time immediately following when I'd been in and out of the hospital all the time after we found out I had cancer. I couldn't stop leading the Sloths, though. I couldn't let any of them down just because I'm sick.

"Now, I'm TeiLuce to keep my identity mostly secret. I run the Sloths, and I left some people back home who have kind of stepped into keeping it up now that I'm here. I also have the whole Irish company since everyone else on my dad's side abdicated the company throne, basically. I'm trying to get rid of it, too, since who wants to run a company like that, but that's probably still a long ways off," she concluded, and Ben and I exchanged a glance.

"That's way more interesting than any story I could have told," I informed her as we soaked in all the new information she'd laid out for us.

"Yeah," Evan said mulling her own thoughts around briefly before yawning. "I'm exhausted."

I got up and stretched, "Okay, bedtime!"

Everyone else seemed to agree and Evan sleepily wiggled into a comfortable spot on the couch to sleep. Ben and I walked into Kodi and Delphinium's room and took up the beds that were there. Kodi grabbed a blanket to sleep on the floor next to Evan.

As the lights went off and I'd relaxed enough, I turned to Ben in the bed next to mine. "Hey Ben, what do you think about all that?"

I heard him sigh in the dark before moving around and rustling the covers, "I don't know. It's a lot."

I had to agree with him. Being unable to confirm any of it made me more frustrated than ever.

"I wish I could talk to her family about it," I confessed

thinking about how angry Evan would be if I did attempt to bring it up to them and then it got back to her.

"Don't," Ben heeded, and I sighed again.

"Yeah, I know," I conceded before rolling over and falling asleep.

12

GLOW STICKS & BLACK LIGHTS

"So, I got these new throwing knives. Wanna try practicing them with me?" Evan asked when I'd come up to her room to visit. She lived across the dorm complex from me, now, but I couldn't complain as she still lived closer than Kodi and Delphinium did.

Rarely did I get solo time with Evan. She enjoyed company and usually always had as many friends around her as she possibly could get, but Kodi had done something stupid to warrant her wrath. So, she'd called me over to keep the company Kodi usually provided for her, and it'd ended up being the two of us.

The chill of the season sunk in faster than I cared to think about since autumn should have been longer than it'd proved to be. We'd found a ponderosa as a target and jumped about to warm up a bit.

Evan already made sure that I'd gotten into *Naruto* and a few other animes that had weapons users in them. They made each weapon seem like an amazing thing to have, and her throwing knives were no different.

Ninjas are so cool.

She pulled out a black case and unrolled it to reveal the knives. They were a beautiful heat-treated steel that made them look rainbowy, and she had five of them in this cute little holder that she let me pick from before we practiced.

We quickly learned that we aren't all that good at throwing knives. We figured that the jagged tree bark surface probably had something to do with the fact that we couldn't get any of the knives to hit right or stick, but it may have been from our lack of a decent throwing arm or the fact that the tree had a tough substance to it.

"Where did you get these," I asked throwing another and failing at getting it to stick *again*.

"A meeting with an unfortunate rival gang member. He had them on him," she explained shrugging a little before trying her hand at throwing another and watching it clank against the tree and fall to the ground uselessly. "We suck at this."

I chuckled. I didn't want to know what happened to the previous owner of the knives, but I had to agree with how right she'd been. We were terrible.

"It's cold out here, too. What the hell?" she commented looking around in the dark of the evening in the valley as if she'd be able to spot the culprit of the cold weather.

"Yeah, it's nighttime in October," I deadpanned. Of course it felt cold.

"Let's go inside, I need something to warm up."

I nodded collecting the knives under the tree and following her back inside and up to her dorm.

Inside, she tossed the knives onto one of her cluttered desks and rummaged around for something to drink in her mini-fridge before handing me the bottle of peach schnapps she kept in there. I admired how she could still even get into the fridge with all the stuff on her floor and around her room, but she managed, and I took a swig of the peachy goodness before handing it back to her.

She took a pull from it, too, before kicking off her shoes and plopping on her bed. I followed sitting on her spare mattress she'd tossed on the floor. While I did that, Evan blinked at me before taking a long drink from the bottle in her hand and then handed it to me while she took off her coat and hat and threw them across the room.

Then she got up and clicked on her black light next to her door before turning off the bright overhead lights of the room so that everything held a deep bluish tone except the shirt I'd been wearing that seemed extra bright in the dimness.

I watched her do all that while drinking, and when she plopped down next to me on the floor mattress and snatched the bottle from my hand for another drink, I didn't argue against it.

"Do you remember last year when you told me that you were jealous of Kayla and I dating?" she asked me taking another quick swig and handing it back to me.

"Yeah," I said remembering too well how she'd basically dated through all the women in her hall last year and how I'd told her that I didn't like her relationship with Kayla in particular because it'd been one of the last and I'd fallen for her by then. "Why do you ask?"

"I'm just glad you said that," she admitted taking another drink of the peachy sweetness that grew ever sweeter with each passing drink. She cringed a bit before setting it to the side with the cap back on.

I couldn't help watching her, then. She looked at me with the biggest, neediest eyes and I melted on the spot. I leaned in and kissed her forehead, and while she seemed a little uncertain about it, she leaned in and kissed me square on the mouth.

I relished in it before she placed her hands on my shoulders and pushed me back and then crawled over me to be sure that I couldn't get back up. Not that I'd fight anything she'd do to me on that mattress. I wanted whatever I could get.

She kissed me sweetly, again, before slipping her tongue into my mouth and making out with me fervently. She tasted like schnapps and melting snow, and I needed her. I'd always need her like that.

I slipped my hands under her shirt and pulled it up over her head and tossed it to the side while catching her mouth again.

She pulled back and slipped her fingers between mine before pinning my hands to the mattress and growling a little at me for trying to do things to her while she had me on bottom.

I sent a wolfish grin her way before she moved to kiss a trail up the side of my neck sucking lightly here and there in the most delicious way imaginable. She sat kneeling over my right leg, and while she drove me forward with her attention on my neck and shoulder, I bent my leg so that it pressed between hers right on the sweet spot.

She cried out a moan right in my ear and I pressed harder against her all while still being pinned. She forced me to stop distracting her by taking my hands and beating them against the mattress again before releasing them entirely and tugging at the bottom of my shirt getting me to wiggle and help her remove it before she went for my bra and got that off, too.

She devoured me after that taking her time kissing and licking trails across my bare skin enjoying the little sounds

I'd make as she went. I turned my head and saw a small glow stick off to the side of the mattress in the clutter that glowed faintly in the blacklight. I grabbed it and used it to trail a light line over Evan's shoulders and back.

She shivered over me and moaned again before taking the glow stick from me and tormenting me with it, too.

I held absolutely still taking sharp breaths every once in a while, as she used the very end of the stick to draw lightly over every inch of my bare skin that she could reach leaving tingles and goosebumps in her wake.

"Beautiful," she mused getting close to my face and then kissing me on the nose.

I closed my eyes and sighed unwilling to part with the moment. "You should try that. It's *amazing*."

She considered me for a minute before moving off me so that we could switch positions so that I could playfully draw lines across her skin with the little light.

"You know a lot about me, but I know little about you," she commented as I kissed across one of her collarbones. "Tell me your life story."

I considered that while I continued kissing her. It'd only be fair after she'd promised to tell me her story, and I'd wanted someone to ask me that for a while. I'd found my opportunity.

I kissed her mouth before moving to lay next to her where she cuddled into me to listen.

"I was almost born in Arkansas," I started holding her and tracing circles over her shoulder. "My family came down to get my parents right before I was born, so I'd be closer to them, and everything happened as normal in a hospital. My dad left us when I was two, right before my brother was born. I don't remember that time at all.

"I consider my childhood pretty normal, though. We

lived with my aunt for a while after that and then we moved downstate to be closer to my cousins. I've never broken any bones and I've always been pretty cautious, though I love traveling and roller coasters. I've had about twenty pet cats in my life, which have always been my favorite over dogs even though we have three dogs now. I don't know, what do you want to know about me?" I asked feeling a little uncertain about where to go with my relatively vanilla life. At least compared to Evan, anything else was vanilla.

She tilted her head back and kissed my chin before wriggling out of my arms and stretching before she moved to her own bed. "That's good for now," she told me crawling into the comforter there and promptly falling asleep.

I wondered if she'd said that to be nice.

13

SHENANIGANS

The vetting process to become an employee of ResLife is a long one. You bond with the other members through a week-long training before classes, and then you barely see any of them again except for holiday parties and when they pass you in the halls of one of the academic buildings.

Even still, the expectations for ResLife member were high being that we were in charge of making sure that our residents were adjusting to life away from home and that they weren't breaking any of the campus rules while they lived there.

That, of course, isn't to say that students couldn't have a little fun and considering the fact that I had broken many rules while I'd been a freshman at Western, I felt a little biased towards the things both me and my residents did out of sight of everyone else.

Just don't get caught.

I made my way from my last class of the day and headed up to the west side of campus to their on-campus apartment. Delphinium had been convinced to stay in and hang out with us again, so we had to, of course, make the most of it.

I knocked on the fourth window from the left waiting for Kodi to ruffle the blackout curtains she'd hung to be sure that wherever she fell asleep in her apartment, she at least wouldn't be disturbed by daylight, and wandered to the door that one of my friends would open for me.

"Hey!" Delphinium said, pushing the metal door open and letting me inside the hospital-like hall of the old apartments on campus.

"What's up?" I asked hugging her as I passed.

"Evan bwought a fwiend fwom class. He seems pwetty cool, but I haven't talked to him much," she admitted joining me on the walk down the dimly lit hall.

My eyebrows rose in surprise. Evan never brought us guy friends. *Very curious.*

"How does everyone seem?" I asked as we neared the door to their room.

Delphinium thought about it a moment before turning to me. "Honestly, Kodi's been testing my patience. I haven't been awound much othahwise."

I tossed that around as she opened the door to their apartment and let me in. It opened to a man with short dark hair and tons of acne from numerous botched shaves sitting across from the open door who'd been talking to Evan on the couch. Kodi moved around the kitchen putting their groceries away and paused only a minute to greet me before continuing on her task.

"Hey! Desi, this is Ian. Ian this is our other friend, Desi," Evan said introducing us and went back to telling him something about the people in whatever class they had together.

Delphinium and I closed the door and moved to sit down. "So, what's Evan like in class?"

Evan shot me a look but glanced at Ian since she apparently wanted to know if he dared answer my question honestly.

"She's pretty quiet, honestly. I've just really started to get to know her. She's pretty nice, though," he finished glancing between the two of us as he spoke.

I considered that for a moment knowing what I knew about Evan myself and the fact that she definitely made a point to say what was on her mind. She could be *nice*, too, but nice all the time? Not a chance.

Before I could comment further, a thunk against the ground sounded to our right from the kitchen.

"Shit!" Kodi cursed, and Evan jumped and rushed to help her.

When I turned, a two liter of strawberry Crush sat leaking on the ground all over the place from a large crack in the side of it.

"Shit," Delphinium said also stepping in to help.

They'd found equilibrium in the bottle where it could sit without spilling more, but we needed a new container if they wanted it to keep some of its carbonation at least.

"What do we have in the fwidge," Delphinium asked Evan who'd stepped over to look.

"Nothing empty...I don't know how you find anything in here, though. Can we empty the last bit of OJ out?" she asked as Kodi grabbed some more towels to clean the reddish liquid from the tan linoleum.

"That works!" Delphinium said holding the bottle like someone would hold a live bomb.

"That's such a waste," I said sitting on the couch to get out of the way of the chaos of everyone else.

"What? Do you want us to put them together?" Evan asked sarcastically from the open fridge as she moved enough things around to pull the jug out without causing an avalanche of food.

"Why not?" Kodi asked tiptoeing to the sink where Evan met her with the almost-empty thing of orange juice and undid the lid so that Kodi could start pouring it in. "It'll make a good mixer."

Each of us considered that a win since we likely had some sort of gross vodka laying around that would need something to cut the flavor.

Delphinium finished her cleaning and stepped on the ground to be sure nothing felt sticky or tacky before she moved to the freezer where they kept the hard alcohols. She removed a bottle of schnapps and a bottle of vodka which both seemed to be our staples for the year.

"Why not both?" Evan said as Delphinium weighed the two bottles in front of her and took to adding both alcohols until the liquids filled almost to the top of the bottle.

"This might be good with cherries, too," Kodi added deciding that if they were going to make something, it might as well be all out.

"Yeah!" Evan agreed getting into it, and Delphinium went back to the fridge to hunt for the jar of Maraschino cherries Kodi kept there.

The liquid in the jug barely touched the top rim, and Evan screwed the lid on to shake it around before setting it down in front of me on the coffee table, taking the lid off again, and asking me to taste test it.

I wondered what we may have done to it if it didn't taste good, but I took the offer and leaned over the bottle to slurp it out since it definitely would have spilled had I tried to pick it up in any way.

Of all our accidental combinations, that mixture tasted best. It had a sweetness to it, definitely, but the tang of the orange juice offset it, and the alcohol flavor still held enough of a presence that you could still taste some of the bitter vodka which meant it had some alcohol strength, too.

I couldn't be sure how we'd ever be able to make it again, but it was *delicious*.

I took another sip to be positive about my decision before nodding to my friends who'd been watching with bated breath to see what I thought. "It's a success!" I called, and Evan stepped up to give it a try.

"Mmm..." she purred.

"I wanna try," Kodi called tossing the broken bottle and washing the pop off her hands.

"That's amazing!" Delphinium laughed taking another drink.

Ian sipped it and found that he couldn't get enough and took a few more sips before Kodi stepped over and took it from him.

"Woah! That *is* good," she said handing the jug back to me.

"I told you," I agreed taking another drink. "We should make this again."

"What should we call it?" Evan asked knowing we'd stumbled upon something magical that we had to patent for ourselves immediately.

We all paused in thought and I considered for a moment what kind of a name might live up to our new concoction.

"What about Shenanigans?" I asked rolling with the first idea that popped up.

"Oh my god," Evan said, "yes!"

"That is so pahfect," Delphinium agreed loudly.

Knock. Knock. Knock.

"ResLife, can you open the door?" called a feminine voice from the hall on the other side of the kitchen.

I looked into the bugging eyes of every other person around me knowing that not only would they be in trouble, but I could definitely lose my job if they knew we had alcohol.

"Shit!" Delphinium whispered.

"Fuck!" Evan cursed before leaping into action along with Kodi who arrived at the freezer first and pulled the alcohol out soundlessly to hand it to her so that she could run it down the hall and into the back bedroom.

I had to answer the door, I knew I had to answer the door. Kodi reached out to get it and I stopped her. Whatever RA was on the other side of that door, I knew them and they knew me. The likelihood that they'd treat this like any other search and raid would be slim to none if they knew more trouble could come to a colleague. Kodi let me push her away.

Opening the door, I put on my best fake smile and found myself having to tilt my head down a bit to look into the blue eyes of Tiffany, ResLife's stout little redhead.

Thank the stars for that, I thought. Not only were Tiffany and I colleagues, but she'd dated Evan's brother's best friend and knew Evan and her brother well.

"Tiffany, what's up?" I asked trying to slow the rapid jolting of my heart against my ribcage. I begged for everyone behind me not to look bug-eyed or petrified and go about doing other things besides staring at the door, but I could only do what I could in preventing her from walking through that doorway.

"Oh, Desi! I had no idea you were here. It was pretty loud, so I figured I'd just check on you guys," she admitted glancing around the apartment over my shoulder, and I slid to the side so that she had proof of our lack of trouble inside.

Glancing in myself, I noticed Evan casually making her way out of the back room where she seemed to register Tiffany, but also the fact that it may have been suspicious that she wasn't out in the main room with us when we opened the door.

I think we both felt the eminent facepalm we were mentally chastising ourselves for, but there could be no crying over spilled milk in that instance.

"Just hanging out right now. Thinking about a movie," I mused attempting to bring her attention back to me.

"What's that?" she asked of the reddish-orange liquid in the labeled orange juice jug on the coffee table.

Shit, what do you call something that's clearly not orange juice? I thought frantically for something but my brain glitched somewhere in the panic. "C-Crush," I stammered knowing I might be able to explain it as a combination with the evidence of the broken strawberry Crush bottle in the trash around the fridge. I just begged that she didn't ask any more questions.

She frowned at it a moment before taking a quick breath and deciding against whatever she'd been thinking. "Just quiet down a bit from now on, okay?" she asked us, and we all nodded. "Okay, have a good night." Then she wandered down the hall and left us to close the door, and we all breathed a huge sigh of relief.

"Oh my god, I'm shaking," Delphinium said from her place on the couch as she chuckled a little to expel the nerves she'd been feeling.

"That was crazy," I admitted wiggling around to loosen all the tenseness I'd been feeling. "Let's not do that again."

"Dude, glad it was Tiffany and not a stricter RA," Evan

said. "I bet you anything that my RA would not have walked away."

"Yeah, well, your RA is too serious about her job," Kodi admitted, and we all laughed feeling far more relaxed than we had moments before, but still not replacing the alcohol bottles in the freezer just in case anyone came back.

Ian hadn't said anything about our near disaster, though. He sat quietly against the wall with a continued look of uneasiness about him.

"Hey, are you okay?" Evan asked wondering if she needed to get anything more for the friend she'd brought into the fray on accident.

"No, no. I think I might go back to my place, though. That was a little too close for my comfort," he told her and Kodi and I exchanged a skeptical look.

"It's not like they're gonna come back," she said attempting to convince him to stay.

He looked at her like she had no idea what they would do or that they definitely could come back but that he wasn't going to be around to see it.

He can leave now, I thought. Ben would have stuck with us if he'd been there, and we only dealt with ride or die friends when it came to trouble.

Evan begrudgingly let him walk out the door to safety.

14

BAX FORT PORN

"Wanna build a fort?" Evan asked us as we lounged around the library. Each of us seemed to have a project or something to complete before Fall Break happened and we were in various stages of work while we hung out together.

"Hell yes," I said with one of my headphones dangling over my ear as I worked in case one of them said something. "When?"

"We should do it this weekend," Kodi said excitedly from her computer cubby on the other side of Evan. "We have a bunch of pumpkin boxes now that it's getting closer to Halloween. They're super sturdy and really hard to break down."

"Save a couple for us and we will," Evan told her smiling.

It'd been awhile since the three of us had built a fort together. Since freshman year at least, and we were already over two months into the new school year. It helped that Kodi basically had her own apartment, too. Delphinium certainly wouldn't be in, she usually spent her weekends at Todd's, so we'd have the place to ourselves.

"I'll have my friend pick up alcohol for us!" Kodi offered since none of us were yet of age to do that.

At Kodi's apartment, Evan and I were waiting around for Kodi to arrive with our boxes. How she'd be transporting them in her little hooptie had been anyone's guess, but she pulled up in her little car with the whole back seat packed to the brim with cardboard.

"Oh my god, Kodi, how'd you even fit in there?" Evan asked her laughing incredulously.

"Magic!" she said grinning happily. "Now, we just gotta figure out how to get them *out*."

With a bit of struggle, we managed to pull the crumpled three-ply cardboard from Kodi's car and into the apartment. It had dirt all over it from the pumpkins, but Kodi could do what she wanted in her apartment. It's not like she cleaned, at any rate.

"So, how should we start this?" Evan asked assessing the space and the boxes we had.

"They're pretty heavy, you think we could cut them apart and use them as walls?" I asked thinking about the structure of them and how much more we'd have if we took them apart.

"With a sheet ceiling? That could work," Evan agreed thinking about our previous blanket forts.

"We could drag the mattresses out and stick them in the middle and sleep here tonight!" Kodi added knowing they had plenty of materials to work with in their room.

"Sounds good to me. Do you have a box cutter?" I interjected hoping she did for ease of taking the boxes apart.

"Yep!" she said bounding into the other room to bring one to me as well as a ton of sheets.

Like that, we started building our first box fort together,

still the kids our hearts knew us to be despite how far we'd come in our time at college already.

The cardboard proved to be much heavier than we thought, and we struggled getting it to stay up on its side that we had to pull out some duct tape to stick a few of the edges together. We added tunnels to both the front door and the hall by the bathroom. The kitchen had been included in the fort's front door entrance, but it got slightly blocked during our execution and became more precarious to get to. We carried the two twin mattresses, the alcohol, and Evan's laptop into the fort before we pulled the sheets over the top for our roof and crawled inside.

As forts are, we were thrilled to be inside like we'd assembled our own secret hideout even though anyone on the outside would clearly know about the fort if they'd seen it.

Because of the cardboard, it'd become surprisingly dark on the inside, too. Kodi, being the last to crawl in, turned out the lights before she made her way inside and took the side closest to the window while I picked the side near the doors and Evan snuggled between us.

We'd been drinking the entire time we'd been building the fort and it showed in Kodi most. Evan and I sipped our drinks while we discussed what we were going to do in our fort now that we'd completed it.

"What's new?" I asked when we'd settled in comfortably.

"Have I ever told you about why I hate the number thirteen?" Evan asked leaning her head against my shoulder.

"Yes!" Kodi exclaimed popping up quickly before she got a headrush and fell back onto the mattress.

"No," I admitted shooting a frown at Kodi before leaning my cheek against Evan's head.

Before beginning, Evan heaved a great sigh, "So, I told you about being kidnapped, right? Well, they took me to this place where there were other kids, too, but many of them didn't last long there and were constantly being replaced. The leader of the ring was Roger. I killed him after a while, but not before a bunch of other stuff happened.

"Roger liked things in a certain way and expected you to follow them or suffer. I once attended a party of his and kept fidgeting around in this ridiculously frilly dress he'd put me in. He didn't show it then, but when we got back to the compound, he took me into a room and removed all of my fingernails for disobeying him."

I cringed at the thought and clenched my fists to protect my own nails from that prospect, growling low in hatred for him.

"He set a kid on fire as an example, once, too," she told us. "It smelled so much like pork that I can't eat it or smell it cooking at all without getting sick.

"Roger picked favorites and already had one in this kid he called Tom. It wasn't the name he had from his family, but he couldn't remember what the real one was, and neither of us wanted to call him something that Roger had given him.

"I had to think about what to name him for a while after that but finally came to the name Hatsu that eventually stuck," Evan explained. "While that was happening was the first time Roger ever raped me. It was horrible, and I choose not to think about it.

"I was nine at the time, and Roger called me into an office where Hatsu already was. He ripped my shirt off my right shoulder and started carving into it with a knife. I was the number thirteen and Hatsu was seven. Roger explained that Hatsu would deliver good news and in the worst of ways I would deliver the bad news which included killing people sometimes. He made me dress in girly clothes to do it, too, since he enjoyed the irony of having a *sweet* little girl coming in and destroying you when you'd expect her to bring good news."

I considered that and wondered if that was the reason that Evan didn't like being girly at all.

"Don't remove my nails! That would suck!" Kodi announced flopping around to change positions before giggling hysterically about the noise the mattress made when she moved a certain way.

"Have you ever watched porn with your friends?" Evan asked us during a lull in Kodi's giggling.

"No, have you?" I asked curiously.

"Of course!" she admitted moving to open up her laptop and search through to find the website she wanted. "What do you wanna watch?"

I considered her a moment before actually thinking about which porn experience I wanted to share with them.

"Oh, let's do that one!" Kodi hiccupped from her place laying helplessly on her mattress.

Bbraaaapp.

"Green," Kodi grumbled as if it were an effort just to speak one word.

"Orange!" Evan said quickly, and I scrunched my face in disdain.

"AHHHHHhhhh," I moaned loudly losing in the best way I could.

"I lost The Game," Evan stated as she scrolled through a few more videos on the screen.

"Well, Kodi has spoken," Evan murmured clicking the

link to a video of one woman being fucked by six different men.

"Woah, that's a lot to juggle," I commented as Evan remained near her keyboard watching for a minute.

"This isn't getting me anywhere," she said exiting out of the page and moving back to scrolling through the videos that were there. Settling on a different one, she opened it and moved back to lay with us.

In the video, three exceptionally attractive blondes all dressed in super scantily clad schoolgirl outfits and standing in what looked like a locker room were all using various toys on each other, and their moans grew with each new thing they did to each other.

I felt transfixed by them. I'd never gone beyond the vanilla of male/female porn before, and this new porn did way more for me than I'd expected.

Evan squirmed a little as another dildo came out before she turned to me and found our faces mere inches from each other. "Umm...do you, uh, know about hentai?" she asked huskily, and I shook my head.

"Oh, it's animated porn. Do you wanna watch one? I think I'll be done after that," she said moving to change from the lesbian porn to something totally different in a video that looked like the animation in anime, but far less innocent than I'd ever seen of anything in an anime series.

We watched a while as a young man had been coerced into bed with two older women and somewhere in there, Kodi managed to fall asleep and let us know with a soft snore before she fell silent again.

As if that were the cue, Evan turned off the porn and closed the laptop before turning and looking at me in the dim light we'd left from the bathroom that streamed in through the sheets. Slowly, she crawled her way from near the couch that we'd built into our fort across the mattresses and knelt over me on all fours. Her blonde hair created a curtain around my face so that I couldn't see anything beyond her and everything that she was in that moment.

I looked into her face, shadowed and longing in a way I'd seen only once before when we'd been at her place drunk and playing with a glow stick.

She smiled genuinely at me and leaned down to plant the sweetest kiss on my lips that I'd ever experienced from her. I let her do what she needed, then, I had no desire to pull anything from her in that moment, and whatever she needed from me had been everything I ever wanted to give.

My absolute devotion to the broken, beautiful woman above me filled my heart and chest and lungs till they were burning, and bursting and I could hold the feeling in no longer.

I cried out into her shoulder as a tear slipped unhindered from my eye and I clung to her with fingers that wanted to melt into her flesh and keep her there with me forever. I'd scarcely loved her more than that moment, but it continued.

She stripped me down to my barest bones and nothing could have been better than the feeling of her expert fingers tracing the nerves beneath my skin and setting me on fire with every movement. She kissed and suckled my neck and shoulder and I tried desperately to muffle the moans as not to wake Kodi who'd carelessly fallen asleep next to us.

She loved me like that. She took her time loving me that way. As indescribable as it felt, she adored me exactly the way I'd yearned for her to in all the time I'd known her and wanted her to be more than my friend. She slid her finger in me and her mouth on mine was all I could do not to shout my desire to the skies for everyone to hear.

I grabbed at her breasts before she started work on my neck again and made me lose track of what I'd been doing.

I groaned into her neck as she worked, using my mouth and fingers in every way I could to show her how much I appreciated what she'd been doing to me in that instant, but she growled at me for distracting her from her task and took my wrists in her free hand and held them above my head to be sure I stop misbehaving.

Grudgingly, I obeyed until she got me where she wanted me to go and let me work again. I took full advantage of her new submissiveness gently moving her so that she lay beneath me naked, pale and beautiful in all that she allowed me to see.

I kissed a trail from her mouth to her chest then moved and licked a trail from her collarbone to her earlobe before sucking on it gently.

She moaned in my ear encouraging me to continue as I followed the trails she'd laid out so nicely on me. I figured they had to be similar since she seemed to know my body so well, so I worked and moved and caressed everything I could while she let me.

Ppppaaaaapaaaaapaaaaaaffft.

Glancing incredulously at Kodi, Evan turned wide incredulous eyes to me and then burst out laughing hysterically at the fact that Kodi had farted in her sleep completely ruining the moment and any future moment we may have had that night. We laughed so hard that my stomach ached with laughing pangs and Evan had started crying in the hilarity.

I rolled to Evan's side trying to ease the hysterics of it,

and she leaned her head against my shoulder and continued giggling.

Kodi woke groggily and grumbled angrily at us before turning her back on us and passing out again. That only made us laugh harder, and we used each other and our shared joy to fall happily to sleep.

15

A LITTLE SHOCKING

One beautiful Gunnison weekend, Evan had to return to the Springs for *business*. Whether that business had to do with programming or *other*, I couldn't be sure, but it seemed weird not having a weekend where we were all together.

Kodi had plans to fix the transmission in her car and took out our only other form of transportation besides the Mustang which had already gotten on the road to the Front Range.

"What would you say to driving to the Springs and surprising Evan?" I asked Kodi who already had black grease staining her hands with a few smudges on her face.

She looked at me carefully to see if I'd actually been serious.

"Think about it! How often would we get a chance like this?" I asked her hoping to convey how fun it'd be to get one over on Evan.

Plus, I missed her.

Kodi's blonde eyebrow quirked and then a slow devilish smile crept up over her face. "Let's do it!"

"Yes! How long do you think it'll take you to finish the car?"

"I don't know. If I worked non-stop, maybe a few hours. We'd get there before dark," she told me musing over her beat up little car that fell apart on her again.

"Great! I'll go get my stuff then," and I left her in the Shavano parking lot and walked back up to Crystal to my room.

By the time Kodi finished fixing her car, or at least what she could fix of it, she'd been coated head to toe in grease. Her bright blue hoodie had black smudges all over it, her short hair stuck together in clumps all over her head because of some that'd ended up there, her skin looked as if she'd rolled around in a fire pit and then lived on the streets afterward, and her hands above everything else were absolutely caked in the stuff.

"Oh, my gods, you look like a hobo," I told her as she walked into her apartment.

She rolled her eyes at me. "Yeah, I'll go shower. Can you open the door?" she conceded moving towards the hall.

"You're showering?" I gasped. "It's a miracle."

"Yeah, I do that sometimes," she admitted wandering into the bathroom and then shutting me out with the latch of the door.

She came out fifteen minutes later almost entirely grease free besides the stuff she'd been unable to (or hadn't tried to) remove from her hands.

"Ready to go?" she asked me rummaging through the stuff in her room and tossing a few things into her backpack.

"Yeah!" I told her shouldering my own bag.

We wandered to the car and I hesitated on it a minute. "It's safe to drive now, right?" I asked her uncertainly. She'd never fixed another one of her cars the way she'd worked on this one and I felt safe to say that she was no mechanic.

"Just get in!" she scoffed as I smiled at her.

We had an awesome drive until about the time we'd gotten outside of Canyon City when the thought of Evan potentially not taking the surprise well struck me.

"Do you think we should have told her we were coming?" I asked considering what we were doing.

"She would have tried to stop us," Kodi admitted, and I knew she spoke the truth.

"What if her parents won't let us stay?" I wondered aloud.

Kodi paused at that, thinking. "We could text her now, we're over an hour out. That should be enough time."

Seemed about right to me, so I pulled out my phone and began.

Hey! Guess what? Surprise, we're in Canyon City on our way to see you!

I sent it and hoped for the best as we continued on our drive. My phone buzzed, and I picked it up nervously.

What?! What were you thinking? How did Kodi get her car fixed? Jesus, let me figure this out.

"I don't think she's happy with us," I told Kodi rereading the text that came in.

"She'll get over it," Kodi said, and I pursed my lips skeptically.

Evan didn't have a track record of being one to 'get over' things like that.

We drove and ended up in the Springs and slowly pulled up to the cul-de-sac where the Adams' house sat. The sun set and the sky held a dim pastel mix of lavender and orange as Evan opened her front door and stood with her arms crossed angrily in the threshold.

"You're both idiots. Whose dumb idea was this?" she asked as Kodi and I pulled our bags from her back seat.

We looked sheepishly at one another. "It was a collective decision," I told her.

She grimaced at me. "Well, did you at least bring the vodka?"

"Shit! I knew we forgot something!" Kodi exclaimed and then turned sheepish again as if she feared Evan might hit her for the blunder.

"Can't even do that right. Figures," she stated stepping aside to let us into her parents' house.

It looked the way it had the last time I'd seen it. Mr. Adams had a thing for trains and there were mini replicas all over the living room to the right of the entry. Evan's parents were on the couches watching a game. I thought both she and her brother favored their dad, though Evan's face definitely seemed a bit rounder than either of the men in her family.

There were still clumps of dog fur lining the baseboards and dishes in their sink as if no one wanted to be the one to volunteer for cleaning or putting things away. The lighting felt as dim as ever even after having come in from dusk.

"Hi Mr. and Mrs. Adams! Thanks for letting us stay last minute," Kodi and I said as we walked in.

Evan ushered us down to the very bottom of their quad-level house where her and brother's bedrooms were. It had boxes upon boxes in it of all shapes and sizes, and she told us to find a comfortable place on the couches in their gaming area outside the rooms.

"I just wish you would have told me before you left because we definitely would have been able to go drinking and you would have gotten to meet everyone," she grumbled as she moved stuff around and tossed a few blankets our way.

My thoughts drifted to the time Evan once said that if you got drunk with the Sloths you'd be initiated into the gang.

The thrill of that sat on the top of my throat waiting to bubble out in a childish laugh, but I had no idea if anyone would consider that a wise move.

"We figured you'd have told us not to come," I told her and Kodi nodded in agreement.

"I *would* have told you to do that," she reiterated growling, "but we'd at least have the vodka and I could have canceled some stuff. As it is, I had to give a bunch of stuff to the others and you're still gonna have to come on a run with me."

Kodi and I exchanged a look. That didn't sound good. That didn't sound safe. *Damn our lack of foresight.*

"When are we doing that?" I asked tentatively not wanting to go with her but knowing that I probably didn't have a choice in the matter at all.

"Get what you need, we're going now," she said checking her phone and marching her way back upstairs expecting Kodi and me to follow.

Kodi watched me as I dropped my bag and I looked at her knowing she felt as nervous and jittery as I did. I flashed her a sympathetic look before we hit the stairs and found Evan slipping on her shoes by the front door.

"See you girls later," Mr. Adams said kindly without turning away from the TV. I wondered if they knew what Evan had intended for the evening or if they knew what she planned on taking us to do during whatever errand she had to run.

"Bye Daddy," Evan snipped out quickly before throwing

open the door and walking out into the quickly chilling night.

We loaded into her powder blue Mustang with the spoiler and the silver stripe over the length of the car. She'd packed a bunch of stuff into the back not expecting anyone to be riding in it until she'd gotten back to the valley.

"Just shove it all to the side and squeeze in," Evan told Kodi as we waited for her to make enough room so that she could get in and that I could push the seat back and get in myself.

"Where are the boys?" I asked noticing that the twins weren't inside when we arrived.

Evan grumbled something inaudible before answering me, "Their biological great aunt has them and is fighting for custody over them at the moment. They haven't been at my parents for at least a month."

The flash of sadness in her eyes was the only indication that she felt anything for that situation, but her focus on the road and the fact that I knew she was still mad at us kept me wisely from speaking more about it.

We drove to a park somewhere decently close to her house and she didn't say a word to either of us until we got there.

"So, I have a meeting with a rival and you two are gonna stay here until I come back. Got it?" she asked.

Kodi and I confirmed that we had no desire to leave our only safe haven in the middle of a very dark park. "Good. I'll be back."

She opened her door and left Kodi and me cramped in the Mustang with all the junk she felt needed to come back to school with her, and for a while neither Kodi nor I said anything. We glanced around the car suspiciously to see if anything noteworthy had snuck up on us and found it just as dark as what we saw through the front windshield.

Evan had wandered off into the trees behind us and out of sight, so we could only guess what had happened with her, only that we hoped she would be coming back.

"Well, this wasn't what I'd expected when we set out earlier," I chuckled trying to ease the tension in the car. As the air outside cooled further, the moisture from our breaths condensed on the windows so that it became even harder to see what might be happening outside. Someone could come attack us and we'd be none the wiser.

"She's probably trying to prove a point. Did you see how mad she was when we pulled up?" Kodi asked from behind me, and I considered that for a moment.

"Yeah, but I've seen her angrier, so this was just mild irritation, I think," I told her and wiggled a bit to ease the cramp forming in my foot.

"I still think she's trying to teach us a lesson. She never wants us to do this again," Kodi intoned, and I couldn't help but agree with her. There hadn't been any real reason for her to keep us locked up in her car here than there would have been letting us stay at her parents' and coming back when she'd finished whatever she needed to do out here.

I looked around the car and remembered all the secret things she'd told us about it. How the RES button on her steering wheel could never to be touched because it had a failsafe tracker in it that called any of the Sloths to her in the instance that she was ever in need of help.

She'd told us she had to use it once after a rival had attempted to kidnap her. She'd also told us she'd pressed it on accident without even realizing it and that a cavalry had arrived and found she'd been perfectly fine.

I'd always wanted to touch it, honestly. The repercussions were too high, which could be the reason I never did, but the drive had always remained.

"If something happened to her out there, would you be able to drive us out of here?" I asked Kodi knowing that I understood the concept of driving a stick but that I probably wouldn't have been able to do it justice if I'd needed to get us out in an emergency.

"Yeah..." Kodi said probably considering what would constitute enough of an emergency that Evan wouldn't be in the car with us.

"What do you think they're doing out there?" I asked not daring to clear the little droplets from the window lest I face the wrath of Evan for possibly scratching her window or damaging her car in *any* way.

The air grew colder and colder the longer we sat. My mind had been allowed to wander and remember just how dangerous Evan could be despite how she seemed every other time we'd known her and hung around her.

I took to thinking about her through each of the other times we'd hung out together. She had so many scars marring her pale skin. So many instances in which she'd been hurt and survived.

I thought about the three clean lines on her ankle that she kept because she thought they looked like she'd been in a fight with an animal. How there were several little nicks here and there over her arms and legs that probably had a million stories to them.

One of her most prominent scars curved over her left forearm and had the cleanest line to any scar I'd ever seen. She admitted it had been an attempted suicide scar done at a time when she'd lost several people at once and how she wondered if life had been worth living if the people you loved could die.

Hatsu had been the one to walk in and find her as she'd done it and she'd been balling her eyes out as he rushed around to hold her arm closed and get her to a hospital.

I thanked him secretly for saving her life since I'd yet to meet him and be able to say it in person.

She'd tried showing us the Roman numeral thirteen that'd once been carved into her shoulder by a malicious man who'd played some sick games with her and other children, but she'd done everything she could to make it go away, especially after Roger had traced over it every once in a while to be sure it stood prominently, and it had been a mere shadow before Kodi and I became privileged enough to see it.

Minutes turned into hours like that, and the prospect of really having to take off without Evan grew larger and larger the later it got. Then, like magic, Evan, covered in *hopefully* mud, opened the driver's door and scared the shit out of both Kodi and me.

"Holy shit, it's cold out here," Evan said clamoring in and starting the engine. "You guys must be freezing in here."

Kodi and I nodded owlishly looking her over carefully and finding nothing notably different about her besides the grime. Still the same lavender coat, slightly muddy jeans, at least she hadn't been hurt out there.

"Look at this cool thing I got," Evan said holding up a pouch that had a rather large throwing star in it.

"Not that that isn't cool, but we already suck at throwing knives, what makes you think this'll go over any better," I intoned with a smirk.

She scowled at me playfully and then glanced at the clock on her dash. "Jeez, is it that time already? I didn't think we were gone that long. Sorry!"

"What were you doing out there?" Kodi asked possibly hoping it accomplished whatever she'd come out to do.

"Meeting with a guy that ended up trying to flip on us. My partner and I took care of it, clearly," she said motioning to the grime in her clothes. "Then we got to talking, which apparently took way longer than I realized, and now I'm here."

I felt Kodi look at the back of my head and I got what she wanted. I have to say that I'd been glad Evan came back alive, as well.

She seemed happier for the meeting, though. Maybe she'd gotten all her frustration out on whatever person had tried to flip on her.

That poor, naive soul.

16

NEAR DISASTER & BILLIARDS

"*I* can't live on campus anymore. This no alcohol thing is driving me crazy," Kodi admitted as we sat around their apartment living room.

"Dude! I know what you're talking about. It's the worst," Evan agreed lounging over an arm of the green couch. "It's almost semester, we could move off campus together."

"Yes!" Kodi agreed excitedly. "Plus, you're quitting now, right Desi? You wanna move off with us?"

"I don't see why not. So long as you promise to clean and not grow fruit flies in the sink like you did in your apartment, I think it could be fun," I said thinking about how nice it'd be getting away from ResLife altogether.

"Oh, and we could get a house with a yard for Addie!" Evan added thinking about her fur-child fondly. I knew she'd missed her since coming to school.

"And more space for activities!" Kodi cheered.

I thought about having a house with two of my best friends and considered how much work it'd be for us to have that over what we had here on campus. Still, it would be fun to be around Evan and Kodi more often.

Quicker than I wanted to happen, Evan had lined up viewings for various houses around the valley ranging in distance from right downtown to five or six miles outside of it. I didn't care much for those being without a car and knowing that relying on Evan or Kodi for a ride to an 8 a.m. would be about as wise as trying to reattach fallen leaves to the tree they'd come off of.

One house we looked at seemed cute enough and super spacious. Only when we had to go do laundry, we had to walk down into a basement passage that took you down a dim hall into a cavernous concrete room with a tiny cobwebbed window peeking above the ground that did almost nothing to illuminate the things that could possibly kill you down there.

It'd been quickly marked off the list.

Then they found a three-bedroom apartment in a complex all the way across town from campus. It would have been fine in the summer but walking across the valley in one of the coldest towns in the continental U.S. would be far more brutal than I'd been looking forward to.

"I like it. Let's do it," Kodi said enjoying the thought of being as far away from campus as she could be while still being in town.

"Yeah, it works for me, anyway," Evan agreed looking at the space.

I hesitated. The reality of having to actually make the move struck me, and I didn't really think I wanted to take that step.

It wasn't that I didn't love my friends, I loved them a lot, actually. I had a lot of friends back on campus in my hall that I'd enjoyed spending time with, as well. I had no guarantees that my friends would keep the space clean and that wasn't how I lived at all. Plus, I didn't have to take care of cleaning anything besides the space of my dorm if I stayed there. The bathrooms and the hall were taken care of for me.

I liked that. This, on the other hand...

"I don't know if I wanna do this, guys," I said looking around at the space.

Two pairs of blueish eyes blinked back at me incredulously.

"What do you mean you don't know if you can do this?" Evan growled.

"Why not?" Kodi asked as a frown creased her brow.

"Just, how can I be sure that I won't be the only one doing all the cleaning? How can I be sure I'll get to classes on time in the chilly hours of the morning since it's still winter?" I asked thinking through everything that I could potentially have issue with living that far away from campus and with two people that I already knew weren't the cleanest. "Maybe it's best that I stay on campus since I'm leaving next year anyway."

Evan watched me, her lip curling furiously, and Kodi scoffed.

"We already said we were moving off campus. The papers and everything are signed."

Well, that's not my fault that you cut it before actually having a new place to live.

I shrugged helplessly. I couldn't do much from there, but there had apparently been much more for Evan to do.

"That really fucks us over," Evan said tersely, and I flinched a bit. They'd figure it out. My comfort had to come first, right?

Living together would be an entirely new ball of wax after all. A whole new level of our friendship. Lines that we'd never crossed before.

They didn't seem to care, though.

"Well, I'm not sure we can be friends anymore with the way this is working out," Evan growled, and even Kodi seemed taken aback by her proclamation.

"Seriously?" I asked snarkily not believing that they would be able to stay away for long. I certainly wouldn't be the one crawling back after this.

Regaining herself and always one to take Evan's side, Kodi crossed her arms over her chest resolutely, "Yeah! You fuck us over, we screw you right back!"

"Idiot," Evan grumbled rolling her eyes at Kodi before glaring at me before turning and stalking off with Kodi right on her heels.

"I can't believe them!" I scoffed taking another long pull from a bottle of schnapps Perez had brought me. We were sitting on my spare bed under the window. The blues and oranges I'd used to decorate the plain white walls of the dorm calmed me a little and I admired how at home I felt there.

How dare they be mad at me for their mistake in signing into a three-bedroom.

No matter what, I made the right decision for me. Thankfully, Perez had been on my side, too.

"Yeah, that is pretty dumb," she agreed with her small sweet voice. Much like Delphinium, Perez could also boast to being the eldest child of a brood which made her patient and understanding beyond all imagination. I admired that in her, too.

"Who just stops talking to someone because they decided not to move in with you? Well, they can have fun with fucking moving by themselves," I grumbled drinking again.

"Oh, they'll come around I'm sure," Perez cooed at me

hoping to ease the tension as I complained to her. She took the bottle from me and took a drink as well.

I sighed starting to feel my alcohol and allowing it to loosen me up a bit more. "You're right. If they want to be that way, I can just enjoy how good life is without them. Here, have you ever played with Photo Booth?"

I pulled my Mac into my lap and opened the funny picture app so that Perez could see it. A filter with a nose swirl popped up and Perez laughed hysterically at it, and I distracted my angry thoughts from my estranged friends with drunk photos and videos spent with someone that actually cared to spend time at *my* place with *me.*

There had been about a month in which I didn't hear a word from either Evan or Kodi because they were so mad at me for not moving in with them. The tension between us grew so much that I wondered if we'd ever mend what'd happened and be friends again. I'd be hurt if the rift remained, but I couldn't say I'd been left worse off to the point that I wouldn't get over it. I made me angry, too.

My phone buzzed one afternoon in late January after our falling out. *Evan.*

We're going to my parents for President's Weekend. Ben said he'd come if you came...So, do you wanna come with us? I don't wanna not be friends anymore.

I considered the text for a minute thinking about how nice it'd be to see Ben now that the occasions were so few and far between. *If it was for Ben...*

Is Perez coming, too?

I had to know what I'd be dealing with, if I'd be walking into the lion's den without an ally or be left in the valley by myself over a long weekend.

Yeah.

Well, that answered my question.

I agreed to come along with them and we were off to the Front Range talking and laughing as if nothing had happened between us. As if we hadn't spent over a month not speaking. Evan had always been so good about ignoring the glaringly obvious issues within her relationships.

Ben was waiting around for our arrival. The Adams' house looked the same as I remembered it. Fur continued to line the baseboards and now it'd gotten all over the upstairs bathroom because her brother had bathed his extremely furry dog up there.

"Hi," Evan called as we clattered through the front door and into the front entry to kick off our shoes and move down into the lowest level of the house.

No one answered her.

"You guys wanna play pool?" Evan asked after we dumped our bags around the mini living room on the lowest level and considered where we'd be sleeping that night. I'd claimed one of the couches.

"Yes!" Kodi said bounding up the half flight to the next level where the pool table lived.

"Well, I guess that's a yes," I said walking up after her to grab a pool stick of my own.

Evan's parents had bought us a ton of alcohol. Kind of them since we were still underage.

Kodi had gotten into mixing drinks with orange juice even though she shouldn't technically have been drinking it since she'd found out she had an allergy to citric acid and it made her tongue itchy. She'd start complaining about it and scratching at it with her teeth and Evan would end up having to get her a Benadryl.

Until then, we laughed and drank and took pictures with the new camera I'd gotten for my trip abroad.

Perez opted out of playing with us to sit on the stairs, drink quietly, and watch us with Addie sitting next to her.

After seriously losing to Ben and Evan, even though Kodi and I had been playing pool in the student center almost every day between our classes, we stumbled downstairs where Perez promptly rushed into the bathroom and threw up.

I cringed wondering how much Perez had drank that caused her to vomit like that, but I knew Evan would already be on the task of taking care of her and making sure she'd be okay.

Kodi laughed and jumped onto the queen-sized mattress laying on the floor of Evan's old room followed by Ben and me. We were smooshed together happily giggling when Evan poked out from the bathroom and hurled herself on top of us to make no room for rolling around at all lest one of us fell off the edge.

Perez came out of the bathroom and stood at the foot of the mattress hesitantly. There had been no room left for her. We'd left barely enough room for the four of us that were already there.

Instead of coming up and lying beside one of us or on top of us as Evan had, she curled at the foot of the bed like a dog partially participating in our fun, but also not at all. It seemed like a very Perez thing to do despite that I felt bad about it. If everyone else ignored it, then I could, too, *I guess*.

"We should totally go skinny dipping in the hot tub!" Evan said rolling to face Ben and leaning over him to talk to me.

"Yes!" Kodi agreed ready to do anything fun and adventurous.

"Yeah..." Ben considered thinking about being naked with all of us. Not like he'd never seen it before.

Evan scrambled up, hopped over Perez's curled form, and rushed into the bathroom to grab a bunch of towels that she started throwing at us.

We all started undressing except for Perez who still seemed like she didn't want to participate.

"I think I'm just gonna stay in," she said sheepishly.

"No! Come out with us Perez," Evan begged not really wanting to leave her inside alone.

"No, really. You guys have fun!" she squeaked insistently.

"Suit yourself," Kodi said throwing off her clothes and wrapping herself up in a towel.

I hadn't been in any mood to deal with whatever Perez seemed to have an issue with right then, either. I stripped and followed Kodi up the stairs to the sliding glass door in the kitchen. Evan and Ben joined us shortly after leaving Perez to do whatever she thought had been more important than being naked with her friends.

"Holy shit! It's freezing out here!" Kodi shrieked hopping quickly between her feet so that she wouldn't have to touch the cold ground with either foot for too long.

"No shit!" Evan said moving to take the cover from the hot tub on the Adams' back porch and scrambling in. Kodi and I followed her quickly before Ben came slowly after us to put his towel down and climb into the superheated water, too.

"You know you can tell boobs are real with the way they float? They sink if they're fake," Evan explained pushing her boobs down and letting them float back up and bulge over the surface.

I tested it, too, pushing my boobs down and watching them float back up through the steam.

"Cool!" Kodi said having tested her own even though we knew that none of our boobs were fake.

Ben put his hands over his own chest and pouted at the fact that he couldn't test the buoyancy of his own non-existent breasts.

The thing I've never liked about hot tubs is the fact that the steam sticks to your face and cools with the air so your head gets cold quickly. I couldn't be sure if everyone else felt that way or not, but I'd sank lower into the water so that my nose sat above the surface and my chin and mouth were submerged. Every once in a while, I'd take warm water and hold it against my ears and nose to keep them from freezing off.

Nothing like naked hot tubbing in February.

We'd climbed out after a while of soaking and found Perez had fallen asleep downstairs killing any amount of fun we could have had down there.

I hoped that she wouldn't ruin the rest of our weekend together like that.

17

A VIRGIN NO MORE

*E*van had always been sweetest with alcohol in her system. Like the calloused walls surrounding her in protection softened enough to let people in. I *loved* the moments her guards came down and she became unequivocally Evan.

Kodi planned a get together and she'd invited a friend from her high school to come up and have some fun with us. We'd never met any of Kodi's friends, and the prospect seemed exciting for each of us.

Perez in her plain blue shirt sat on the floor in a corner saying nary a word for the who knows what numbered time since she'd joined our group. Her hair grew below her ears and she'd tinted it auburn in her latest adventure in hair coloring experiments.

Delphinium had her long blonde locks hanging down around her face as she chomped at the piece of gum in her mouth and the excess saliva smacked around with it. She'd already had a drink in her hand and laughed loudly at Evan's recalling of some crazy adventure she'd had over Spring Break can home.

Evan busied herself around their kitchen making a mixed drink or two since she definitely wouldn't make food if she could help it and handed them off to Perez and me. She'd finally gotten her hair back to blonde after the horrible purplish brown she'd had it in for the past two months. She looked so much better in that color.

I leaned back against the green couch they'd moved into this new apartment that seemed identical to the one Kodi had in Shavano. I'd joked with them that they'd stolen it, but they insisted that it had been a gift from Evan's Uncle David.

"Hey! This is Juan," Kodi said bursting through the door to their apartment. A taller man stood trailing in behind her that had cleanly shaven everything on his head and had no remarkable features at all. He seemed curiously plain, in fact.

She introduced all of us by name as she clamored inside and dumped her jacket on the chair next to the door with her keys and skipped into the kitchen to get them both a drink.

"What was Kodi like in high school?" Delphinium asked sipping from the bottle in her hand.

"Did you even do anything besides band?" Evan asked thinking about how boring her life must have been there.

"She wasn't so bad," Juan admitted sipping on the drink Kodi fished from the fridge for him.

Kodi preened at the compliment. "Yeah, plus, band geeks are crazy."

I had to agree with her there. Everything I knew about band kids from my own high school experiences told me that they were wild, and everyone knew some insane story about band camp.

Evan and Delphinium nodded in agreement, as well.

Seemed that no matter how far apart your schools were, band kids were bred the same.

As Delphinium drank more, she inched closer to me. After about three drinks, she laid her head on my shoulder and snuggled her face against me. I could smell her flowery shampoo in her hair that had a nice sweetness to it. I would have liked it any other way than being pinned between an armrest and an affectionate Delphinium, but all I could do in that moment was look helplessly around at everyone else.

"I miss Todd," she told me before nuzzling into my neck and kissing me there.

"Woah there, killer!" I said squirming around to get away from her advances.

"Todd's the best, ya know?" she mumbled and pulled out her phone to drunk text him. I had to wonder if he'd come and get her if she seemed obviously drunk in her texts, and I had to say that I kind of hoped he would.

"Well, I'm gonna go now," Perez said finishing her drink and picking herself up off the floor.

"What, you're leaving now?" Evan and I asked together equally as baffled about why Perez didn't want to stay and play with us. *Again.*

"Yeah...I'm pretty tired and it's been a long week. It's no big deal, though! You guys have fun!" she squeaked moving towards the door.

Kodi couldn't be bothered with anything that happened around her and Juan. They were deep in conversation and Juan had his hand on her thigh tracing small circles as they spoke.

"Do you need us to drive you back over to campus?" Evan asked concerned about letting her walk all the way across town with a little alcohol in her system.

"Of course not, I'll be fine. Stay here and have fun,

okay?" She quelled Evan's protests and managed to slip on her shoes and jacket quickly.

"Well, bye Perez," Evan said sadly wishing she'd stay and have fun with us, too.

"Yeah! Bye Perez," I said wriggling out from under Delphinium and going to hug Perez before she left.

"Bye guys! Have so much fun, and, uh, keep an eye on them," she winked and pointed at Kodi and Juan wrapped up in themselves to even notice we were talking about them. Then she slipped out the door and left Todd in her wake who quirked an eyebrow when he caught sight of Kodi with a guy.

"Todd! Babe!" Delphinium cheered stumbling from the couch to the door and falling into his burly arms.

"What'd you guys do to her? How much did she drink?" he asked Evan and me nearly supporting Delphinium in his arms as she melted all over him in drunken happiness.

"We do what we can," I admitted gathering a few of the things I knew were hers and handing them to him.

"Did'ya have any more than this?" he asked Delphinium holding her coat and hat in front of her face so that she could see them.

"No," she said in a persistent whine as she'd started kissing his cheek and pulling on him to get him to move towards their car.

"Well, thanks," he said to Evan and me as he followed his girlfriend to catch her before she attempted the stairs alone.

"Bye Delphinium," Evan and I called after them before shutting the door and turning back to find Kodi and Juan staggering to their feet as well.

Evan and I exchanged an amused look and giggled furiously at the prospects of what they were going to do after they made it back to Kodi's bedroom.

"Use protection!" Evan shouted as her door clicked shut and then she crashed on the couch next to me.

"A virgin-less Kodi is weird to think about," I mused chuckling a little bit more.

"Who would ever want to have sex with Kodi?" Evan queried, and I knew exactly what she meant. Kodi had been great as a friend but too gross to want to fuck.

"Anyway," Evan said drunkenly moving over my lap to straddle me as we sat on the couch. "We can't leave you out."

I considered her as I stroked circles and patterns over her back and sides and she leaned her head against my shoulder happily. "You don't have to do anything if you don't feel up to it," I told her enjoying the feeling of her warm breath against my chest.

"I'd feel bad if we didn't," she admitted kissing my neck affectionately. "I know how much you enjoy it, anyway."

I nodded truthfully. She had been right about that. I liked fucking her a lot.

"Still, I don't mind this either," I said continuing to trace her curves.

She nodded into my shoulder. "This is nice."

We sat like that in silence enjoying our company in absolute contentment where she'd lean up to kiss me every once in a while, and I'd continue drawing on her back. Then disaster struck in the worst possible way.

Evan started having an attack.

I'd never experienced one with her before, but Kodi had and Kodi had been otherwise occupied. I guess I had to go it alone.

Evan's attacks had something to do with her cancer and her immune system that caused her immense pain. She cried into my shoulder and shook all over from the stabbing sensations that wracked her body, and I helplessly held her there on my lap cooing soft nothings to her to distract her mind in any way I could.

After a few minutes of that, she promptly shot up with her hand over her mouth and rushed into the bathroom. Kodi told me a bit about what they were like after she had one and how sometimes the pain became so intense that she'd throw up, so I remained calm as she jumped off my lap.

I followed her into the bathroom and knelt on the floor beside her to brush the hair from her face and continued offering my support to her as I did.

"I'm so sorry," she said as she cringed, and another wave passed over her.

"No, it's ok. I'm here," I told her rubbing her back again.

I turned as a door opened and Juan came stumbling out of Kodi's room and turned looking at us frustrated before turning and vomiting into the bathroom sink.

I cringed and opted out of breathing for a moment while Evan still occupied the toilet. She too seemed pretty disgusted by him in that moment.

He turned the water on and it didn't seem to want to drain at all. He shrugged at me before trotting back into Kodi's room and shutting the door in his wake. He didn't have any pants on.

"You know, if I wasn't so grossed out by that I'd say it's pretty damn ironic that he just threw up in the middle of having sex with Kodi," I told her as her face sat in the toilet bowl again.

Her laugh echoed against the porcelain and I knew from there that she'd be alright and Kodi's life would definitely suck tomorrow having to clean up the mess in the sink.

PART III

SENIOR

18

———

NIPPLE PIERCINGS

*P*erez came to the little valley airport to pick me up after I'd flown into town for the first time in over a year and I couldn't have been more excited to see her. It'd been a year since I'd seen any of my college friends, and even though things felt a little different on my end, I didn't think that I'd changed so much that I wouldn't be able to pick right back up where we left off. A year studying abroad will definitely change you, though. I certainly did miss them!

"Desi! My sexy pirate is back to me!" Perez squeaked as she shrank down to give me a low hug around my torso that happened to be her trademark hug I'd received many times before I'd left.

She'd started referring to me as a spy initially, but I'd quickly corrected her that pirates were way cooler and that I preferred a little booty.

I squeezed around her hunched shoulders and beamed at her. "Hey! How are you? How is everything? Where's Evan and Kodi?"

She talked hurriedly about everything going on, about our apartment and how she'd seen Evan and Kodi and how they'd helped her move her stuff into our new place.

They were working.

Explained a lot about why they'd miss their first opportunity to see me.

Perez had already moved into our new apartment and had been living there for a week before my arrival and seemed to like the space quite a bit.

I listened to her chatter away in her soft higher pitched voice while we climbed into her little red Jeep and headed to my storage unit to pick up a few of the things that had been left there over the time I'd been away.

Hopefully, we'd move everything if we had the time, but I couldn't be sure we'd be able to make it in only one load. Even if not, I still had the blessing of almost an entire August day in the mountains and the sun still sat high overhead. We had plenty of time to work with by the sound of things.

It took a couple of trips to get my stuff from my storage unit and through our front door. The fresh mountain air felt light and familiar, and something about near perpetual sunlight brought a smile to my face that wouldn't have gone away no matter what.

We moved things around in our place. Right as the door opened to the apartment they'd left the pull-out couch. Perez informed me that it'd be best not to move it again. She'd nicknamed it "The Metal Nightmare" for its weight and hadn't touched it since.

I thought our new place was cute and perfect for the two of us. You walked in and ignored the ugly blue carpet in favor of the cedar rafters in the ceiling. The kitchen had been separated from the living room with a high-top counter on the left and down the short hallway were two bedrooms and a bathroom.

Since they'd stayed over the summer, Kodi had been kind enough to get a mattress and a box spring for me so that I wouldn't have to hunt around for them once I arrived. They were queen-sized, too, which worked out perfectly for me and I'd have to pay her back for them the next time I saw her.

Perez started growing out her hair since the last time I'd seen her so that she could officially pull it back into a ponytail. It didn't do much of anything to help define her neck and chin, but she could look however she wanted if that's what made her happy.

She helped me move my stuff around and unpack a little. Thankfully, I'd organized my stuff when I'd packed it up, so unpacking came down to pulling things from their boxes and sticking like things together in the same place around the apartment.

"I know everyone's excited to see you," Perez mentioned as we pushed my bed into the back corner of my bedroom and dropped it onto the ugly speckled carpet. Perez had already chosen the left room across the hall from mine, which only left me with one option. Despite being so close to our friends, we never really hung out anywhere but Evan and Kodi's, so Perez and I hadn't needed to worry about any kind of furniture besides what we'd be using for eating, sleeping, or doing homework on. It left us tons more room than every apartment the others had lived in.

I liked it.

"Are we going over there tonight?" I asked moving a small chest up next to my mattress for a side table since I lacked a bed frame to need anything taller.

"Yeah, I think they get off around eight, so we can get something to eat and go over there."

I nodded. Eight wouldn't arrive quite as soon as I'd like, but the same day felt better than tomorrow.

With only a few things left to do, including decorating, it seemed the perfect place to stop to run to the store for groceries, then over to Mario's for dinner. All the while, Perez told me about her adventures with our other friends during my year away.

"It seemed like Rah and Kodi were gonna hook up officially there for a minute, but something happened and Kodi got really angry at her. I don't know why, but it seemed like her attachment to Evan might have gotten in the way or something. They both have a strong attachment to her. Oh, and Ben was here for the semester, but he dropped out again. Oh, and I got a job and a new tattoo!"

I listened to the latest news on our friends and smirked. Things hadn't changed here and that felt refreshing. I could pick things up where I left off.

I did remember hearing about the thing between Kodi and Rah, though. I hoped whatever it was and whatever it turned into, it wouldn't cause too much strife in our current friend dynamics.

We ate happily before Perez received a text from Evan telling her they were home and waiting for us.

"Oh! We need to go! They're so excited to see you!" Perez exclaimed as we finished our meal and grabbed the checks.

I wanted to jump out of my skin with excitement.

Perez drove us in her little red Jeep through the familiar streets of our little town and back to Mountaineer Village to the other side of the complex where Evan and Kodi lived.

"Are you ready?" she squeaked with anticipation. I wasn't sure which of us felt more excited for me, but I beamed at her and nodded. We walked up to the second floor and she knocked rapidly before stepping back to let me be in the way of the door.

"Oh, my god, Desi!" Evan greeted throwing open the door for me. She looked the same as I'd left her albeit with much longer hair.

Still beautiful.

We hugged briefly, her smelling like stale cardboard and pizza before Kodi walked out of her room at the commotion.

"Hi, Desi!" Kodi said in her same humdrum way as if she'd just woken up. She hugged me more enthusiastically than Evan had, smelling equally of used pizza boxes. "You owe me \$40."

I laughed at her but pulled the money out of my pocket for the bed all the same. Least I could do since she'd gone through the trouble of finding it for me.

"In honor of Ben, you totally just lost The Game," I told her, eyes glittering with mirth.

Per usual, Kodi made a beeline for the fridge to grab beers for the group. I looked around the common rooms of their apartment and it seemed like they had way less space than Perez and me, but it may have been the fact that they had tons of stuff crowded around all of their furniture making it seem like the walls were closing in on the space.

We drank the beers and Kodi started on mixing too-strong drinks in their colorful plastic cups. Dishes still existed all over their kitchen and coffee table and 'pigsty' seemed the only word able to describe the general feeling of the room, but none of that mattered to me at all. Evan and Kodi, my best friends in the whole world minus Ben, were there with me after a whole year and we were finally all legal drinking ages.

"Here's to a super late happy birthday!" Evan toasted to

me holding her still full glass while I'd practically polished mine off by that point. We toasted to me and laughed heartily at the true lateness of it. It'd been over a month ago.

Being well on my way, I let Kodi refill me and I chugged it before scowling at the lingering bitterness of the vodka she'd put in it that the juice couldn't even hide the flavor of. *Definitely too strong.*

Confident in my drunkenness and the fact that I knew exactly what it took to turn Evan on, I sauntered over to her as she sat on a stool by the counter.

I knew where we *could* go. I knew from every other experience I had telling me that we were going to fuck as soon as we were both drunk enough. I counted on that, honestly.

I ran my hand across her back and nuzzled and kissed across the side of her neck and jaw. She gasped, shivered, then pushed me away.

"I need to be way drunker for that," she told the room before chugging her own drink and having Kodi load her up with another one.

To prompt her further, I let my hand continue tracing circles and patterns across her shoulders that made her keep shivering and squirming. "Go sit down and I'll deal with you in a minute," she told me taking another large swig of the new drink Kodi gave her and cringing at the flavor.

Satisfied, I wandered back to the green couch where Perez had perched herself to watch us. I'm not sure why Perez never seemed keen on being in the throes of action within our little group of friends, but she sat quietly sipping whatever horrible drink Kodi had given her.

Without even finishing her second drink, Evan turned wickedly in my direction and my skin smoldered wherever her eyes lingered.

Yes, please, I thought watching her coyly make her way

from her stool to sit across my lap. I smiled wantonly grabbing her hips and pulling her closer to me.

I enjoyed her straddling me the most. She fit so well in my lap and I reveled in the moment before she took hold of the bottom of my shirt and lifted it up over my head. She captured my lips in a kiss I'd longed for since I'd last seen her as my shirt landed to the side somewhere.

To keep with fairness, I rid her of her dingy NJROTC t-shirt, too. The bras quickly, desperately, followed, and soon the two of us sat in the middle of the living room making out with nothing but pants in our way and lust-filled eyes.

"Well, I think I'm gonna go..." Perez announced from her corner of the couch. She broke Evan's adoring concentration when she said that which had given me a chance to look around.

Kodi managed to set up her gaming console without a word and started playing something like Skyrim. Perez had finished her drink and moved to get up from the couch.

"No, stay!" Evan cried grasping out and pulling Perez closer to us so that she could join in the fun Evan and I were having. She seemed hesitant at first, but Evan could be oddly encouraging when it came down to it.

I'd been perfectly ready to let her go, honestly. If she didn't feel like being a part of everything or get involved with Kodi, why did I need to make her stay? Evan would never allow that, though. She always put her friends' well beings above her own. It was the nature of the beast. Nothing I did would have prevented her from pulling Perez in.

Evan started by kissing her and putting her into the same form of undress the pair of us were in all from her position on my lap. I watched.

Never one to fight anything, Perez allowed her clothes to

come off and her mouth to be occupied by both me and Evan in alternating goes. I couldn't remember her bra coming off, but Perez didn't have one on then and something about testing the sensitivity of her nipples seemed enticing to me. While Evan made out with her, I took her nipple into my mouth and sucked hard.

One of the most distinct and unforgettable moments of intoxication for me is the feeling of those metallic bars from Perez's nipple piercings clacking against my teeth as I sucked on them. I recalled her getting them. She'd asked me to come along for moral support. I couldn't have done it, but the drive to put them in my mouth had been more than I could resist.

"Come to my room, I need space," Evan said to Perez, getting up off my lap and pulling her in the direction of their hallway.

No, stay...

I woke up feeling like I'd suffocate in the heat of the room. I'd been sweating under the pilled blanket over me, and I pushed it off all while realizing that I was completely naked on a mattress that didn't have any sheets on it. My grogginess from the early morning dissipated and I looked around not recalling the space or how I'd ended up there.

What the—

I flopped back onto the mattress and scrunched my eyes tight trying to reassemble the foggy pieces of memory left floating around in the darkness of the previous night.

Okay, so Evan and Perez left, and Evan gave me Kodi to keep me company while she was gone...Evan came back to Kodi and I fighting each other for dominance which was super fun but could have knocked someone's teeth out. Maybe that's why my face hurts? Where did this mattress come from?

I racked my brain trying to jog out a few hazier memories, but nothing more came out. I went for finding all my clothes instead.

A door creaked from the hall and I turned to find Kodi, in all her groggy, bed-headed glory, creeping her way from her room and paused to find that I, in a state of half-undress, had been watching her. Clearly, she hadn't expected me to be awake, yet.

I glanced at the time on my phone.

6:30 a.m. Fuck me...

"I don't think I've ever seen you alert and active this early before, Kodi," I taunted as she stumbled into the bathroom. Of all of us, Kodi enjoyed sleep the most and wouldn't give it up unless the building was actually burning down.

"Yeah, well, I never asked for a bladder," she countered before closing the door on me.

When she came out, she wandered over and plopped down on the couch tiredly rubbing her eyes like a child. "You wanna go get breakfast?" she mumbled.

Based on the slight headache forming between my ears, that sounded amazing. "Yes!"

We glanced down the hall at Evan's closed door knowing how angry she'd be if we woke her for food. I could just hear her chewing the two of us out for being idiots that had no concept for the sleeping patterns of kings. So, we dressed quickly and left to find some nice hearty grub to kill whatever alcohol had been left over in our stomachs. Sunrises in the mountain summers were nice enough that we opted to walk and made our way downtown.

"So, how much of last night do you remember? I'm not even sure how I ended up falling asleep completely naked," I admitted rubbing at my neck slightly embarrassed.

Kodi looked at me nonplussed, "Yeah, you were way far gone. So, do you remember Evan bringing you her mattress?"

"Not at all."

"Well, what about us *tongue wrestling*?"

"Vaguely. That's pretty hazy."

Kodi thought for a minute about how to order and lay everything out for me. "So, we were making out pretty intensely for a while and then Evan seemed to give up on keeping Perez around and left her in the bedroom to come out and check on us. When she saw what we were doing, she stopped us and started coaching me on how to have sex with you since she apparently thought I was the one not doing it right."

"To be fair, we were both pretty aggressive there," I chuckled remembering the feeling of my face after waking up that morning.

"Yeah, well, don't fight me and we'll be cool next time," she suggested as we walked.

"Probably not gonna happen, but nice try."

She laughed, "Well, Evan still felt the need to coach and decided it'd be easier with a flat surface, so she went back to her room and grabbed the mattress off her bed and brought it into the living room. Meanwhile, Perez left, thankfully, and Evan made you lay down so that she could keep teaching me. We kind of tag teamed it, actually."

I could dig that. "Hmm...like the very last thing I remember from the whole night was her coming out of the room and being like 'No, no, Kodi what the fuck are you doing? You're going to hurt her!' and then you stopped fighting me. That's it. Next thing I knew, I was waking up in your living room that's a damn oven for that early in the morning."

Kodi sympathized with me. She'd been all too happy to take the west-facing room in their place. Something about that happy morning sunshine didn't sit well with her.

Definitely could go without drinking that much again, though.

19

MARRY ME NOT

Danielle Rah and I had been working out for days after I'd convinced her to start coming to the fitness center with me since I didn't want to go at it alone. It always took a little prodding on my end, but I'd appreciated the time with her and getting into better shape after all the drinking we'd been doing since the year started.

She'd unceremoniously filled the space that Perez seemed to be leaving as she pulled further and further away from the group after I'd come back from my year abroad, but it wasn't my job to be sure the girl maintained her friendships.

Rah was a friend of Evan's from high school. Though she was two years younger than the bulk of our group, I enjoyed knowing that each of the friends that seemed to step into the place of Delphinium in our group always gravitated more towards me in the end. Rah was no exception.

The two of us had been getting closer after she'd gotten over the initial fear that I wouldn't like her and that she'd be kicked out of the group. Apparently, they'd been talking me up with all the adventures we'd shared over our years of friendship and she'd become intimidated by the mere idea of me.

As flattering as that was, I'm glad she quickly got over it.

Rah was an interesting one, though. After realizing that she'd technically known Evan the longest and therefore held the most sway over Evan's decisions, Kodi had started treading lightly around her and that wasn't a normal thing for Kodi to do. Evan had introduced Rah to us by her last name because of their time in ROTC together and it's stuck with us as we got to know her. She came from Germany originally and her mom had married her stepdad who'd been stationed over there at the time and then moved back to America when he had the chance.

She walked uncannily flat-footed, like a duck, and never went a day without straightening her dense, dyed-auburn curls. Of all of her features, she hated her hair the most because of its tight curls and kinks that came from her father's African American heritage. Her mom's genes had some influence over her, though. Her skin was more of a *caramel* color than true brown, being sure to pronounce every syllable of the word, and her almond eyes were more rust-colored than chocolate. She had the same issues we all did with our weight and it hadn't taken much for me to convince her to join me at the gym.

She could even claim being as feminine, or even more so, than me.

That said a lot, considering that I'd been hanging around no-makeup wearing, unflattering women all of my college career before she'd come around.

Rah and I hit things off immediately when we'd met at the beginning of the year and I was glad to call her a friend most of the time. Her copper-tinted brown eyes slanted happily above the high apples of her cheeks and she retained the propensity to laugh even in the gravest of times. I admired her for that, her easy nature, and her ability to make friends.

She'd walked over to my place so that we could start our journey up the mountain to the fitness center, but the clouds seemed foreboding and the chill didn't sit well with us for being early October when it seemed to rain the most. We figured after sweating from our workout, it'd be extra not fun as the evenings started to cool down, and we decided to use the people we knew that had cars to escape that fate.

Come to the fitness center with us. I'd texted Evan hoping to get a response.

She could be pretty fickle most of the time. She liked participating in things like drinking and camping and adventures, but she also didn't enjoy giving the satisfaction of partaking in things unless she'd suggested them. I wondered if her mind warred with itself often on whether to spend time with us or pretend to be too cool for our activities.

Fine, but we're driving.

For the first time in a long time, she came to workout with us and insisted on driving up the mountain without either of us even having to ask. I'd never known her to be one for strenuous activities, but she didn't have to be at our altitude. Walking up and down the mountain for classes would usually get the job done.

We checked in and set up on a group of treadmills. While I prefer ellipticals, there hadn't been three open all together, so we started walking with a headphone in one ear and the ability to listen to our conversation with the other.

Our three treadmills were in the first row looking out over the library lawn and parking lot on the second floor of the fitness center, though we couldn't see much as a cold mist had slowly crept in, and the clouds hung low, heavy, and gray in the usually sunny skies.

The fitness center sat in the middle of the Escalante Complex. Colorado and Dolores Halls were on the right, and Tomichi and Crystal Halls were on the left. Evan and I were all too familiar with Escalante with it being our home for a year and a half of the beginning of college.

A lull had befallen us as we walked before Evan cleared her throat and glanced at me. "Let's get married," she suggested from my right that caught me off guard for a moment.

I considered Evan from the corner of my eye and glanced over at Rah who stood looking a little stunned on the other side of her. I wondered if she'd been serious. She seemed to be, at least.

"Okay, but I think we should date first," I told her not denying but also not wanting to rush into anything. I'd known her long enough now that her mouth ran away with her thoughts sooner than she sometimes took the chance to think about them.

"Really, let's just run away to Vegas and elope," she insisted as she pulled out her phone.

I waited as she sat on the line before someone answered. "Daddy, what would you think if I ran away to Vegas and eloped with Desi?"

Why she decided to ask *her* parents for permission, I'm not sure, but I think she hoped she'd made a sound decision in asking me then.

I couldn't hear anything but muffled talking from his end since the workout equipment around us had been drowning out all the quieter sounds, but I knew that he couldn't say much to counter her if she really wanted it.

"Okay! Love you?" she said. I considered the way she'd asked them for love instead of delivering it outright. *Might that have anything to do with any of her childhood issues?* I'm sure there were plenty of familial things I'd never have the chance to help her through, but I held on to the speculation all the same.

She hung up and put the phone back on the ledge of the treadmill as we continued walking. "He said he doesn't care."

"So, date me and I'll marry you," I said as our time ended, and the treadmills came to a stop.

I watched her hesitate on the answer.

Why? I'd seen her date Kayla, Rachael, Kodi, and CJ. The only people she hadn't were Ben and me, and it baffled me as to why considering she loved the two of us most of all.

"Date me."

She continued to look skeptical.

We started on the weight machines and floor exercises. Rah said absolutely nothing while we worked, choosing to stay out of the decision-making that ultimately had to be done by Evan though Evan begged her to give some sort of advice on what she should do.

I didn't mind letting her think about it, but I wouldn't let her escape the decision, either. With each change of machine, I'd cross her path and said it again.

"Date me."

"Date me, Evan."

"I love you and you love me and that's why we should date."

"We *should* date."

"*Date me.*"

Eventually, I'd said it enough times with enough favorable arguments, that she crossed the room to stand in front of me while I did a butterfly machine.

"I do love you," she began, "I don't know if this is gonna work out, though...What if we break up and it's horrible? What if we aren't friends anymore?"

"Do you really believe that'll happen?" I asked earnestly.

She frowned at the floor before meeting my eyes. "No."

"What's the problem, then?"

She shook her head once at me before glancing at Rah and looking me square in the face with seriousness like she'd decided to enter into a business deal. "Fine, yes. I'll date you."

I beamed at her as we continued with our weights and Rah congratulated us on our new relationship.

What I'd wanted for years had finally come true for me, and my stomach fluttered about excitedly.

We finished all our workout and Rah had to run back to her dorm for some meeting or dinner plans that I hadn't paid much attention to. Evan offered me a ride home in the rain in her old black Tacoma. I'd been glad for the forethought on driving then.

We parked in front of my apartment where we'd be parting ways for the evening, and we both looked at each other with hesitation and knowledge of what came next before I opened the door to leave. I couldn't leave the car without a kiss.

Why I hesitated after I'd experienced kissing her dozens of times before that moment, I can only guess. I remembered our first kiss happening while CJ had been courting her and how he hadn't been moving fast enough for any of us. I'd told her to kiss me from my place on Kodi's bed and she'd jumped over from Kayla's bed excitedly and tackled me with an amazing kiss. She'd complimented me on it, too.

Why couldn't I be so bold there in the truck?

Probably because every other moment leading up to that had been affection for a friend, someone I loved dearly but couldn't consider anything more.

This time, we'd gone a step further from where we'd been and closer to where each of us wanted to be. It meant something that she asked to marry me, that I wanted the same from her, and that we'd started dating promptly after her confession.

Finally, after avoiding eye contact and worrying my lip, I looked up hopefully and she leaned in and kissed me. She wanted everything I had to offer her, and she let me know through that kiss and each small kiss after that.

Crazy enough, that's the only time I'd ever kissed her while we were both sober.

20

A GYPSY & A PIRATE

"What are you being for Halloween?" Rah asked me knowing we'd planned on going out and that I'd go all out for one of my favorite holidays.

I considered it for a moment before telling her. "I got this really pretty green corset with gold embroidery. It came in the mail last week. I'm just waiting on this cool black skirt I ordered that kind of looks like something a pirate would wear."

"That sounds awesome," she admitted. "Can I see it?"

I shrugged knowing I'd need her help putting it together anyway, so we made our way back to the apartment Perez had been slowly moving out of.

"Is she gone, yet?" Rah asked as we moved inside, and I kicked my shoes off by the door.

"Almost. Says she'll be gone by November, so we'll see."

Rah considered me a minute knowing I felt begrudged towards Perez for bailing on me the way she had. "Well, where's the corset?"

I smiled gratefully at her for taking my mind off my

roommate drama and wandered back into my room to grab it out of my closet and put it on.

"So, the lacing isn't tied since I can't do it myself, so maybe we can lace it up now, and I'll just use these snaps to take it on and off," I suggested holding it up around my waist.

"Oh, my goodness!" Rah swooned over my costume piece. I knew how she felt, I did the same thing when I took it out of the box.

She got to work pulling on the laces up my back so that they held the corset snugly against my torso and I braced myself against the counter so that she could get a better hold on it.

"Do you want this to be super tight or just tight enough?"

"I'd like to breathe, thanks," I told her holding the best posture of my life with the help of the ribbing sewn into the piece.

"This looks amazing on you. It's stunning," she finished and twisted me around to look at me.

"I'll be wearing a different shirt under it, of course," I confirmed feeling a little uncomfortable with her compliments. Rah always had the nicest things to say to me.

She laughed at me. "Well, I figured you weren't wearing this!" She was referencing my pink shirt I'd been wearing that clashed miserably with the bright true green in the corset.

"I just can't wait to see it with everything else," I admitted stroking my sides happily enjoying the curve it made with the ribbing.

Halloween weekend came faster than either of us could grasp. Rah decided to be a fairy and do some fun sparkly makeup around her eyes that made them pop brightly.

She'd come over to help me in case I needed it getting into the corset and admired me fully after the whole ensemble had been put together.

"You literally look so amazing," she told me looking me over. "Are you going for a pirate or a gypsy?"

I considered her for a moment. I hadn't really thought about gypsy as a costume, but something about it did remind both of us of Esmeralda from *The Hunchback of Notre Dame.*

"I don't know. Which do you think?"

She put her hands up in surrender and took a step away from me. "It's your costume, hon."

"Let's take a picture and ask my mom what she thinks," I suggested handing my phone to her.

She took the picture and sent it off to my mom to receive an almost immediate response.

Gypsy for sure.

Well, Mother has spoken.

"Gypsy it is," Rah confirmed glancing at the text over my arm.

"Cool! Do you think Evan'll wanna come with us?"

I started slipping my ID, cash, and a credit card into my bra so that I wouldn't have to carry anything while out drinking. *Too bad the costume didn't have a secret pocket or something.*

Rah nodded fiercely. "We should invite her if anything, but I can't imagine she'll wanna stay home when she sees you dressed like *this!*"

I laughed at her slightly embarrassed before we finished up and made our way from my apartment to Evan and Kodi's across the complex.

As soon as Evan opened the door and saw me, she stared

with predatory eyes that roved my figure hungrily. Well, Rah had been right about something, at least.

"Hey, we came to see if you wanted to go out with us tonight," Rah said glancing slyly at me as if to tell me *I told you so.*

I smiled at her in acknowledgment.

"I have no idea what I'd wear," she admitted pushing Addie back from the door so that she couldn't escape into the night, "but I definitely want to go out with you." She looked pointedly at me, and the butterflies fluttered around in my stomach excitedly.

"You don't *have* to dress up. You can be minimal like me," Rah told her motioning to her small fairy wings and glittery makeup as Evan moved back into her room to rummage for something to wear that might even come close to what I had on.

"What about this haltered corset thing?" she called waving a black piece of fabric out her door.

"Oh, let me help you!" Rah told her and flashing me a grin before she moved down the hall to Evan's room.

Addie and I watched each other while we waited. Evan's dog had been fine most of the time that I'd known her, but Evan had started training some bad habits into her recently. After Evan and Kodi started smoking pot in their apartment, they'd given Addie some secondhand by blowing the smoke in her face. If they were drinking on top of it, Addie was allowed to have the alcohol, too.

Though bad for the dog, none of that bothered me so much as Addie's obsession with the plastic pop bottles left all over the house by her owner who drank nothing but soda all day long. Addie would find a bottle and offer it to Evan for fetch and after playing that for a minute, Evan decided the most fun follow-up to that was the *attack game.*

Play was simple: dangle the bottle over another human, usually the one sitting closest, and tell Addie to get the bottle. Being a rescue with a checkered past and no qualms with getting what's hers, Addie would do exactly that, and when I was the victim, Evan liked to take special care to be sure her dog snapped somewhere close to my face at least once while the bottle was in her hand.

Despite having dogs of my own, I'm still more of a cat person on a normal basis. Evan's torture of us under the guise of a game with her dog put a sour taste in my mouth for the creature who'd taken to lying in the hall to wait for her master to come out.

Evan lesson: Even my dog could kill you if I wanted her to.

Ten minutes later Rah came out waggling her eyebrows at me as if to tell me I'd definitely enjoy whatever outfit they'd come up with.

Evan stepped out after her wearing a pair of tight black jeans, a flowy white shirt, and the black halter corset over it.

"I wish I had a hat," she admitted looking entirely like the pirate of my dreams.

You should wear those jeans more often.

"You look perfect," I told her, and she beamed albeit a bit uncomfortably at the compliment.

"So, where are we going?" Evan asked expecting us to have a plan of attack for the evening.

I turned to Rah knowing that she wanted to hit up a party somewhere. Maybe we'd go to a few!

"Who's driving?" Evan asked again, and I surrendered knowing that I didn't have a car to drive.

Rah conceded to driving if only for the fact that she kept glancing between us and catching us ogling over the other.

She prided herself on being some kind of matchmaker, at least.

We took off towards a house on Wisconsin St. where one of Rah's friends had been hosting a Halloween party. It didn't look like any of the other house parties I'd attended, not exceptionally busy or anything, but we'd started on drinking and we wouldn't stop after that.

People, men especially, would watch us as we walked into a room and I saw a few of them give us a once-over approvingly. They were the main providers of our alcohol after they came over to make conversation with us.

"Hey, whatever you are, that looks awesome on you," this super drunk guy dressed in a ghillie suit without the head-piece said walking over to me and handing me another beverage. I turned the can and saw the blue ribbon and hoped that wouldn't be the only thing I'd drink all evening, but no one said I needed to *savor* anything.

"Thanks! I'm a gypsy," I told him tapping the can against his and drinking swiftly.

"Beautiful is what you are," he said leaning in closely so that I had been the only person to hear what he said.

I smiled brightly at him for the compliment. Some drunk men were so kind.

We got into a conversation about the other costumes he'd seen and whether we were standing in his house or not. He denied it, and then Rah had to shout over the music to get our attention about heading to another party at the corner of Denver and Wisconsin.

"Yeah, let's bounce!" I yelled and let Rah lead us out of the house.

"It was nice to meet you!" ghillie suit guy called, and I turned and quickly gave him a kiss before walking down the stairs after my pirate girlfriend and our fairy guide.

"Still allowed to hook up with other people while we're dating, right?" I asked finally being able to talk without shouting at each other.

"Yeah," Evan said grabbing my hand and swinging our arms as we made our way up the street to the corner and the most infamous of the party houses in town.

Once inside, I encountered a guy who'd spent much of his time around the residents that lived in my hall over sophomore year.

"Jake! Nice costume," I said admiring his rendition of Zoidberg minus the tentacles which seemed to have come off sometime earlier in the night.

"Woah, you look great!" he told me giving me a hug. "You need something to drink?"

"Yeah!" I said waving Evan and Kodi after me into their tiny kitchen. There were people everywhere dressed in all kinds of things all the way down to almost nothing. Some had even pulled out their ski gear and were walking around as ski bums in various stages of undress since they all seemed to be getting hot the more people seemed to walk through the door.

Jake, digging into his fridge that seemed fully stocked with various alcohols, grabbed a bottle of Firewhiskey, uncapped it and handed it to me after he'd taken a swig of it himself.

"Cheers!" I told him taking a pull from the cold bottle and handing it to Evan. The cinnamon burned my throat a little, but it definitely tasted better than a few other alcohols I'd tried that night.

He then handed each of us a beer before giving me another drunk hug and walking back into the room that I imagined could have passed as a living room in any other house but had been converted into a dancefloor with a DJ booth that had a person in a DeadMau5 head standing over it.

"Dance with me?" I asked Evan as I bumped cans against theirs and drank the Buds he'd given to us.

Not perfect, but still better than some of the stuff I'd been drinking that night.

"This music is terrible, but sure," she agreed and Rah followed us into the dark dance area where we laughed, mostly at Evan's inability to dance (which she freely admitted to), and had a great time before Evan grabbed the back of my neck and pulled me so that she could talk right next to my ear.

"Wanna go to the Last Chance?" she asked me, and I would have been down for anything at that point.

"Rah, are you ready to go?" I asked her as we danced through our third song.

"Yeah!" she yelled, and we immediately made our way out into the blissfully chilly night and back to Rah's car parked up the street. "So, where are we going?"

"The Last Chance. It's a bar on the other side of town near the airport," Evan told her as she released my hand to climb into the front seat of Rah's car. I climbed in behind Rah, but she hesitated in starting her car and going.

"Oh, can I get in? I'm not 21," she said pointing that crucial piece of information out to us that we'd forgotten having drank so often with her.

"You should be fine, we'll just tell them you're our DD and have them mark your hands or something so they know."

She seemed placated by that and started her car to take us across town to a bar I hadn't been to, yet.

We parked and walked past the outside of a relatively nondescript, cedar-sided building lit by a single outside light near the front door. We handed our IDs to the bouncer to find that though he hesitated on letting Rah in, with the right idea and the fact that she had been driving us around, he pulled a black marker from his bag and put big Xs on the fronts and backs of Rah's hands and let us all in.

The inside of the bar looked like most every other bar I'd seen. A large oval bar attached to the back wall sat in the center of the open room, pool tables were on the left side and a dance floor on the right. They kept it well-lit to prevent any trouble from starting, which created an interesting atmosphere for all the drunk Halloween celebrators, but everyone seemed to be having a good time. Plus, it was *packed.*

"Hey, there's Delphinium!" I said excitedly waving in her direction until she saw me and almost reluctantly waved back. Todd noticed us when she'd waved. *That'd certainly be interesting.*

Evan directed us towards the bar where we finagled our way in and called the bustling bartender over for a round. He nodded and moved off to get what we needed while Evan slapped her credit card onto the counter. "Will you put that on a tab, I'm gonna go talk to Delphinium," she told me before slipping out from the herd of people around the bar and moving over towards the pool tables where we'd last seen them.

I did as she asked and took the two pints carefully and tried making my way through the crowd without spilling. It worked, mostly, but there were way too many people around for all of it to arrive safely.

"Hey guys! Fancy meeting you here!" I greeted handing Evan her beer and taking a sip from mine.

She and Todd seemed to be in a serious discussion for the occasion, so Delphinium pulled me over and started up a conversation of our own while Rah hung back a bit to listen.

"I heard you're getting married! Congratulations!"

"Yeah!" she gushed. "Todd pwoposed this summah. Did you see?"

She held her hand out to me and a little white gem sparkled back at me. I considered calling it a diamond, but I knew they didn't have any money, so that would have been very much out of the question. It didn't sparkle like a diamond, anyway.

"Oh, it's so pretty!" I told her smiling.

"Yeah, I told him we have to wait until aftah I gwaduate which won't be for another yeaw, so it's not a big deal," she admitted though I could tell she'd be a little bit happier if they did it sooner than that.

"What do your parents think?" I asked since I thought we were way too young to be married at only twenty-one years old.

"Oh, they love Todd. My mom's supah excited and has been sending me all of these things about weddings, but it still won't be for a while, so we won't be this young."

I mulled that around for a minute and while I did, it seemed that Evan and Todd had concluded whatever they'd been talking about.

"Hey Baby, are you ready to go?" Todd asked as Delphinium moved over to him to stand under his arm.

"Yeah Babe!" she agreed before turning back to all of us. "It was good seeing you guys!"

We watched them walk out before Rah turned to us exasperated. "I don't know how you guys stand her! She's so annoying and whiny!"

Evan and I exchanged a knowing look. "She's cool when

she's not dating anybody," Evan told her and seemed to have been placated by whatever she and Todd had discussed.

I danced in my place while we stood there drinking, and Evan let Rah take little sips off her beer while the staff had their backs turned. Not like the bartenders were going to notice much of anything with how busy they were.

Soon, we'd gotten into our second round, which definitely did me in. Evan made the executive decision that we should go home, since she'd also been well on her way, and Rah ushered us outside seeming a little sad that she hadn't been able to drink with us while we were there.

On the way to the car, which wasn't a far walk at all, I took Evan and kissed her deeply before walking closely the rest of the way and touching her coyly in places that I knew made her shiver and moan to the point that she had to hold my hand to keep it from turning her on further.

Instead, I took the opportunity to truly work some magic by pinning her against Rah's car and making out with her there until she pushed me away breathlessly.

"Okay, get in the car," she gasped holding the door for me and then climbing in to straddle me as she pulled the door closed behind her.

Rah groaned a moment clearly envious of what had begun to transpire behind her seat, but we paid no mind to it as we kissed and caressed in ways I hadn't experienced with her since we'd started dating.

This is my favorite Evan, I thought excitedly as Rah put the car in drive and took us back to Evan's apartment first. She parked, and it took Evan and me a moment to untangle ourselves, but we managed long enough to thank Rah and say goodbye to her, walk up their front steps and into their place before we started touching each other again.

"Jeez, how do I get this thing off?" Evan asked fumbling with the corset.

I looked ruefully at her before I sucked in and pushed the front so that the clasps slid and popped open. Once that came off, she took to pulling me along into her bedroom.

She kept the light off and I did my best not to trip over all the clothes and things I knew were mounded in heaps aside from the little trail from her door to the bed that she kept clear except for a stray sock here and there.

She shed a few more of her clothes and mine and then threw me onto her bed with nothing but my black skirt on. She tried climbing on top of me, but I fought her for it this time and flipped her a few times before she'd settled so that she stayed on the bottom.

A little shocked, she struggled and tried to flip me back, but I was taller and stronger and kept her there until she gave in and let me start for the first time since I'd met her.

Not just anyone could get Evan to lose control like me.

21

A DEATH AMONG THEM

"What would you say to someone from the gang coming to stay with us?" Evan asked Kodi, Rah and I as we sat around their little apartment watching another episode of *Bones* on Netflix. It'd become Kodi's favorite since she'd gotten so involved in her anthro major, and Rah and I couldn't care either way what we watched since we talked most of the time while it was on not paying attention.

With that poorly timed query, Kodi paused the episode and turned to her looking quizzical. We all did, honestly. She'd never invited anyone to come meet us before, and here she had someone coming to stay.

"What's up?" Kodi asked her as she scrutinized Evan propped up on the barstool by the counter and knowing that Evan must not have much of a say in where this Sloth stayed, or they'd be headed to the cabin like all the others.

"He just needs a place to stay," Evan said casually, and that seemed fine enough to me. But Kodi still watched her a moment more before agreeing.

"I guess that means I can't crash on your couch now,

huh?" Rah asked having been practically a third roommate for Evan and Kodi since she stayed over so often.

"That'd be great," Evan admitted turning to her.

"So, who is he and when does he arrive?" I asked pulling at the ends of my long hair. They'd started breaking with the cold air moving in.

"Tonight," she said, and I wondered why she'd waited so long to ask about him staying. "Do you wanna come to dinner with us when he gets here? I know everyone's been wanting to know more about you since we started dating."

I considered her and all that I knew about the Sloths before answering. I wanted to meet them ever since they'd started mysteriously showing up in town to wreak havoc and then leave without a word. Now would be as good a time as any, I figured. "Sure, where are you going?"

"Mario's, I think. Probably a little later, too," she said and then bit her lip in thought clearly warring with whether she should mention something else. "Don't say anything about anything you know, okay? I'm worried he's gonna start reporting on it to the others."

I hadn't dreamt of it, and I assumed that no one else had either. "Not a word," I said, and Rah and Kodi nodded.

"Thanks!"

With Rah and Kodi having to work that evening, anyway, there weren't any hard feelings about me being the only one with an invitation to dinner.

Sure enough, the evening rolled around, and Evan loaded us into the Tacoma and started the drive into town. Apparently, whoever came would be meeting us at the restaurant.

"I'm nervous for you to meet him," Evan admitted as we pulled into the parking lot and I grabbed her hand and squeezed it reassuringly.

"What can they do? I'm dating their boss," I told her thinking no one really could say anything about Evan's choice in partners.

She smiled uneasily before climbing out of the truck and waiting for me to come around so that we could walk into the old wood-paneled building together.

"Hi, just two of you?" the perky brunette hostess asked us as we walked in.

"There are three, actually. I think he's already here," she said, and the hostess told us to take a look around to check.

About four booths in on the far side of the room in a little cubby sat the man Evan had been expecting.

"Oh, you're here. Desi, this is Mike," she introduced and a man taller than me with dark hair and scruff that seemed a few days old looked back at me with interested dark eyes. All over, he seemed pretty tired, though.

I held my hand out to him politely and he shook it.

His hands were rough against mine.

"So how was your drive?" Evan asked uneasily, clearly knowing something that I did not.

"Fine. Nice that it hasn't started really snowing, yet," he said raspily.

"Good, good, and how long are you staying?" she asked again, and I wondered why exactly she didn't know that.

"I think a week. We'll see," he intoned, and I got the feeling that there wouldn't be any way to negotiate around it.

Evan sighed audibly. She looked clearly uncomfortable with the whole thing. I couldn't blame her. She'd managed to keep us away from them for practically three and a half years, and that meant something.

"So, I hear you two are dating," he said casually after the waitress came to take our orders.

Evan nearly choked on her drink.

They certainly were forward.

"Yes," I said as casually.

"When did you start?" Mike asked taking a sip of the pop he'd ordered.

I raised my eyebrows questioningly at him. I figured he'd already know that from talk. "The beginning of last month," I told him.

He shrugged approvingly at the thought.

"How are things back home?" Evan asked trying to steer the conversation away from her and I and onto something a bit more neutral.

Mike shrugged again. "Fine. Just getting things together now," he said clearly speaking about something that only he and Evan were meant to know about since he provided no detail beyond that.

Our food arrived, much to Evan's relief, and we ate in a tense silence. Part of me wondered if Mike felt any of it or if it had been Evan's extreme distaste for the situation as a whole. I wondered if we'd ever end up meeting any of the others at the rate this meeting seemed to be going.

I allowed Evan to steer all conversation after that. Mike asked the pair of us a few more questions, but mostly allowed his boss to direct where she wanted him to go. That seemed fine for both of us since we quickly ran out of conversation topics with the stunning lack of anything in common besides the fidgeting blonde to my left.

After the check came, Mike grabbed his and Evan got ours, though I told her she didn't need to since I could definitely handle it, and then we got up and walked out quieter than ever.

"So, we'll meet you back at the apartment," Evan said parting with Mike for the few minutes it'd take to drive back. He got into his little silver sedan and took off, and I waited for Evan to turn around and talk to me.

Instead, she turned and leaned her whole body against mine forcing me to wrap my arms around her smaller frame affectionately to keep us from toppling over.

"I don't think that was bad," I told her reassuringly as she stayed leaning against me breathing steadily.

"It was fine," she admitted as she continued to relax against me in the parking lot.

"So, what's the deal, then? Why's he here?" I asked her kissing the top of her head.

She gulped and reached her arms up to hug me, too. "Don't tell anyone else this, but Remi died."

I froze where I stood still holding her but unable to think about what that meant for not only the Sloths, but for Evan. Remi had not only been a huge part of the organization, but also of her life as a whole.

"How?" I asked starting to rub small circles into her back.

"Suicide," she said sadly, and I held her even tighter then.

I knew then why Mike had come. She'd done something similar before, so why would it be so hard for her to open a new cut in her arm to add to the scar I knew already existed there?

We drove back to the apartment in silence. She lost herself in thought which she scarcely let herself do around any of them. I couldn't say anything that would have made a difference to her then, either. Things whirred around chaotically in my head, too.

We parted with a kiss and I told her to let me know if she needed me.

The weekend passed quickly, and a text came through while I'd been reading through some homework.

Wanna come for a drive?

It seemed Evan needed me, and I figured this would be one of those moments where she wanted the company as she escaped life for a minute.

I replied and wandered out to grab my coat and boots and headed for the door where the old black Tacoma pulled up outside.

Kodi sat crammed in the back seat (which didn't exist since a subwoofer had been installed back there), and I frowned at her before hopping in.

She needs some heavy artillery tonight it seems.

"What's up?" I asked as we drove west towards Blue Mesa.

"I just needed to get away," she said, but the way she said it seemed flat and numb.

I said nothing more as we went until she parked in the same pavilion area we'd used for Delphinium's birthday freshman year, climbed out, and made her way to the frosty shore of the reservoir.

"What's going on, sweets?" Kodi asked clearly as alarmed as I had been when we had to jog to catch up with her.

"What would you do if I just walked into the lake?" she asked turning on us as soon as she reached the waterline.

Kodi and I both paused considering her seriousness. I saw it there in her eyes.

"What do you mean? You aren't going to do that!" Kodi chuckled obviously not seeing what I had.

Evan scoffed at her and said nothing.

Kodi got it then and her laughter died instantly. "I

wouldn't let you," she told her, and I mentally facepalmed again and again.

That's not what you say to a suicidal person, stupid!

Evan turned to me expectantly as if she were challenging me to say the same things Kodi had.

"I wouldn't stop you," I told her honestly, and she seemed to relax after I said it. "I'd be sad, and I'd wade in to retrieve your body, but I wouldn't stop you if that's what you really wanted."

Evan considered me for a moment thinking about what it meant if I did everything I said and if she could really be the one responsible for that.

"Doesn't the blackness look inviting? Like it could swallow you up in an instant and that'd be it. Hypothermia wouldn't take that long to set in either," she mentioned toeing the edge of the water with her boot.

"I would walk out and get you all the same," I told her standing out of reach to prove that I wouldn't be able to get her before she'd decided to take the plunge.

She heaved a sigh and scrunched her eyes closed as if she were preventing tears from slipping out of them the way I knew they probably needed to.

"Great! Now let's go back to that car!" Kodi said shivering and Evan started toeing the line again.

Certainly, I'd been cold out on the shore. I'd been holding back shivers ever since we'd left the truck, but I would suffer in the freezing cold a hundred times over if it meant I'd saved her life. Clearly, Kodi didn't see that or she'd have kept her mouth shut.

I growled at Kodi internally as she pushed Evan away from us, and I could have tackled her and started throttling her if I'd been anywhere but on the brink of preventing Evan from walking into the freezing, mountain-fed lake.

"I've considered how easy it would be. Just take off my coat and run in till I couldn't touch anymore," Evan said staring longingly into the darkness.

I considered for a moment what to say next. "That would be pretty easy. It usually is, right? It'll be hard to fish you out from there, but I think I owe it to your parents to take you back to them," I told her, and she looked sadly into the darkness still and sighed again.

Another Evan lesson: Death is only okay if I'm the one killing you.

She walked around in a circle considering me and not even bothering to look at Kodi as she stepped up to the water again in thought.

Clearly, Kodi thought that this had become a moment that she could present the thought of leaving as she, again, cheerfully told us to walk back up to the truck. To which Evan, who still sat finely on the edge, seemed to walk in enough that the soles of her boots submerged in the black water.

I glared hatefully at Kodi for speaking hoping that no one else got into trouble like this and expected her to help them out. She had no fucking clue what she was dealing with.

"Why is this so hard?" Evan asked tilting her head to look up at the sky. It became one of those rare cloudy nights, and no stars could be seen over the area which made it seem even darker and less inviting than if the stars shone brightly overhead.

"It'll be hard explaining to everyone why we didn't stop you when we take your body back. I'm sure Addie will be sad not having you around anymore, but I meant what I said," I told her not daring to move any closer for fear that she'd run. She looked so much smaller in those moments by the lake.

She stepped out of the water again and looked to me the way prisoners appeal to their executioners: Helplessly pleading.

"So, let's go back to the car now!" Kodi suggested again and Evan growled at her furiously.

"Can't you just shut up for once in your damn life? If you wanna go to the fucking car then walk up there! Jesus," Evan snarled, and I thanked her for it internal. I'd been wanting to do that since Kodi had first spoken.

"Fine, fuck, it's balls cold out. Let's fucking go," Evan conceded and joined me in the walk up the hill. She grabbed my hand and held onto it for dear life. I let her even if it meant I'd be the only thing anchoring her to the ground.

22

THE SOURCE OF EVIL & MOLDY CHEESE SMELLS

"Uh, Desi, can I talk to you for a minute?" Perez said propping herself up on one of our barstools while I worked around the little kitchen in our apartment making dinner. She'd taken to wearing grungier clothing as the days went on that only made her look boxy and bulky and a little more like she'd lost all faith in trying for herself. I questioned her self-worth once more as she settled in with a tee shirt that was at least two sizes too large and she avoided looking anywhere but at the table.

"Sure, what's up?" I asked closing a cheap wooden cabinet that held some of our spices after grabbing the salt and pepper.

"Well, um, what would you say to me moving, to me moving out?" she stammered quietly, and I stalled in my cooking shooting her a quick look.

"You wanna move out? Why?"

"Well, a friend invited me to come live with them and the rent would be way cheaper for all of us if I did..." Perez said, and I considered her thoughtfully. "It's definitely not about you at all! I love you, I just need to save money."

It always came down to money.

I frowned wondering what her moving out would mean for me. Certainly, I wouldn't have to worry about her running off to find random truckers and men to hook up with around town anymore. I did worry a lot about that lifestyle path she'd chosen, since it definitely wasn't healthy in the least and probably didn't supply her with the *emotional* satisfaction she clearly craved.

The sacrifices people make for attention.

"Please, say something," she begged after I'd been silent for too long.

I sighed heavily, unable to hide my disappointment. "I can't stop you if you want to break the lease and move out. What am I supposed to say? You do what you need to," I told her going back to cooking my dinner over the old gas stove.

"You really mean that?" Perez asked earnestly, and I glanced at her again.

"Yeah! We're friends. Why would I not support your decision?" I asked her. I definitely couldn't say no if she absolutely had to go, though I questioned her ability to save herself money no matter where she ended up living. She was one of those people that just wasn't good with her finances.

"Thank you!" she squeaked hopping off one of our barstools and moving around the counter to give me a low hug around my middle.

I hugged her back before watching her scurry off down the hall to her room to start preparing what she'd need to move out.

After about a month of Perez being out of the apartment, our complex manager called me to ask me what I'd think about filling the other room in the apartment with someone new.

My lease stated that I technically only rented half of the apartment, so it didn't cost me any more to have it empty than if it were filled.

"What are they like?" I asked thinking that I actually enjoyed living alone and having the space how I wanted it.

"She's an older woman from Crested Butte, and I'm just checking your comfort levels on this since it's your space first."

"Can I talk to her before I say anything?" I asked thinking about how much I might be able to glean from my potential future roommate.

The apartment manager gladly gave me the information to contact Susan. She seemed nice enough over the phone if only a little spacey. I couldn't tell if she existed in another world all the time or if our conversation caught her at an off moment.

I texted the complex manager to tell her that she seemed okay and I'd be fine with Susan moving in if it were easier for her that way, and she thanked me for it.

One thing I learned from my conversation with Susan: *you can't tell how people affect the space until they're confined in it.*

A portly woman with fully silver hair and a waddle moved into my apartment. She had kind eyes for a few days before they slowly grew wearier, assessing me more by the day. I'd assumed she'd be something of a matronly figure and offer peace through food and full bellies, but the more her presence lingered, the more the smell wouldn't go away putting me off my appetite completely.

At first, I wondered if it came from some of the old musty things she'd moved in with her. Like they held an odor that couldn't be helped as if it'd been trapped in the material as time wore on.

I questioned a few times why there never seemed to be anything except a bar of soap in the shower. I wondered if she took all her shower soaps and things back into her room when she'd finished with them and brushed it off as nothing more than that. A few more candles could drown any horrible scent thrown at them.

Susan usually always seemed uneasy around me, though. Like she had a secret she didn't want me to know or she didn't like me as a whole and attempted to hide that from me behind fake smiles and small talk about the days we'd had. It'd usually always come around to this one friend that she had that carved healing stones and that I should speak with him about it sometime.

Whatever that meant.

She'd moved in with a massage table that she'd offered me a session on, but that made me feel about as comfortable as sitting in a car on a freezing night while your friend heads into the woods to kill someone. She'd been so shifty around me, though.

On top of that, Susan ran her own business of *healing* people from that massage table. At least that's what she told me. I couldn't complain about it if she kept it out of our place, but each time I'd come home from class where the apartment smelled of gross cheese and a strange person, usually a man, would be splayed out on the massage table while she'd stick crystals over their bodies became a bit too much for me to handle.

No doing business in our apartment.

She'd gotten in trouble for that.

It never stopped her.

"Hey, do you guys want to come over?" I asked Kodi and Rah knowing that Evan had gotten into something that made her a little crankier than normal and not something that any of us could sanely be around.

"Sure!" Kodi agreed as they followed me from campus back to my place.

"I have to warn you, it stinks when you first walk in."

"Stinks? Like what?" Rah asked huddling a little further into her jacket. I couldn't blame her. November could be one of the worst months in the mountains when there isn't any snow on the ground.

"I think it smells like moldy cheese, honestly," I told her thinking on the rank smell I had to walk into each night after class.

"That's weird," Kodi mused. "Do you know what it's from?"

"No idea. It came when *she* moved in," I said trudging up my apartment steps to the door.

"Ew, god, I know what you mean!" Rah said as I opened the door.

"Oh, I didn't know you were having company," Susan commented airily as she wandered from her room into the kitchen to grab a snack from the fridge. "I'll just be in my room, then."

After she'd gone, Kodi turned to us still standing in the doorway. "I know where the smell is coming from. There's a fungus trapped between her fat rolls that she's not cleaning properly."

"Ewwww! That's just nasty!" Rah groaned moving further into my apartment but fighting herself the whole way.

I cringed in agreement. It had to be from an unclean woman.

We got down to wiping off all the surfaces and working on the ham and swiss pinwheels we'd decided to make for dinner that we could only make at my place since Evan would not go anywhere near pork.

When they were finished, we pulled out some beer I had stashed in the fridge and got down to drinking and enjoying our treats.

I tried drowning the knowledge that the smell lived permanently on my roommate in alcohol. While it didn't exactly work in that way, drunk goggles do a lot for me, too.

Apparently, they do a lot for Kodi, as well, since she'd started standing so close that our arms touched and then she put her arm around my back to hold me in place.

"Rah, I don't think you should be here for what comes next," Kodi said pulling me over to the couch.

She looked as if she couldn't believe she'd been asked to leave our little gathering, but Kodi had already claimed me as her own and had started kissing a trail up and down my neck making me shiver.

I looked sympathetically at Rah before Kodi gained my full attention, and the message she'd been trying to send to Rah had been made clear: *Get out or you'll be forced to watch us having sex without you.*

Kodi would not be extending an invitation.

Rah definitely understood, but I knew she'd be hurt and that I'd need to make it up to her in the future. Until then, Kodi started removing my clothes on our ratty pull-out couch as soon as the door latched shut.

Ignoring most of the other gross things about Kodi as she worked, I accepted that she wanted me and let her. At least she *didn't* smell like cheese.

23

HINDERED BY MISFORTUNE

Some living situations are unfortunate. Kayla and Kodi freshman year did not belong together, and they mostly assumed the school lacked any other match for them at the time. Kodi and Delphinium sophomore year didn't need to happen, either, but that was a mistake in putting a neat person with Kodi in the first place.

Me and Susan, well, it'd been a month and a half of living with her, and like a well-meaning terrorist, she'd started creating chaos in my life the moment she moved into my apartment.

Thankfully, Evan and Kodi were doing me the grandest of all friend favors by breaking their current lease and moving into a new apartment with me as soon as spring semester started up.

Moving in together had been a long time coming, anyway. We'd tossed the idea around our sophomore year before deciding to go with it until the logistics of moving in the middle of the year and the prospects of getting to campus from the edge of town in the winter and relying on

Kodi and Evan to get me there were too much for me to continue in the search.

Me backing out did not sit well with them, though. It'd almost caused the end of our friendship since they'd already signed themselves out of their campus accommodations. We didn't speak for nearly two months afterward.

If it's not one thing, it's another, and it was a miracle they'd even considered moving for me after that.

I'd left several details of our move unresolved before winter break came around and ignored the aching drive to figure out more as I hopped a plane to Costa Rica for the month. Upon returning to the valley on a late afternoon flight where the skies were already getting dark because it was January in the North, Kodi kindly drove her little beater to pick me up even though her car was practically crumbling apart as it sat in the lot.

Kodi's misfortune in finding decent vehicles was laughable. Every one of the cars I'd seen her drive found her as their final owner if only for the fact that they were already half duct tape when she decided to buy them. I couldn't tell if her own handiwork, taught to her by her non-mechanical father, did any good for her cars besides. One of her cars, that she'd attempted to fix herself, even died on me after I borrowed it for a class trip on the outskirts of town.

I walked out of the spit they considered an airport and felt my nostrils give a jolt of surprise as the warm cedar smell from inside froze with the crisp below-freezing temperatures of valley winters. That, coupled with the bite of the air stinging my face, gave me the right mind to walk back into the airport for the next flight to someplace tropical.

Where's a beach when you need one?

Kodi climbed from her tri-color sedan she'd parked in one of the nearest spaces and waved quickly to catch my attention. I couldn't see much of her beyond the black ski coat, gloves and blue knit beanie in the dark, but she jumped about to keep warm as she waited for me to lug my bags over the snow-packed lot to meet her.

"Desi!" she greeted cheerfully. It being true winter at 7,700 feet above sea level, she shivered in the cold along with me, but she seemed glad to see me back in the mountains. I could tell by the large dimples that formed exactly in the middle of each cheek peeking above the high collar of her coat and the mischievous twinkle of her eyes. The glint usually meant something about trouble, too, but I couldn't imagine what kind of trouble we'd try for in the dark winter evening.

"Hey! It's freaking *cold* here! How's everything?" I asked as we settled my luggage into the car and climbed in ourselves. I glanced around, and the interior of her poor car looked exactly like her bedroom: shit everywhere. I couldn't be sure how she found anything in there at all, especially if she threw her papers around her backseat like a mini tornado.

I sniffed disdainfully. *Stale fries and...pizza?*

I couldn't complain about the mess, though. At least her car had heat and potential to get me back to my apartment without us having to give it a running start like a *Flintstones-*mobile.

She shrugged. "Fine. Evan's sick which is why she isn't here, but you can see her if you want."

I looked at her skeptically from the passenger's seat. Her blue eyes lit mischievously at the thought like she'd hoped I'd been asking for the trouble that her idea brought.

"Ha, so funny. I'll pass thanks!" I snarked back.

Kodi and I had plenty of experience with an under-the-weather Evan. She caught a 'man cold' like the grass grows green. While cantankerous on any given day, you could multiply her angry, needy, uncooperative nature tenfold and still not get the kind of person Evan could be. Best to avoid her at all costs lest you want to get wrapped up in Evan-sitting for hours at a time, forced into hearing her whine for snacks from her bedroom if she wasn't cursing you out for waking her up by sitting around too loudly.

"Yeah, just let me know when she's feeling better," I shuttered rolling my eyes and imagining all the other ways I'd dreamt of returning to my girlfriend that didn't involve her being sick.

Sometimes, I wondered how she could be an absolute mess with something as simple as the common cold and walk around with cancer and seem completely fine most of the time.

Kodi nodded likely wishing she had the same luxury that I did in going home to my own place even if she knew what Susan could be like. I'd certainly be missing it after we moved in together.

Evan and I started dating back in October and she'd worried about keeping in touch before we'd left for the winter holidays. With me in Costa Rica and her to see her family in Ireland, we'd never be able to call or text as we normally would without exorbitant cell fees and that would have been a first for us in our relationship. It would be true testament to the strength of our bond no matter what since we'd never spent that much time away from each other as a couple.

We'd managed to settle things with an app, and I'd

received happy updates from her and the fun she was having in the Ireland snow. There were no worries in my mind that we'd come out of the break with the same affection we had going into it.

"Did you have a good break?" I asked Kodi, changing the subject.

"Yeah," she shrugged, "same family stuff."

I nodded. She had both of her parents and her sister, and Kodi didn't enjoy or get along with anyone in her family besides her dad who stood as a beast of a man with a bear of a personality to match. It was only because her mom wanted her to be more feminine than what she'd been raised to be by her dad, but there were probably more underlying issues feeding the family tension as well. I wondered if Kodi could have turned out any differently with such a grizzly man providing most of her child-rearing.

Maybe, since her sister had...

She flipped on the radio to indicate that she'd finished with the conversation, and we drove the short five minutes back to my apartment in the near silence between us. That seemed to be the way the two of us hung around each other most of the time, anyway.

That's exactly how *I* liked it, at least.

"Do we know what's happening with the new apartment?" I asked before opening the door to the cold and leaving her for the evening.

She sat idling in the lot thinking about the news of our new place before answering me, "Only that it should be ready in the next few days."

I pursed my lips and remained silent. I'd been hoping to move in immediately, especially since we only had a few days before classes started up again.

"I'll come over this week to help you pack," she offered as I climbed from her beater.

"Thanks," I smiled before closing her car door and watched shivering in the cold as she drove off around the lot to her apartment which sat kitty-corner to mine in the complex.

I sighed, lugging my bags up the flight of stairs to my second-floor abode, semi-grateful to be back to regular, everyday life, though I'd never stop thinking about how nothing compared to sunny coastlines and the crash of waves.

The smell of hot molding cheese hit me first.

I'd forgotten about the smell and it seemed to have intensified with the lack of someone there to air the apartment and bring better smells into the rooms during the weeks I'd been gone. My eyes watered at the offensive odor and I held my breath and fanned the front door to make sure I'd have enough fresh air to survive the night.

I looked into my place and found the same blueish carpet, ugly blue sofa, cedar-beamed ceiling, and *bare* white walls. The second shockingly horrible thing to hit me upon opening the front door being that the once-colorfully decorated space of a college student's apartment now held three dull frames with computer prints of birds and flowers with the worst peace reminders I'd ever laid my eyes upon.

My internal monologue remarked that they should have said something about bathing regularly since she seemed to have the peace thing down.

But really, what happened to all my decorations?

The source of the stench and the bane of my current existence waddled from her bedroom at the brush of the door across the carpet as it opened, as if anyone else would be walking into our apartment. Where I could tell she was about to fake-smile at me as she had every other time we'd been in the same room together, this one died before it could even become a smirk.

Must be something about my face.

She looked mostly the same as I'd left her. All over-the-hill gray hair pulled away from her face and jowls that'd make a bulldog jealous. What looked like a poorly sewn quilt-turned-sweater covered her plumpness from the chill outside; though, I couldn't tell how she felt chilled at all with how stiflingly warm and cheesy it smelled in our place.

I was suffocating.

My eyes burned with the stench and my personal fury, which filled the space enough that I'd be surprised if our neighbors couldn't feel it. I felt my hands shaking with a rage that I usually reserved for the devil himself, and Susan, being so "in-tune" to emotions, didn't need any of her energy crystals to feel what boiled beneath my skin. The fire in my eyes and the oozing anger radiating from my person was enough to let her know I'd drag her down to Hell with me if I had the chance.

"How was, how was your trip?" she stammered in her crinkly old lady voice as she grasped the wall for support and a wave of fury washed over her and the small space.

I felt mildly surprised that the carpet didn't catch fire as I walked across it. "Fine," I bit out hoping she'd catch fire if I walked on her, as well.

I dragged everything into my room and did a quick glance to be sure that she hadn't touched anything in there, too, though I still had no idea where she'd put all my decorations from the living area. I snarled at the thought of her having thrown them away.

I glanced around while I stood in my doorway and found all my patches of fabric, wall hangings, and inspirational remnants of a dismantled calendar still hanging where I'd left them a few weeks before.

I closed my bedroom door, breathed a little easier, opened my window a crack to let even more fresh air into the room, and started unpacking.

Thankfully, the cheese smell hadn't infested my space.

Pulling my toiletries from the suitcase, I left my room for the bathroom across the hall with hopes that Susan would remain out of my sight for the rest of the evening.

She didn't.

As soon as I'd made it into the bathroom to put things away, she cornered me with that same hand continuously braced against the doorframe to ground herself from being burned alive under my fiery death gaze.

"Sher-Sherice said you're moving out," she mentioned of our complex manager trying to justify her actions. "I was getting things ready for you."

Yeah, sure, ya liar. Get OUT of my sight.

I said nothing as I attempted to keep the snarl from my face and not tear her head from her body. Her saving grace in that moment could actually have been her nasty cheese smell and the fact that I didn't want to touch her or her blanket-turned-sweater and become contaminated myself.

Shame.

"It's all in that box out there. You can check," she tried again to placate me, but I didn't want to feel anything but rage towards her, so my internal inferno had no need for quelling. Especially from her.

I rolled my eyes at my reflection as I replaced the last of my toiletries in my drawer and turned mechanically to face her rotund frame taking up the space in the doorway. She'd made it impossible to leave unless she made her peace.

Fine.

"I'm sorry if I did something wrong," she said, finally, but it justified nothing unless she knew of her misdeeds and maybe learned a thing or two about boundaries.

Sorry is such an empty word, anyway.

I quirked my eyebrow at my reflection in agitation and my lungs shook with every inhale. I knew I'd have to calm myself if I didn't want to full-on, lion's rage attack her. *We couldn't have that…*

What's reasoned out with yelling that isn't solvable with well-placed scathing words, anyway?

I closed my eyes and counted to ten before deciding to speak. "It was wrong," I breathed trying to keep my tone from rising in any way. "You CANNOT," *calming breath*, "just touch other people's things without asking them. You have *no right* to replace what's here until I'm gone. *None.*"

"I can tell you're pretty angry about it," she sighed fully supporting herself against the door as she sagged under the weight of my scolding.

Pretty angry? Ha!

Try livid.

Her look of sad disappointment that I assumed came from my lack of appreciation in what she'd probably thought was a good deed made me snarl internally. I quirked another eyebrow with a deadpan look but said nothing as I would not let her attempt to guilt me into accepting her actions as something justifiable.

How dare she think she can guilt me into anything!

She'd probably end up cleansing her mind with the crystals overnight, anyway.

I wondered if she thought the crystals were an honest replacement for an actual soap and water bath. I couldn't say, but I certainly didn't want to know that much about her, either.

Her gaze dropped, and her eyes grew sad, and she waddled her way into her room. Again, I hoped she'd stay there for the rest of the evening.

If I had my way, I certainly could go without seeing her for the rest of my life.

24

PANIC & A MOUTH THAT DOESN'T STOP

It'd been a few days since I'd returned home from winter break and I still hadn't seen or heard from Evan. Kodi had been integral in helping me get many of the things around my apartment together, and she and Evan were going to do as they'd done every time I'd seen them move up to that point, throw shit in boxes and hope for the best when it got there. All last minute, of course.

As she had every other day that week, Kodi came over to hang out with me, help me pack, and get away from Evan who seemed to be feeling more stressed and ornery about the move as the days passed. That, on top of her cold, only made for an unpleasant place for Kodi. I couldn't blame her for wanting to get away from everything as often as she could.

"I heard the apartment's ready. Do you wanna go look at it?" Kodi asked me from her perch on the faded blue pull-out in my living room. It technically belonged to her and Evan, but it was such a pain in the ass to move with all the metal inside that we'd opted to leave "The Metal Nightmare" in the apartment and let Susan deal with it at a future time.

"Yeah! Should we ask Evan to come?"

Kodi thought on that a moment. "She'll only say she's busy and not want to see it with us. She was kind of grouchy this morning, anyway."

I considered that a valid answer since she rarely did anything besides lay in her bed for days in hopes that her cold would get better as often as I'd told her it'd only be worse rolling around in your own nastiness day and night.

We clamored into our winter gear and left my place to wander across the complex and grab our new keys from the complex manager. We found our new ground-level apartment in the building across the lot from mine and down from Kodi and Evan's.

It had all new lightly stained hardwood floors, and the previous tenants left an old sunken couch and a large, low coffee table in the living room that they'd started covering with stickers. It seemed to be the only evidence that anyone had been there before us at all.

Kodi and I walked in further glancing around the small apartment kitchen that had a white fridge and oven like the ones each of us had in our own places. It had a decent amount of space without the counter-bar placed between the kitchen and the living room that our two-bedroom apartments had. I liked the exposed cedar beams on the ceiling, too.

"Do you wanna pick our rooms?" Kodi asked excitedly as we wandered down the hall. We passed a full bathroom with a bathtub on the left, and the three bedrooms all sat with their doors at awkward angles to each other at the end of the hall. We walked through each finding that the one on the left was what should have been the master with its own shower and the other two were meant to share the bath in the hall.

"Since you've been sharing a bathroom all this time already, would you mind if I took the master?" I asked her as we met back in the hall.

Kodi shrugged not caring about having a bathroom to herself. "I want this room," she pointed to the middle of the two that had far better lighting than the smaller one on the right, "and Evan can have that one. Works out fine."

I shrugged figuring that the two of them could figure that out as soon as Evan got involved. We left satisfied with the new place and made our way back to my apartment intent on getting as much together as we could to move in.

Evan had been texting Kodi bossy messages all afternoon by that point. I'd been surprised she was even awake, but she seemed to be yelling at Kodi for being dumb or something and I felt a little bad for her.

Then a text came for me.

We need to talk.

I considered this showing Kodi and she looked wearily at both my phone and me before shrugging slightly. "What are you going to say?"

My mouth quirked to the side in thought. **Sure! Are you free right now?** I sent back excited to be in her presence again.

I showed Kodi who frowned at the phone again but said nothing.

Yeah.

I hopped up and paid little mind to Kodi trudging behind me. "Are you cool with this?" she asked me as we threw on our winter gear and slipped into our boots.

"Yeah, why wouldn't I be?" I asked shrugging into my large black coat.

She struggled again, still not saying anything but followed me all the same.

We walked across the parking lot all the way to Evan and Kodi's apartment. We clamored up the wooden stairs to the second floor, and I knocked on the door before Kodi stepped up and opened it with her key. Evan sat tensely on the green couch with her black lab mix, Addie, amid a mess of things in their apartment. It seemed they were at least trying to pack.

Besides her posture, she seemed relatively normal to me. She wore a ratty old t-shirt with holes worn into the armpits and a pair of black basketball shorts. She'd tucked one of her knees up under her chin and played with her bare toes. She hadn't showered for a little while, it seemed.

"Hey!" I said happily. It'd been forever since I'd actually seen her, but she seemed the same as I'd left her. Slightly unkempt, definitely unwashed, fully Evan.

Evan smiled uneasily like she'd sat on a raw egg and broken it but felt too embarrassed to stand and clean it up.

"Come to my room," she told me, and I followed her from the living room down the short hall stealing a curious glance to Kodi before I went. She closed the door behind me and offered for me to sit down on her bed that actually had sheets on it while she took up post in a black swivel chair in the corner.

You couldn't walk in her room. There were dirty, and probably even clean, clothes all over the floor and an even further myriad of clutter strewn through that. I had no idea how she found anything, but I couldn't judge her on her method of organization. I didn't have to live in it, so it meant little to me.

Evan watched me look around her room before my gaze settled back on her. I smiled. I did love her, after all.

She sighed deeply and looked away. Something troubled her. Maybe she needed to talk about it? I'd do what I could to help.

"So..." she started, "things haven't been the same since you came back."

I frowned but continued listening.

She hastened, "You used to be up front and corner us into talking about things, but you haven't been doing that and I liked that about you. I don't know if it's because you went to Spain or what happened, but you changed and I don't like it."

"What do you mean?" I asked knowing that I had in fact changed but feeling like we'd had a whole semester since I'd returned to figure out that we were the same group of friends we'd been before I'd gone, it hadn't crossed my mind as being a big deal.

"We should break up," she explained, and a strange spiraling vortex opened in front of my vision, and the words stabbed at my heart like a cat clawing at my chest that I was unable to stop or pull away from.

"W-what?" I choked out in shock.

Things were fine a moment ago!

She took a deep breath and sighed again. "Yeah, I can't do this anymore."

Unable to think, I sat for a moment trying to make the cogs in my brain turn and being unable to do so. I wondered blankly why I hadn't started crying.

I remembered how she'd started planning out our future children together right after we'd started dating and how we'd named them. She'd liked the name Luxe for a girl. Our future daughter vanished before my mind's eyes in that instant. All four of our future children gone with those simple, horrible words.

"Are you okay?" she asked, though I wondered if she truly wanted to know or if she saw it written all over my face. I couldn't feel my face, anyway, so what did it matter what she saw there?

I frowned at her but said nothing. Suddenly completely aware of how small her bedroom was and how much I did not want to be in it anymore, I stood up from her bed. Her bed held too many memories for me to be there at all.

She stood up, too, frowning at me and searching my face for something that I don't think she found. She sighed again and let me walk out.

Kodi stood awkwardly in the living room like I'd interrupted her pacing.

She looked concerned and it dawned on me that she'd known what had been coming for me. She knew and she didn't tell me. Hadn't warned me about it in the least! *Let me walk into it even!*

That hurt possibly worst of all and the beast that usually safe-guarded my heart grabbed at it with both paws and gnawed furiously on the edge of it like cats do with feather toys.

Damn.

I shot her a look I hoped conveyed her betrayal, and she shrank at it knowing that I knew what she'd let me walk into. That I'd been blindsided and she'd let it happen.

Some friend she'd turned out to be.

"Well, Evan just broke up with me," I stated flatly.

Kodi nodded and said nothing.

"I'm going back to my place to pack," I said to the room, though I said it more for me in doing something methodical while I put my head on straight again.

I walked out of their apartment and back to my place where I placed every last item in a box except the bed I slept on and the clothes I'd be wearing the next day for moving. Nothing felt real in the least.

By the time I'd got down to it and pretty much everything besides my bedding sat boxed and ready to make the trip across the lot, darkness fell, but I still hadn't sorted any of the day's events out in my head.

I could feel the devastation sitting on my chest and filling up my throat like an enormous cotton ball. Still, I hadn't cried.

As the evening wore on, I received another text from Evan asking again if I was okay.

Can I talk to you? I asked back, and to my relief, she agreed.

As I had earlier that day, I climbed into all of my winter gear and made my way across the parking lot to Evan and Kodi's. The sky was a deep blue and the stars were drowned by the orange glow of the street lights illuminating the lot and the piles of snow pushed in various directions out of the way.

I knocked and Evan answered the door and welcomed me in. Her brow creased with concern as she looked me over and I shed my coat, hat, and gloves as I entered. However I looked, I imagined it didn't seem good to her if she made that face. Her blue-green eyes seemed puzzled by the lack of whatever she'd been searching for in me that she still couldn't find.

I say lack because I felt useless.

"I'm sorry about earlier," she told me as we sat down beside each other on the gross emerald sofa.

I smiled half-heartedly at her. I couldn't tell if she meant that. She wouldn't have done it otherwise, I don't think. Instead, I said nothing and looked at her forlornly.

"I was a little shocked that you were so gung-ho about

coming over after I sent that text," she admitted uncomfortably.

"I didn't know that's what you were going to do," I told her.

She looked taken aback, "You didn't know?! There's nothing that says break up more than 'we need to talk'! How'd you not see that?"

I shrugged. Now that she said it, I realized the truth in it, but before I never dreamt she'd actually break up with me. We were in love! "I figured we'd actually get the chance to see each other and talk now that break is over. I couldn't have dreamt otherwise."

She scrutinized my face again, still searching. "Yeah, I'd been texting Kodi the whole time after that asking for advice. I'd been expecting you to keep avoiding me which would have given me more time to prepare."

"Keep avoiding you? Kodi told me you were sick! I was giving you time to get better to be sure I wouldn't end up catching whatever it is you have," I admitted surprised that she'd thought I was avoiding her but glad to clear everything up all the same.

She relaxed a bit as I livened up with the conversation. "I just saw Kodi leaving to go to your place all the time without an invitation, I figured you hated me and didn't want to be together anymore."

That couldn't have been further from the truth, but I suppose we hadn't been inviting her because she'd been ill and probably wouldn't have showed anyway. Didn't mean that I shouldn't have extended the courtesy.

"Kodi's been helping me pack. I've been telling her about how I couldn't wait for you to feel better and how she needed to tell me when you were so that I could see you again. Why didn't you just talk to me?" I asked.

She frowned a moment in concentration looking distantly at nothing somewhere near the ground. Slowly, a smile crept its way over her mouth and the knitting between her unkempt eyebrows eased. She seemed to conclude something and I'd be curious to know about it.

"If it's cool with you, I'd be cool if we called this a break instead of a breakup," she informed me at last.

My heart soared, and I beamed with excitement from ear to ear. "Yes! There's so much I need to catch you up on now that you're here. How was Ireland? Did you have a good Christmas?"

Without letting her answer, I continued word vomiting in my relief. All floodgates had been opened. "It's so cold here after being on the beach. I wish you'd been there. I know you didn't feel good the last time we went, but beaches really are better."

She smiled and then laughed at me. I considered it absolute music to my ears, so I kept talking and telling her all about my break and what'd been going on for me since I'd flown into the valley.

"Kodi's been weirdly helpful lately. All my stuff is pretty much packed, and I heard the apartment is ready, so we can start moving in! Kodi and I have been talking about stuff when we break from packing and she told me about her holiday and some theories she had about the Sloths and how she doesn't believe some of it and-"

The smile dropped from her face, and she looked shocked as if someone had dropped a glass and it shattered around her. Her sudden change of mood gave me pause, too. *What happened?*

"You guys don't believe me?" she whispered incredulously. The happy color had drained from her face almost instantly and she looked a little sick. "You don't believe what I've told you about them? About my *life?*"

I backpedaled in my brain trying and failing to come up with something to rectify the situation I'd found myself in. My mouth opened and closed helplessly like a fish and no words came out. I found myself faced with the whole reason I didn't talk much summed up right then.

"Just some of the things you've said…Proof of the—it was Kodi that brought it up!" I stumbled over my thoughts and found that I couldn't make heads or tails of anything as my brain shut off for the second time that day. I grasped at straws and found a large dense wall building itself up between Evan and me. The same wall I'd been working years to tear down.

"It's safe to say we're done. I need to be alone," she cut me off coldly and waited for me to put on my winter stuff and walk through the open door she was holding for me.

I looked at her pleadingly to let me explain, but the wall stood too tall for me to climb in that moment. I could do nothing for her then. How could I if I couldn't even help myself?

I left, furious with myself and Kodi for bringing up notions of possible falsehoods in every story she'd told. Damn my mouth. Damn her for not seeing how much I *loved* her.

Maybe she did and that's what the whole thing had been about in the first place?

I trudged hopelessly down the stairs and into the cold winter night. I needed a lifeline in that moment. Anything that'd convince Evan that I wasn't the bad guy. That I'd always be on her side…

I pulled out my phone and texted the one person that might be able to help me, SexyBears. He was a Sloth that'd gotten a clone of Evan's phone and started texting me around the time Evan and I had started dating. I'd never met him or any of them face to face, but I needed to know they were there. That they were real.

What a time to be alive.

Hey, can I talk to you? I asked him through text.

Hey, yeah what's up? He asked me back.

Perfect, word hadn't gotten to him about what'd happened between Evan and I. Sure, it would get to him eventually, but I could hope I'd gain a bit of sympathy, or something, before then.

Some stuff happened today and I need someone to talk with about it.

I waited and waited and dared not move from the cold. With the numbness I felt in my head, I couldn't feel the chill, anyway.

My phone buzzed.

WHAT THE FUCK HAVE YOU DONE TO HER? DON'T FUCKING TEXT THIS NUMBER AGAIN OR I'LL FUCKING HUNT YOU DOWN AND KILL YOU FOR HURTING HER!

I could have screamed at the sky in my frustration if not for worrying the many neighbors in the apartments surrounding me. News had arrived.

Confused, heartbroken, blacklisted, and crushed into the shell I stood in, I stumbled back home in the cold to weep at my loss and prepare to move in with someone I felt sure would hate me for a long time to come.

25

NOISY NIGHTS

*R*ah came over to help us with unpacking the rest of our stuff and for help with some computer-type homework. She'd been over every night since we'd moved in over a week ago and Evan had taken to recording her making high pitched noises that'd been coined as summoning the aliens that'd come and take her away to her home planet.

"I don't know what it is about you, but your alien summoning weirds me out," Evan said harshly to Rah from her perch on her green couch. The sun had set and the fluorescent lights in our apartment drained the coloring in the room.

How Rah ended up living with us after Evan, Kodi and I moved in together, I'm not entirely sure, but she made our inherited leather couch her resting place each night for at least the first month and a half we lived together.

Despite the breakup and collective meltdown, I figured that after we'd moved in together and I'd gotten away from "Stinky Cheese" Susan things would settle down for us. I hoped that even after her fury at Kodi and I for spending time discussing the merit of everything she'd ever told us, wrangling the room Kodi wanted from her, and forcing us all into helping her deep clean everything in their old apartment for inspection, that she'd settle in and we'd manage to get back to some sort of normalcy.

I forgot how much Evan enjoys holding a grudge.

"I'm going to bed, guys," I muttered removing myself from our sofa and stretching a bit. It'd gotten late, and I hadn't gotten used to the new environment enough to sleep soundly. On top of that, my bedroom door sat right next to the door of a murderer.

"Yeah, I should do that, too," Rah said laying down in my place, but Evan and Kodi made no indication of moving anywhere.

"Night!" Kodi called.

Evan scowled at me for leaving the conversation despite having classes in the morning.

I rolled my eyes mostly ignoring her as I turned to walk down the hall.

She could be such a petty bitch sometimes.

"Kodi! Take Addie out for a walk. It's kind of cold and Rah and I are busy," I heard Evan demand as I wandered my way from our living room. I didn't envy Kodi then, but I always wondered why Evan didn't take care of her dog herself. If my dogs were around, I'd be mortified to even mention someone else taking care of them besides myself.

Pushing open my door, my room remained the same one Kodi and I had agreed on when we'd come to look through it. Apparently, Evan didn't mind continuing to share her bathroom with Kodi. Worked for me.

Shutting myself in for the evening, I went about my usual bedtime routine of showering, brushing my teeth, and tucking myself in for a nice night of rest.

"*Ppft.* Ahahahaha, are you kidding me? What the fuck!" Evan's spiteful laughter and loud banter with Rah came floating through my bedroom door. I could tell she was being loud on purpose. She had this tone to her laugh that sounded more like a forced seagull cry than the actual happy beauty that her true hearty laughter rang with. I wondered if Rah could tell she'd been using her to get some sort of passive aggressive revenge on her roommates. If anything, she'd be forced to stay awake on the couch until Evan decided to go to bed herself.

Unfortunately, their midnight or later cackling had been the biggest perpetrator in my lack of sleep. I couldn't say how many nights it'd been going on for, but they sat cracking up down the hall and as far as I could tell, Kodi must have gone to bed, as well.

Through several attempts at conveying how much I needed my sleep and trying to be civil about things, I had no idea how to make them stop. Did I suffer and ignore them until Evan got bored of the game and dove into some other spiteful activity that might work better for her? Had it come down to my mom's grade school advice of ignoring it and it'll go away like those bullies that'd taunted me throughout my school years?

How do you stop a bitch on a mission to ruin the lives of her roommates without being evil yourself?

I had no answers, but I couldn't retaliate in the same way she'd decided to attack. Open retaliation could mean extended misery for everyone involved, and I couldn't handle being even more miserable than I already was with the situation. Might as well draw the Xs over my eyes now if that was the path I tried to take.

Since I'd also been angry with Kodi for getting me into conversations that'd caused all the pettiness we were currently experiencing, I'd started putting a little more of a distance between us.

I found I needed an ear to lean on, though. Someone to speak of my woes to that'd have some sympathy for me during all the backwards BS I had to deal with.

I turned to social media.

Noisy roommates at three in the morning are so great! I wonder if our neighbors are having similar issues this evening?

I posted it with a tag on Evan, Kodi, and Rah and waited to see what would happen. Sometimes there were perks to public forums.

Things quieted down in our apartment soon after that and I managed to drift off, thankfully.

I woke the next morning before any of the others since I seemed to be the only one of us with enough of a drive for school to make my morning classes. Evan and Kodi were lucky if they made it out of having morning classes, Rah usually followed whatever kind of day Evan had, so her education had been somewhat screwed from the start.

I couldn't be responsible for their lives, though. If they had morning classes and chose to sleep through them, their fault and their degree at the end. I'd be damned if I didn't make it through in four years, though.

Once a self-motivated student, always a self-motivated student.

A drawback for Rah living off of our sofa always seemed to be the fact that she'd be woken up as I shuffled around the kitchen for breakfast in the mornings. Her loss not going to bed on time or moving back to her dorm at night to sleep. I gave her credit for sticking around as long as she had. I'd be annoyed by me if I were her.

I made the walk through the cold mountain morning to

hit sculpture first, not checking my phone until I'd arrived in class.

I unpacked and warmed myself by the furnace before unlocking my phone and opening the app to check on the internet world.

Several new notifications and a private message?

My heart dropped a little as I imagined what probably came of my post last night.

Hesitantly, I opened the notification center and read through the list. Several people had liked it. I suppose that's something.

Evan, Kodi, and Rah had all commented on it several times. *That's not good.*

I sighed at my inner self as she chastised me for acting out as I had. Best to get it over with, though. I read the first comment.

Sorry! Rah wrote as I knew she probably would.

Kodi: **I didn't hear anything...**

"Of course you didn't," I mumbled at the phone. I swear, Kodi could sleep through a natural disaster and it would be the best sleep of her life.

Untag me from this immediately or take it down! Evan commented angrily which made me sneer at my phone.

Why? I retorted. **It's not like anything I say means anything to you.**

I was reminded once more of the fact that Evan has issue with coming off as anything but sweet and pleasant in the eyes of the masses and had to appreciate my accidental fortune in turning to social media for my answers. I left the post as it was and moved to see what kind of message I'd received. Hopefully, it'd be better than Evan. Anything was better than Evan right then.

From Evan Adams. *Damn.*

I don't care what you do on fb or how you post whatever stupid shit you decide people need to see but don't drag my name into whatever petty bullshit you post there. Your childish shit is on my last nerve. Cut it out or we're done. Never tag me in shit like that again!

Evan Lesson: Passive aggressive is only okay when I do it.

I closed my eyes afraid that I'd burn holes through my screen with the rage I felt. God forbid she face her own damn music! I couldn't have responded to her even if I'd wanted to, though. I still needed her to live with me.

26

THE BACON FALLOUT

"Mom!" I greeted as she parked her rented lime-colored Fiesta outside of our apartment. "How was the flight?"

"Hey Des," Mom smiled climbing out to give me a hug and a kiss before we moved inside. I beamed at her familiarity. The fact that she kept her hair short and I got my height from my dad were the only real differences between us. Mom tended to wear more makeup than me, as well, and never went anywhere without a shade of red lipstick.

Evan's black lab mix came to greet us at the door and Rah sat on the couch but got up to greet my mom as she came inside.

"Mom, this is Addie, Evan's dog, and this is Danielle, but we call her Rah. Rah this is my mom, Francesca," I introduced before I gave my mom the grand tour of our apartment. She'd come to check on me after dealing with Susan and then the quick decision to move on top of that. She also knew about the breakup between Evan and me, and though she'd been glad for it, she cared enough about me to still worry about my well-being.

"Honestly, this isn't so bad," Mom admitted as we ended up back in the kitchen, "besides the mess."

I glanced away embarrassed. Evan and Kodi never had been clean even in every other apartment they shared, and they had way too much stuff for what little bit of space we could work with. I'd settled for them in an emergency and Mom knew it, but I know she preferred me living there over "Moldy Cheese" Susan no matter how much she disliked Evan.

"Where are they?" Mom inquired wondering if she'd have to run into my roommates.

"Kodi's in class and should be here in a few hours. Evan's at work and shouldn't be here until later."

"Good," she said. "Wanna go get some food? Do you want me to make you some potato soup? What do you have to eat here?"

How very Mom of her.

I showed her my cupboard of food I had separate from Evan and Kodi's and my section in our fridge. I'd expected her to come in and say something like that, so I'd purposefully left things a little more barren than I normally would have to capitalize on the opportunity.

"Des, have you been starving here? Let's get you stocked up on groceries," Mom concluded as I'd gotten into the bare minimum and definitely needed some more of the essentials.

We made our way to the store in the little Fiesta. I told her we could have walked since the store and my apartment were back to back practically, but Mom argued that she didn't want to walk all the groceries back to my place after we'd finished, and I couldn't argue with her logic.

As we walked through the store and Mom had me grabbing various things off the shelves, we came to the point where we were standing in front of the bacon and she picked a package up.

"Evan doesn't like pork," I said slightly panicked hoping to get her to put the package back down.

"Who doesn't like bacon? I'll leave it on the side so she doesn't have to eat it," she bargained thinking that'd solve all our problems.

"No, we can't cook it in the apartment, she'll get mad," I tried explaining to her knowing that Evan's rage for that faux pas would most certainly fall back on me since I clearly had no control over my mom in her eyes.

"She doesn't even let you have bacon in the apartment at all?" Mom asked her eyes burning a little in anger before shaking her head. "Well, Evan can get as mad at me as she wants, but potato soup tastes way better with bacon, and since I'm the one making it, it's gonna be how I want it."

I sighed in defeat. It wouldn't work that way, but I admired her blind courage all the same.

I remembered the first time Mom ever met Evan after she and I first became friends and how Mom had turned to me and told me Evan seemed like she'd been hiding something after Evan had left and that she didn't trust her for a minute. Her mistrust of Evan happened to be the whole reason Mom didn't like her in the first place, but it seemed that the list continued to grow, and I hadn't noticed until we were grocery shopping four years after their initial meeting.

I guess the bonus would be that Evan couldn't boss my mom around even if she tried. I'd seen her interact with Kodi's parents and she always tried to make a good impression on them.

Maybe she had a thing for deceiving parents?

We finished shopping and headed back shortly after

where Rah had been cleaning a couple of things that we hadn't been able to finish before Mom had arrived.

"Have you seen *Frozen*, yet?" I asked Mom while she started on the soup and I put things away in the spaces designated for me.

"No, is it good?" Mom asked pulling out the bacon and placing it on one of our baking sheets for it to cook in the oven while she worked on the stovetop.

Rah glanced at me when she saw it and I could only shrug helplessly in return.

"Oh, my goodness! It's so good!" Rah said longingly. She'd introduced me to *Frozen* and Evan had been sucked in, too, despite the fact that she hated all things Disney if only that she'd become so calloused to happy endings.

Being an avid Disney fan, Mom definitely wanted to see it and told us to get it set up so that we could watch it while we cooked and ate dinner.

"I'm sorry, but I'll probably have to leave and go to work before this is over," Rah told us getting Netflix set up so that we could watch the movie.

"That's fine," I insisted smiling.

"Thanks for hanging out with us," Mom told her as she handed her a bowl overflowing with soup topped with cheese and crumbled bacon bits.

I took mine happily, it being a huge family favorite for not only us, but our extended family, as well. Though we called it soup, it resembled chowder more, but the semantics were forgotten entirely as I took the first steaming bite and had to wrestle with a too-hot potato chunk in my mouth.

Rah made happy eating sound from her perch on the couch while she juggled the remote to press play.

Near the end, Rah did have to leave and felt truly

remorseful leaving my mom and I before she enjoyed Mom's reaction to the ending. Mom had definitely been surprised. Once the movie finished, we cleaned the bowls up and Kodi walked in.

"Mom, this is Kodi, I can't remember if you've met yet or not," I confessed introducing them.

"Hi Kodi, I'm Francesca," Mom said. "Do you want any soup before we put it away?"

Kodi greeted her uneasily but agreed to the soup and ate it from the couch while we moved around the kitchen cleaning.

I can't say why Kodi always seemed so skeptical about meeting strangers, but it annoyed me when it came to our parents.

As if we weren't already living with a volatile human. Evan made everyone else seem like cotton candy and rainbows in comparison.

Mom left for her hotel shortly after that with promise that we'd make our way out to do something fun the next day before she left. I agreed and kissed her goodnight.

"It reeks of bacon in here," Kodi told me looking wearier still and I shrugged.

"I tried but my mom wasn't having it, so we'll just have to deal with it when she arrives," I said thinking about how bad it might be once she got back. Things were finally returning to a kind of peace in the apartment, too. I'd have to start working for it again.

Sure enough, Evan walked through our door and despite us propping the windows in attempts at airing everything out, the smell of bacon hit her so fiercely that she stopped dead in her tracks in the threshold like she'd run into an invisible wall.

"*What* did *I* say about *bacon*?" she growled removing

clothing from her body forcefully and looking about for the things that were hers in our living room.

"I tried, but my mom wasn't having anything to do with it. I couldn't get her off of it without revealing why you don't like it and I figured you didn't want me to do that, so she stuck to her guns and made it," I explained jumpily hoping she wouldn't get too angry at me.

She continued stomping about and grabbed her hat and scarf that were hanging over the couch and sniffed them. "Great, these fucking *smell* like it. I can't wear them and it's fucking cold outside!"

She was shouting as she marched down the hall to be sure her door had been closed, which it thankfully had been, before she came back out to stand menacingly before me.

"One of you needs to fucking wash these," she demanded coming out and throwing her bacon-smelling garments at Kodi and I. "I'm not even sure I can fucking sleep here tonight."

"Where will you go?" Kodi asked as a frown of concern creased her brow.

Evan rushed around some more grumbling to herself angrily and grabbing things to stuff into a backpack before she called Addie to her side at the door. "I'm going to the cabin. When I come back on Sunday, I shouldn't find any trace of bacon or anything with bacon in it. No pork at all!" she snarled pointing her finger dangerously at me.

Fuck, fine! You can stay in the mountains for all I care, I thought grumpily.

She stomped into her boots and marched out the door, slamming it in her wake. Kodi gave me a look like I'd committed treason on the government. "That's mostly the reason I wanted you to stay in your own apartment. It was nice having a place where I could go cook ham if I needed it."

I shot her a look thinking a separate apartment had been all my hopes and dreams come true in that moment. "So how do we do her laundry?"

Kodi waved me off. "I can do it. We probably need to do laundry, anyway. Plus, she can't have fabric softener, she's allergic to it."

Oh, yeah. I forgot.

I shrugged believing that worked for me fine since I didn't want to do Evan's laundry, anyway. She would have found a way to make it seem like I'd messed that up, too, and then I'd be found dead somewhere for the three strikes she'd racked up against me.

I thought about her laundry for a moment, though. I wondered if the fabric softener issue had been the whole reason she never slept with sheets on her bed, but I brushed it off knowing that she never washed her sheets enough to have any clean ones to put on the bed in the first place. Instead, she slept in a sleeping bag and never ever washed it or took it off her bed unless we'd decided to go camping.

Kodi got up from her place in the couch to rinse her bowl and stick it in the dishwasher. She never did that unless she'd been forced into it. She must have felt bad for me right then.

"Tell your mom thanks for the soup and tell her not to bring anything else like that into the house again. It's really hard to deal with Evan," Kodi admitted moving into the hall to collect the laundry.

"Yeah," I agreed wondering if Mom would even be back in our apartment again before graduation. I hoped not for her sake, honestly.

27

THRUSH & MISTRUST

I awoke one morning to my tongue aching dully. I studied myself in the mirror in my bathroom concerned as I opened my mouth and looked under my tongue to find small white patches forming there.

What the hell are those?

I frowned further at my reflection before checking again. I tried scraping them off with my teeth, but they stuck pretty good, and I felt more confused than ever.

I considered myself thinking about all that I knew about weird white growths and wondered frantically if I'd contracted an STI. Bug-eyed and hands shaking, I rushed into my room to pick up my phone and Google through to see what it might come up with for me.

Please don't be an STI. Nothing serious, I thought as I pulled up my browser and searched based on the only observations I had for whatever the little patches were that ailed me.

Going straight into images, I found that whatever the first few people had caught were way worse than what I had with puss and bumps and a manner of grossness that looked nothing like what I had in my mouth. Then I found one that had some similarities to me.

"Thrush?" I thought aloud. "What's thrush?"

Going back to the search bar, I typed in the new word that I'd only ever heard in reference to birds.

A bloom of Candida albicans in the mouth as a fungal infection...Okay, what causes it?

I searched further to find that it could be caused by an excess of antibiotics that kill the bacteria that usually keep the fungus in check or a seriously poor diet full of processed foods could make things a little wacky, as well.

For a split second, I considered Evan and Kodi and how they knew that I couldn't take antibiotics because of an allergy.

Could they be feeding me the smallest doses in hopes that I'd die? Was I being poisoned?

I shook the notion off knowing they wouldn't stoop so low, but I also considered my diet and didn't actually think I ate all that bad.

I scrolled through my contacts until I found who I'd been searching for.

"Hi Mom," I said after she answered which was as an extremely unusual instance for her since she barely ever answered when anyone called. In fact, I hadn't even kept her as my emergency contact because of that.

"Hey Sug-sug, what's going on?" she asked me sensing with her Supermom powers that I seemed a little panicked.

"Mom, I think I have thrush!" I said distressed.

"Like the kind that babies get?" she asked over the line, and I could tell that she seemed to ease with the knowledge. Clearly, she didn't think that was serious.

"I don't know. Yes? Do babies get thrush?" I wondered.

"Yeah, it's pretty common for babies actually. How do you think you got that?"

I considered for a moment and told her what the internet had told me. She scoffed at the idea of an excess of antibiotics, further confirming that it couldn't be that my roommates were poisoning me. Had to be the diet, then.

"Well, keep me posted on how things go. I hope it goes away soon. I love you!" she said immediately easing my worries and hanging up after I told her I loved her, too.

Walking out into the kitchen, I found Rah playing around on her phone and my roommates gone to Monarch to ski for the day as they had been for the past few weeks. I had the day off, so it seemed Rah and I were hanging out as usual.

"Wanna know something weird?" I asked her recanting the morning I'd had discovering my new issue.

I looked through my cupboard and in the fridge thinking more about the diet I'd had since starting the year. *Not what you'd consider exemplary.*

"That is weird. Do you know what it's from?" she asked after I showed her the underside of my tongue and she cringed a bit. *If only she'd seen the pictures on the internet. This was nothing!*

"Well, I thought for a minute that Evan and Kodi were trying to kill me with antibiotics, but I think I just need to eat more good for me foods," I explained chuckling about it a bit. Seemed like an easy fix.

I glanced around our apartment common room and found it as filthy as last weekend before Rah and I had cleaned it.

She saw me look and sighed knowing what I'd been thinking and definitely happy, albeit begrudged, to help me do it at this point. It'd become another bonding experience for us that had brought us closer together than anything ever had before.

It was like the enemy of my enemy is my friend, but it only applied while we were cleaning the apartment, which didn't discount the fact that it got cleaned by us every single weekend.

"Do you wanna clean their bathroom this time? We all use it, and every time I go in there, I fear touching anything beyond what's absolutely necessary," I asked moving to the bathroom door and opening it to find the dim light illuminating dusty boxes and toiletry items I'd never seen either of them use in my life.

I looked back at Rah who also looked into the bathroom disdainfully. "Yeah, it definitely needs it," she mused looking at me and stretching her way off the couch.

Without saying more, we both got to work on the usual things. We'd picked up a bit of a routine since we'd started tidying together, and it worked that she'd start on the living room surfaces while I quickly did my room and my bathroom.

Neither of us bothered with Evan and Kodi's rooms. They had some propensity for rolling through their spaces like a tornado, and we both figured they'd be angry if we went in and touched anything they had in there. As it happened to be, we'd touch as little as we could working at putting together a paper pile for Kodi and a pile for Evan and setting them out of the way so that we could clear whatever sticky, colorful, or otherwise dried-on bits sat around our common room after we'd removed the piles of crusty dishes from the coffee table and mopped the floor of residue.

Naturally, because of Addie, Evan's medium-sized black dog that she *rarely* bathed and who shed over every surface of our apartment like a furry nightmare, giant dust bunnies were lining the baseboards that had to be swept up and vacuumed before we could do anything about the sticky stains from some forgotten spills. I swear Addie's fur-dust could have been collected and made into a sweater every weekend we cleaned, though.

Usually, Rah would attend to the floor while I'd get the things Kodi had cooked and let dry on the counters and stove. Then Rah and I would tag team the mountain of dishes that we'd have soaking while we did everything else since *no one* had taught either Evan or Kodi that dishes clean way better if left to soak or the food's been rinsed out of them.

After four hours of aggressively taking out our frustration towards our missing apartment friends on the grime in our place and jamming to Panic! At the Disco, 30 Seconds to Mars, and every song Rah and I knew and could sing together, we came down to the shared bathroom we'd decided to add to our regimen that day.

"Are you ready for this?" I asked her as we peered around what should have been a spacious room but lacked that with the mildewed boxes that'd picked up the moisture from every shower the pair had taken in there. They'd gotten extra rank once Evan had decided to close the door of the bathroom after she showered without leaving a fan on inside.

"It needs to be done," she agreed holding her container of Lysol wipes and a spray bottle in her hands.

Deciding not to waste any more time, I went in and tackled the toilet while Rah got after the sink with its dried-on toothpaste, remnants of fur and hair and dust caked around the edges of the porcelain, and a stunningly empty soap bottle.

"Ewwww! What have they been washing their hands with?" Rah cringed holding the empty bottle up to me.

"Dude! How long has that been empty?" I asked horrified.

"Too long, I think," she admitted placing it gingerly on top of the overflowing trash can to the side of the vanity that hadn't been emptied in months.

I grimaced and started on the toilet. They had an ugly black seat cover that looked like shag carpet. I wondered mildly if they thought that would be enough to prevent them from having to clean it, but my thoughts were stopped cold as I lifted the seat up to find a fine black film under the bottom-most seat.

"What the fuck? Is that black mold?" I shrieked stepping back a moment to look at it.

"Oh, my god! It is! That's just nasty! How does anyone live like this?" Rah asked me as I considered the mold a moment and knew that it affected all of us if I let it stay there.

Taking my toilet wand and thanking my stars that I'd gotten one that had replaceable heads that popped off when you'd finished using them, I grabbed one from my bathroom and started scrubbing fervently at the mold.

It came off fairly easily, and I used the wand over every surface on that toilet before dusting the top and closing the lid again and leaving it.

Rah seemed to agree with my sentiments after that, and we decided to never clean their bathroom for them again. *Disgusting!*

Satisfied with the rest of the work we'd done around the apartment, Rah and I crashed against the sunken couch in the living room to enjoy our hard work before Evan and Kodi came home and ruined all of it.

"Wanna watch a movie?" she asked me as I laid my head in her comfy lap so that she could play with my hair as she'd taken to doing after she told me it looked beautiful all the time and that she wanted nothing more than to touch it.

"Sure," I agreed letting her up so that she could flip on Netflix. We found an obscure movie with Jared Leto in it and immediately agreed to watch it having bonded over our love of 30 Seconds to Mars and our attraction to their lead singer.

We watched happily, Rah playing with my hair all the while, and finished with absolute confusion because the entire movie was obscure and jumbled. My roommates crashed in shortly after that carrying their gear and looking angrily at us.

I rolled my eyes and continued enjoying my time with Rah as Addie came in and greeted us before making her way back towards the bedrooms.

"Hey, how was the mountain?" Rah asked them being far friendlier than I felt.

"It was fine. I see you guys cleaned again," Evan commented looking over our handy work without an ounce of emotion on her face.

"Yeah, when are you gonna stop that?" Kodi asked kicking off her boots and wandering into her room to drop all her winter gear.

"Never!" I called knowing it'd be *filthy* if Rah and I didn't do anything. I turned back to Evan. "Oh, and guess what? We went to clean your bathroom to be nice and all, but we found black mold under your toilet seat, so that's probably not happening again."

I saw her glance at Kodi who'd slouched her way back into the living room. "I don't believe you. No there wasn't," she told me seriously and with no room to argue about it.

I saw it, Rah apparently hadn't. "Yes! It was so nasty. What have you guys been doing in there?"

Evan's cheeks flushed ever so slightly, but her mood flipped so quickly that all color drained immediately, and she stood defiantly against us. "No. Mold."

Rah seemed to get it then and backed down. As per usual, no gratitude fell from either Evan or Kodi's mouths about having a clean place now. Nothing about thanking us for getting rid of the mold after we'd found it either.

Some part of me wondered if they thought we'd stop cleaning if they continued complaining about it, but I did it for my own benefit more than anything else.

If that had really been their intention with their bitching, I had only one thing for it. I would not stop. *Not on their lives.*

28

AN ENGAGEMENT & A BREAK

As senior art majors, we were required to set up a senior exhibit of all the art we could make for a collection that we'd present as a final example of how far we'd come as students in our undergrads. They usually took place in the spring and the first group happened in March.

James had volunteered for that group, and word on the street had been that he'd planned on proposing to his girlfriend after his presentation.

"I don't understand why he has to do it here!" another senior grumbled from the pottery wheel as he prepared another piece. "It could be just as good *anywhere* else and not distract from what everyone else is doing."

I had to agree with him there. I'd spoken to James about why he planned on doing it over his exhibit. He'd been begrudged to do it there, too.

Apparently, his girlfriend wanted it to be in the most public, captive audience setting she could get her hands on. That definitely meant an auditorium of art students, faculty, and whoever happened to come watch the proceedings.

Part of me knew he been making a terrible mistake. I

couldn't help remembering James telling me that his girl-friend knew nothing of his kinks or the son that he never saw. Certainly, there's something to be said about loving someone, but those are some huge things not to know about a person you plan on marrying.

Exhibition came before any of us could register it. James opted to go last since nothing would be able to follow a proposal no matter how hard you tried. With my friends and fellow students sitting around me watching, one after another of the senior presenters got up on stage to talk about their artwork and what'd inspired them.

Several people, including me, grumbled curses and pleads under their breath that James wouldn't have the courage to go through with it as his turn had come around.

I watched him walk up on stage wearing an oversized gray suit with a black shirt under it and a black and red tie. For the first time in a long time, he hadn't been wearing a hat.

He could have definitely gone without the suit jacket and been fine, but someone somewhere had told him he looked good drowning in it, so he kept it on. I wondered if he felt more comfortable in baggy clothes.

James had chosen photography as his emphasis and had pulled inspiration from our little valley in producing giant panoramic pieces. He talked about the people that had pushed him. Thanked the people that'd kept him on track and worked alongside him to get everything done, and then he called his girlfriend up onto the stage.

"So, this girl has been an absolute inspiration to me. It's been a rocky road, but I'm glad that we've finally made it here," he said into a mic he'd picked up from the podium, and then looked nonchalantly at a young woman who was wearing a backless patterned maxi-dress and heels that made her steps clunk as she attempted to walk in them.

It seemed to me that James had tried dressing up far more than she had, but I still couldn't believe he'd decided to go through with it. This girl was the same girlfriend that'd cheated on him freshman year. Her sister was the exact same girl that James slept with in revenge for what she'd done. I know he didn't see it as fully as I did, but every part of my mind shrieked *mistake*.

"Adrienne," James said holding her hands and then taking a knee causing all the fabric over his slender frame to look even bulkier than when he'd been standing, "I love you, baby. Will you marry me?"

She hadn't even been surprised, honestly. She didn't cry or put her hand over her mouth in shock like she couldn't believe he'd finally asked her. She smiled without her teeth and agreed, taking the ring from him and slipping it on her finger without his help.

Hello ball-buster.

Everyone started clapping and cheering. The whole theatre erupted in a cacophony of congratulations and happiness. All except the small group of ready-to-graduate art majors in the corner who knew James and knew what a mistake he'd made.

The stupid things people do for love, I thought standing to leave the auditorium.

She'd never know what kind of a person he could truly be. She'd never know that throughout their second round of dating that he'd texted me with requests for turning him on and getting him off. That he'd gone beyond the porn fetishes and entered into wearing lacy thongs, owning dildos, and sending me pictures of various objects shoved in his dickhole.

She would never know that about her future husband.

Soon after that, shit hit the fan for the women in my little group of friends. I want to say it happened for many different, vast, and valid reasons, but there are only two reasons that I can truly imagine and honestly believe: Rah owed Evan money that she apparently needed far more than she'd initially let on, and the stress of graduation suddenly sat so heavily on our minds that some of us couldn't handle the pressure any longer.

It started with Rah being unable to afford our trip to Las Vegas for Spring Break. Ben couldn't come because of some unforeseen inability to take so much time off in such a short window since he'd planned on coming to watch graduation, too. That meant it would end up being Kodi, Evan, and me if Rah didn't join us, too.

As it stood, Evan agreed to front Rah the money and they'd set up a monthly payment plan after we came back so that Rah could pay her back appropriately even though she couldn't pay her back all at once.

As I'd been informed, Evan seemed cool with that. In all honestly, I thought it worked out perfectly if they were able to work that out together, but it didn't stay that way.

On our way there, we decided to check out the Grand Canyon. Evan, apparently, was the only one of us that'd already seen it, and she seemed to think that one hadn't *lived* until they had.

We were camping at a little sight in a tent in March. That alone says a lot about the kind of weather we'd definitely be facing if our track record with tent camping was anything to show for us. We froze throughout the night, and Evan insisted that we wake up as early as possible in order to catch the sunrise over the canyon.

Exhausted and already packed up for the journey to

Vegas, we all decided a nap before we left was a perfect idea and hunkered down in the car we'd borrowed from Evan's parents for the journey.

We'd put way too much in that car, though. Between the camping gear and the luggage and the car snacks and all of the other miscellaneous things we had to work around for comfort, I'd accidentally kicked a jug of orange juice that'd popped its lid and started leaking all over the floor mat.

"Shit!" I grumbled opening the rear passenger door and pulling the leaking container out with me.

"What?" Evan hissed glancing back from the driver's seat tiredly before the scene register, and she flew from her seat to push me out of the way and check the damage the orange juice may have caused.

"Where's the lid?" I asked holding the half-empty jug at arm's length while it continued dripping and Evan dug around under the seat before turning with a snarl and throwing the cap at me.

"Why the fuck is there orange juice all over my dad's car?" she growled accusingly.

I frowned at her. "It was an accident. It was under my feet and I didn't realize it. Why wasn't this in the cooler?"

"I don't believe you! This better not do any damage or you're gonna pay for it," she threatened, taking the mat out and shaking it for what little good it did now that the juice had soaked in.

The way she growled at me and the fact that she was so mad over an accident took me back a moment, but I tried not to let it ruin my mood for the rest of the trip.

Somewhere in the spilled orange juice, the molding car mats, and the blowfish tablets that made our hangovers *way* worse than they had been, Evan decided that the original payment plan wouldn't work out for her and Rah once we returned to Colorado. As if all the nipple tassels and strippers and the zombified burlesque dancers singing about how eating penis doesn't make you gay weren't enough to rip us away from our assured comforts.

"I'm gonna need you to pay me back before the month ends," Evan said in the most no-nonsense way I knew.

"What do you mean? We agreed to monthly payments," she reminded Evan thinking they'd come to a miscommunication. She frowned in confusion.

"I don't remember that, but I need it for bills this month, so I'm gonna need you to pay me back."

Rah glanced at me for help as we sat around our living room posed in various shades of studying and homework. I frowned sympathetically at her in return. Unfortunately, I couldn't interject into their conversation to come to her aid, though. I was already trying to get over my own stuff with Evan to really do much good.

"But we agreed to the monthly payments because you knew that I didn't have the full amount of money for it, let alone to actually go to Vegas in the first place. You knew because I told you! I would have never agreed to go if it wasn't for our agreement," Rah explained growing a little more flustered the longer Evan sat on her green couch looking nonplussed.

"You have until the end of the month," and nothing more could be said about it even though Rah's chest rose and fell more rapidly than it had before the news.

Evan lesson: I make the rules that work for me unless it's in writing.

Having no place left to turn, Rah went to the only people she knew had money, her parents. They were reluctant to give it to her at first, not liking Evan to begin with, but as the days passed and Evan became more forceful in her demands for the money no matter what it took for her to get it, Rah's parents had eventually had enough of the whole thing.

"So, my parents are driving up to the valley today. I really want you to meet them," Rah told me considering that she might as well make the most of the situation. Clearly, they were coming to bail her out.

"Sure! What time will they be here? You thinking something special?" I asked her wondering just what Rah's parents might actually be like. I'd heard plenty about them already, and Rah had a lot of shit to deal with in them as a whole, but I'd definitely meet them if only to learn a bit more about her and where she came from.

"Maybe dinner? I don't know exactly what time they're gonna get here, but my dad is adamant about taking care of the money thing before anything else to get Evan off me," she explained, and I nodded in agreement. It'd gotten pretty bad from my end, too.

Rah and I had taken to using all the beautiful sunny days to walk up to the soccer fields next to the apartment complex or the park a few blocks down the road to vent about all the frustrations presented to us by my roommates.

Almost always, we'd invite either Evan or Kodi to join us, too, but they usually declined in favor of video games, naps, or just sheer laziness. Most times we'd take Addie along so that she'd get some kind of walk in for the day since no one else seemed to have the energy or drive to take her and walk off the fat slowly turning her into a sausage roll. Rah and I felt bad for her even if she didn't always behave for us.

Rah provided a sounding board I'd desperately needed for several things as the semester, and my college career, came to a close. I'd tell her all about a professor that seemed to enjoy giving presentations far too close to the last day of classes and how life seemed to get scarier the closer I came to being thrust into it. Adulthood was not a thing I looked forward to facing.

In turn, Rah would tell me all about the woes of her life, her family, and our mutual friends, and we'd enjoy the relief that came with having someone graciously understand us and sympathize. I didn't have that with anyone else, and Rah became a life raft for me pretty quickly.

I loved her and appreciated her immensely for every moment we spent together, too.

I didn't know what to think when Rah's parents arrived, though. They were as opposite in looks as I could have imagined. Her mom looked pale and blonde and short and full of curves. Her dad was dark and tall and lanky and reminded me a bit of Eddie Murphy in the face.

Her mom had been kind and overjoyed that Rah had a friend like me and seemed to appreciate my role in Rah's life immensely. Absolute gratitude.

Rah's dad, on the other hand, who wasn't her real dad but who'd raised her, had quite the personality.

Rah told me about his propensity for running around on her mom and that they'd threatened divorce more times than she knew how to count. He seemed to prey on women with self-esteem issues and held himself up pompously with no sign of a humble bone in his whole body.

None of that would have mattered if he hadn't been horrifyingly using Rah and her mom in any way he could craft into his favor. Rah told me he'd force Rah to write out pages of the dictionary if they didn't clean the house to his perfectionistic standards which became the whole basis for why she no longer enjoyed reading.

That alone is the sole reason Rah's dad and I would

probably never be friends. Rah deserved so much more than what he brought into the relationship. Or didn't, actually.

Dinner went swimmingly, though.

"I can' believe that girl think she can boss anybody around the way she does," Rah's dad, Sly, grumbled from his side of the booth. "Unacceptable."

Sandra, Rah's mom, nodded, "She has no idea who she dealin' wit'. Nobody does that to their friend and especially not to my baby girl."

I had to agree with them. I'd have never dreamt of doing what Evan had done to any of my friends. Her lack of consideration for people had grown into the main difference between us, that's for sure.

"Don't you borrow anything else from her, ya hear, Danielle?" Sandra said chastising her daughter. It sounded weird hearing her real name used over Rah.

"Why you call her a friend, I'll never understand it," Sly growled angrily. I got the feeling they'd had a similar conversation with Rah before based on how frustrated they were. My own mother had said similar things to me.

"Honestly, I don't really know right now, either," Rah agreed partially in honest opinion and partially to placate them so that they'd stop discussing the bane of our collective existence.

"So, Desi, what do your parents think about Evan?" Rah's mom asked me earnestly, and I smirked accepting the new topic.

"I only have my mom and she's hated Evan ever since she met her. Doesn't trust her at all, honestly. She's on your same page," I admitted thinking about the last time Evan and my mom had come in contact.

"Good, I like her already," Sandra said decisively as our food arrived at our table.

We ate happily for the rest of the meal and enjoyed lighter conversation than the Evan-bashing that'd occurred once we'd sat down. It being only a quick trip for them, they climbed back into their little car and headed back towards the Front Range soon after we finished our meal.

Rah sighed in relief of their exit. "Sorry about that, they really don't like her and won't shut up about it sometimes."

I considered Rah for a minute. I couldn't help but agree with her parents in that moment. Rah had been hurt by Evan for no reason besides a reneging of their deal. If anything, Rah should have been the one being mean.

I remained silent in favor of wandering back to Rah's car and hopping in.

"So, what do you wanna do now? I'm not really in the mood to go back to campus and I can imagine you don't really wanna go back to your place, either. Wanna take a drive?" Rah asked me climbing into the driver's seat.

"Yeah, wanna do Blue Mesa again?" I asked thinking about all the other great times we'd had there as the weather grew more beautiful and warm by the day.

Rah agreed and put her car in drive to take us to the reservoir as the sun began to set. The only unfortunate thing about the sun going down was that the nights still felt cold, so we weren't able to stick around for very long. Only to wander around from stone to stone and admire one of the cliffs we'd jumped off of at the beginning of the year. The water had dropped far below where we'd jumped from, but it still felt thrilling to think about.

"Do you want me to drive you back to your apartment?" Rah asked me as we settled back into her car.

I didn't want to. Not really.

"No, wanna go back to your place?" I asked and then felt my phone buzzing along in my pocket.

I looked at Rah who shrugged back at me and let me answer it.

"Hello?" I said accepting the call.

"*Listen,*" Evan began, "*I don't know what the fuck you're playing at picking sides or whatever fucking bullshit this is that you have going on with Rah, but stop it fucking RIGHT NOW. It's annoying and you're becoming more useless to me the longer this goes on! Got it?*"

I swayed, taken completely off guard by the call, and took a moment to process all that she'd said.

What fucking side?

I exhaled angrily. "You think after all this time of Rah and I taking walks and inviting you and taking Addie and *everything* that I'm taking sides? You think I'd willingly do anything with anything that had to do with you if I'd fucking picked a *side*? You're making things up now and being a bitch about it. I have nothing more to say," I said hotly not believing that she actually had the gall to call me about it.

Evan clearly felt taken aback by my counterpoints as she paused a moment over the phone where I could scarcely hear her breathing before she scoffed and hung up the phone.

I let my own phone drop in my lap and growled before the reality of her accusations overcame me, and the tears fell quickly from my eyes.

"Oh, don't let her get to you like that," Rah said with concern. "Nothing she says deserves your tears."

I couldn't help it. The overwhelm of everything had been too much to bury, and I let it roll over me in horrible, body-wracking sobs.

Rah let me sit in the parking lot of Mears, her dorm complex, to clear some of my tears before we walked inside to her dorm. I cried for a long while after we'd gotten through her door, too.

I wondered, honestly, all that could have been saved with the existence of a contracted payment agreement instead.

29

A UNIQUE TRIO

"*D*o you wanna come home with me this weekend?" Rah asked me as we sat on the swings in the big park near Highway 50. It was a longer walk to get to this park from our apartment, but it was also nice to switch up our scenery for a bit.

"That sounds amazing," I said still recovering from Evan's call a few days ago that'd caused a huge rift in our friend dynamic. What she'd imagined had been happening with me taking sides and the whole reason for her call in the first place had actually caused sides to start forming in the group, and I couldn't help it. I felt betrayed by her accusation.

"If I invited Ben, do you think he'd come?" Rah asked me hopefully.

"Never hurts to ask," I told her thinking about how much I'd missed him. I'd called him after my call with Evan and he'd calmed me down immensely, and I could imagine that he'd come see me if he thought it'd mend something within the group.

And just like that, Rah and I found ourselves on another

amazing road trip full of singing, laughing, and chattering about our friends and how to solve our problems that all seemed to stem from the same person.

"I have a new song that I think you'd like," I told her taking over the aux cord and scrolling to find the one I'd been looking for.

I sang along with Tegan and Sara's "Closer" and Rah's eyes got big with excitement.

"Oooo! I like this a lot!" she cooed listening to the song further.

I laughed knowing she would.

"So, Ben's parents moved his family to Manitou Springs?" I asked her looking at the GPS again.

"Yeah. A little while ago. He wants us to pick him up there," Rah explained having received a text from him that he did want to come hang out with us at Rah's parent's house for the weekend when she'd asked.

We pulled up to the traditional middle class-looking house in a cute little neighborhood. The neighborhood had been nestled in a canyon area at the base of a mountain and all of the houses seemed to have some sort of brick and green siding.

"So, this is his house, huh?" I asked opening my door and stretching from the drive.

"That's what the GPS says. He's not answering his texts though."

"Huh, I wonder what's up. That's pretty typical Ben, though," I admitted thinking about all the non-communication moments I'd had with Ben in the past.

We walked up to the front door and rang the doorbell, and we listened but didn't hear much of anything going on inside except the appearance of a fat little pug in the foyer.

"That's weird," I mused as Rah ogled over the little dog. I

rang the doorbell again to be sure, but no one came rushing to the door at all.

"Is he actually home? Where could he have gone since we texted him?"

I considered that, but I didn't think he'd have left knowing that we'd be there to get him in the half an hour it would have taken us to get to his house since we'd texted him.

"Maybe the military already came to claim him and we're too late," I joked knowing that Ben had already signed on to become some kind of soldier. I tried not to think about how that'd kill the person that he was to me, but some emotions, when they're real, aren't as easily forced down.

Glancing at Rah, I could see that she had similar thoughts, but growing up as a military brat herself meant she probably understood the implications even more than I did.

"Or he could be sleeping," I pondered changing the subject and ringing the doorbell a few more times to attempt waking him up if that had been the case before I marched back to the car frustrated that he hadn't answered, yet. *Where could he be?*

Rah looked helplessly at me. "Do we just leave, then?"

I didn't want to do that. I shook my head at her thinking before I paced back and rang the bell again, hopefully.

I saw Ben poke his head around the corner of the upstairs hall and scowl at me.

I raised an eyebrow at him incredulously as if he thought his frustration had been warranted.

What had he been doing in there?

He kept the scowl as he rushed down the stairs and opened the front door to let us in. "What the heck? I was in the shower," he complained, and his hair had a little dampness to it, still, proving his point.

"Well, how were we supposed to know that? Not like we can hear that through the door," I growled back at him. "Besides, why would you wait until the last minute to shower? You had all day to do that before we arrived."

He shrugged. "You could have given me a little more warning than telling me you were in Canyon and then just showing up."

Rah looked sheepish. I felt too frustrated to feel more than that. He could have showered sooner or told us that's what he'd planned on doing in case we arrived before he got out, but I sighed knowing arguing over Ben's habits were no way to start the weekend with him. "Alright, do you have everything you need? Are you almost ready to go?"

"Your dog is so cute!" Rah told him leaning down to pet the little pug.

"Yeah, let me grab some stuff. I'll be back down. Oh, and you lost The Game."

Rah groaned and I rolled my eyes at him. "Sure just hurry up! I'm excited!"

We loaded Ben's things into Rah's little car and got underway to her house. It looked similar to Ben's if a little cheaper in material and without all the brick Ben's house had.

"Danielle, just park on the road so that your dad can pull into the garage later," Sandra said from the front porch while she held a squirming black and white Shih Tzu in her arms.

"Sassy!" Rah cooed to the little dog but she did as her mom asked.

We unloaded and made our way into the house and followed Rah upstairs where she showed us her neatly made room and the spare room that had a large sectional sofa in it that could definitely have slept three like a king bed.

"So, someone can sleep in here with me or you can share the spare room. They're both connected to this bathroom," she explained dropping her bags and turning her attention to the medium whiteish dog. "Skippy! My love!"

Ben and I looked at her and then to each other. Rah's bed was only a full which meant that'd be some snug sleeping compared to sleeping on the spacious bedroom sofa in the other room. We both moved our stuff in there and walked back in to find Rah cuddling more with Skippy who somehow managed to look uncomfortably awkward despite her tail wagging.

"Danielle, can you come down here please," called her mom from the base of the stairs.

Skippy got up and trotted over to the stairs and down at the call of her mom even though it hadn't been for Skippy herself.

"Yeah, be down in a minute," Rah called back before looking at Ben and me expectantly.

"I hope you don't mind," I said as we made our way downstairs again. "I think it'll be a little easier to sleep in the other bedroom. You should come over and join us."

"No, that's okay. You do what you need to be comfortable," she reassured me, and we landed in the living room.

Rah's mom asked her something in German that I couldn't even begin to guess at and Rah answered her question.

Rah's fluency in German and English impressed me more than I cared to admit. I wished I knew another language like that.

Ben went to petting the dogs who looked at him uncertainly for a minute before actually letting him touch them. Sassy seemed even warier than Skippy before she decided to warm up to him, but Ben had always been a dog person despite his own mystery and preferred silence.

I plopped down on the couch waiting to hear what the plan would be.

After dinner, the three of us wandered down into their basement to watch movies, drink Jägerbombs, and be sure that we wouldn't disturb Rah's parents as they started getting ready for bed.

Rah wandered upstairs for something, and I'd decided to crawl over Ben's lap and straddle him. He didn't mind much and let his hands rest on my thighs while I kissed trails over his neck and jaw before we started making out.

We heard a thumping down the stairs and turned to find that Rah had rejoined us.

"Oh, I didn't mean to interrupt," she blushed looking away from us which was amusing since she'd definitely seen me make out with our friends before.

"No, join us, Rah," I said reaching out to her until she grabbed my hand and let me pull her into our makeout session.

"I mean, there's always sex," Rah suggested after we'd been kissing each other for a while. She slid down onto the floor mats and looked up at the pair of us hopefully.

She'd never had sex with Ben or me before, so that had been a bold suggestion on her part. I couldn't blame her for wanting that, though. I always wanted that with Ben.

"I can't. The Communists are invading the funhouse," I admitted bitterly referring to my period, but they already knew what I meant. I mean, I knew bleeding was better than the alternative, but talk about *extremely* poor timing.

"Oh, no," Rah said sadly.

"I know. It sucks," I griped tucking my feet up under me and scowling.

Ben sighed sadly with the loss of opportunity.

"I mean, you guys can always do it without me. I don't mind," I told them hopeful that they'd take the opportunity to enjoy each other in a way they hadn't before since Ben usually always got involved with me or Kodi before Rah ever had the chance to steal him.

Rah looked suggestively at Ben with the same hope, and he seemed to consider her for a moment before shrugging.

"Yay!" she cheered scooting a bit closer to him so that they could kiss again. It seemed tentative now that it was meant to take them further than the making out we'd been doing before, but they had every right to feel apprehensive about the newness of the experience. I'm sure Rah would definitely start to feel a little nervous even if she wanted it.

"Woah, wait. You don't mind that I'm watching?" I asked wondering if they wanted me to wander for a minute while they did it.

"No, you're fine," Rah said as Ben laid her back against the ground.

"Stay," Ben told me undoing his own jeans and freeing himself. He stood proudly, and I couldn't help looking.

"Okay..." I agreed leaning back against the sofa. I wouldn't call myself a voyeur by any means, but the prospect of what I'd be witnessing on that couch seemed thrilling and totally taboo to me, and my stomach fluttered a little bit.

Rah undid her pants and removed them completely so that Ben had access to her and he thrust into her expertly as he had every other time I'd known him that way.

She groaned happily.

I knew the feeling. I'd told Ben he had a great dick on many occasions.

I watched his well-muscled bare ass move with each thrust, and the point where his dick entered Rah and the way it seemed to thicken while it was in her was directly in my line of sight. It looked so erotic, and I'd been so turned on that I started rubbing myself through my pants getting off on the sex as it played out in front of me like live porn.

Rah moaned again and Ben seemed to thrust faster with the encouragement.

I couldn't blame him. It moved me further as they went until I cried out a moan of my own along with Ben who came in her almost at the same time.

He laid tiredly on her for a minute before he clamored back and let her get up to take care of herself as she moved to a bathroom.

Ben wiped himself off on the inside of his boxers and put his pants back on watching me the whole time.

I considered him for a minute while he watched me. "So, how was it?" I asked him.

"Good. How was it for you?" he countered having obviously heard me.

"Hot," I said wondering if he'd be down for a little shower sex later.

"Okay, that was awesome! I'm so tired now," Rah admitted popping back into the room.

I agreed. I felt tired, too. Tired of all the crazy shit that I'd experienced in the valley and school as a whole. I could sleep for a hundred days and still probably not be over my own emotional exhaustion.

Ben seemed to agree with her on the physically tired part, though, and considered going to bed an awesome idea.

We moved upstairs, and Ben and I laid on the bedroom

couch under our large shared blanket enjoying our company until sleep overtook us.

The next morning I woke up with the light of the day and Ben sleeping heavily next to me as we had every other time we shared a bed together. I knew he hated being woken up in the morning, but I started snuggling into him and kissing him softly every once in a while, as I attempted to wake him.

He grumbled with the disturbance, and I nuzzled him happily.

"Hey, Ben?" I prodded after he'd blinked a few times and scowled at me before flipping so that his back faced me. "Hey, do you wanna shower with me?"

He looked over his shoulder considering me for a minute and being all too familiar with our showering habits if we managed to bathe together before he sighed. He'd always be down for showering with me.

I dragged him to his feet and we locked ourselves in the bathroom and stripped, and I climbed in to turn on the water so that it'd warm up before Ben climbed in after me.

I started kissing him again once we'd climbed in together and he stood tiredly letting me and the water wake him up a little more.

"Do you wanna have sex?" I asked moving to the back of the tub.

Ben moved to the floor of the tub with me and mounted me before thrusting in much the way he had the night before with Rah. The suction of my wet back against the tub floor made a loud popping sound with every thrust Ben made which must have been the way the tub was shaped since we'd never experienced anything like that before in our sexy shower times.

I laughed a little with how horrible it sounded, but I

hoped no one else in the house could hear it, too, since no position change would silence it.

I thoroughly enjoyed showering with Ben, though. As a general rule, showers were always more fun with other people.

After making it downstairs and finding Rah and her mom chatting in the kitchen, Rah walked over and pulled me to the side where her mom couldn't hear us.

"You know we could totally hear you having sex in the shower, right?" she asked me seriously.

"You could?" I asked flushing in embarrassment.

"Yeah, my mom was even asking what the noise was and I had to play it off as something," she told me giggling a little.

"Sorry," I said sheepishly thinking about how we probably could have been a little quieter or moved at least.

Oops.

"In other news, Sassy got out and we've already cased the neighborhood in search of her. We're thinking about going to the humane society next to see if she's there."

"Oh, that sucks. Do you want us to come with you?" I asked knowing we didn't have anything better to do.

"You don't mind?"

"Not at all, but let me eat breakfast first," I said wandering over to the kitchen where Ben followed along to find some food, as well. I knew we'd find Sassy somewhere. I mean, there were certainly coyotes and that'd always suck if it came down to it, but I imagined that someone probably picked her up and went to see if she had a tag or not.

Not a big deal for us.

30

FORTS & ORGIES

"Do you want to meet one of the Sloths?" Evan asked Kodi, Rah, and me as we lounged around our living room watching *Arrow*.

Kodi glanced at me before looking at Evan. "A *real* Sloth?"

"Of course a real Sloth, Kodi," Evan deadpanned before snarling and Kodi looked back at me again for another bout of silent communication that seemed to be our main mode of talking to each other.

I did want to meet more of them. I hoped to meet all of them, honestly. I'd been beyond curious to know what they were all like and how they had been faring since Evan had passed the mantle of TeiLuce after she realized she couldn't handle it while being four hours away at school.

"When?" Rah asked her curiously.

"Tonight," she told us completely unphased by the fact that she'd basically dropped a bomb on us last minute. It reminded me a bit of the time Mike came up after Remi killed himself. I looked skeptically at her then.

Kodi looked at me with a pleading hope in her eyes that

I'd back her up with anything that needed to happen or maybe even to say no? I couldn't be sure.

"I'm not going anywhere tonight, so it's fine by me," I told her thinking that I would finally get the proof I so desperately wanted about all of it. I needed everything Evan had told us to be real so bad.

Kodi understood that, too. Maybe she'd been hoping for the same thing and that we'd both find clarity in this person's arrival.

Evan looked smugly at us, satisfied that we'd agreed and wandered back into her room to nap until she'd gotten word that her friend arrived in town. Kodi and I exchanged unspoken words as the time ticked on and we grew more and more agitated and nervous about the meeting with another dangerous person from the gang on top of the one we'd been introduced to and the other we'd been living with the past few months.

What if this person didn't like us? What if the order went out and we were put on a hit list on the spot?

I never put death past any of the Sloths. A reaper followed them wherever they walked as far as I could see. Plus, Evan had only just decided how she'd planned on killing me last week after she'd found out I didn't like the feeling of wet plastic on my skin.

She'd been plotting my death since meeting me. I know because she'd tell each of us how she'd planned on killing us if she'd ever had the need to. According to Evan, Kodi would be run over repeatedly because of her constant stupidity, Ben would die being strangled because he never came directly out with anything, and Delphinium would be shot a few times executioner style for her betrayal. And the list goes on.

She struggled with me, though. No deadly scenario ever

seemed exciting enough whenever she thought of me dying. She'd brood over it completely at a loss over what would be a good enough death for me. It'd been a safety net for me, really.

Then, she finally knew. Right at the end of school, too.

After she'd said that she'd wrap me in plastic and throw me in some large body of water, I couldn't help imagining all possible scenarios in which I could leave clues to her murdering me. How she'd get caught simply for being so cocky about it. As if I wouldn't fight back against my own demise.

Talk about hauntingly colorful imagery.

Who plots the deaths of their friends?

Knock. Knock. Knock.

While I'd been thinking about Evan's more wicked ways, an arrival sounded. Evan rushed down the hall at the sound of the door, and Kodi looked at me with concern lining her features. I couldn't say that I felt all that thrilled about having another potentially lethal person in our apartment, either, but it would have to be now or never for certain.

Evan paused glancing excitedly at the both of us, "Are you ready?"

As ready as I'll ever be, I thought bracing myself for whoever happened to walk through the front door.

Evan unlocked the knob and twisted it quickly to fling the door open and hop out of the way.

There stood a skinny man with mousy hair. His face was thin and angular, and he looked like he might be shorter than me by a few inches. He'd flung a backpack over one shoulder and he had on a pair of jeans, tennis shoes, and a gray shirt...

Ben.

"Surprise!" Evan said jovially presenting him to us.

"Ben!" Kodi said standing and I rushed to the door with her.

Addie came barreling over and leaned her large body against Ben's legs in greeting. Her stubby tail wagged furiously in her happiness.

She moved when I came in and threw my arms around him in a delighted greeting and kissed him for the time we'd been apart though it'd only been a few weeks. He grumbled begrudgingly as usual but smiled at us.

Kodi stepped in and hugged him happily.

"You lost The Game," he told her, and I couldn't even be indignant enough to groan.

"I figured you'd be here closer to graduation," Kodi said moving inside so that he could come in, as well.

"I'll be here for ten days," he told us which meant that he'd be around until a few days after graduation, too.

Yay!

"How was the drive?" Evan asked as he settled onto our brown couch.

He shrugged in indifference to the drive and Evan nodded in agreement. The drive from the Front Range could be that way.

We stayed up late talking. Evan admitted that she had no idea how the surprise was going to work, but that she needed to keep us around for it without spoiling it. Apparently, the only way to do that was through the Sloths, but Ben was way better than them. The four of us had weathered so many things together, and we were all going to be adults in the world together. That meant a lot more to me than someone else that might kill me in the grand scheme of things.

It being the beginning of the weekend, nothing made

more sense than ending where we'd started as friends, with a blanket fort.

With all the spare sheets that I don't believe left Kodi or Evan's closets all year, the fort went up quickly, especially with Ben, Evan, me, Kodi, and Rah there to get it together.

We pushed our coffee table into the kitchen and set all of our alcohols on it. We'd spent a crazy amount to stock for our time before graduation, and we drank it happily.

Sitting in our fort together, trading off on dying playing hard in CoD, I remembered the time we'd played spin the bottle with Kodi, Evan, Ben and me.

"Hey, you wanna play spin the bottle?" I asked as Ben and Evan destroyed the enemies on the screen.

"Yes!" Rah cooed in agreement.

"Definitely," Kodi chirped.

The three of us turned towards Evan and Ben who were completely engrossed in their game.

"Yeah, yeah, let us die first," Evan said as another smattering of bullets burst from her animated gun.

Satisfied with that answer, Rah popped up and wandered behind the sheets to find an empty bottle in the kitchen. Not hard since we'd already polished off at least five beers.

"Fuckfuckfuck!" Evan growled having died and dropping her controller unhappily. "I have to say that if this game is as rigged as the last game of spin the bottle was and Kodi and Ben continue being the only ones making out, I quit."

I nodded, "Agreed, they were at it practically the whole time."

Kodi grinned cheekily at her fortune before Rah reappeared in the fort with a rinsed out brown bottle that one of us had torn the labels off to test if the Fates would still decree us as virginal if it came off in one piece.

It hadn't.

Evan and Ben moved away from the sleeping bags laid out on the ground so that we could clean a space on the hardwood where the bottle would spin unhindered.

"We should make it more interesting like last time," I said thinking that making out was all well and good except I preferred doing it without any clothes on.

"How?" Evan asked having paused mid-spin.

"What about taking a piece of clothing off if it lands on you?" Rah asked combining the drinking games she knew.

Strip spin the bottle seemed interesting enough to all of us that Evan spun so that none of us could back out and it landed on Rah.

Rah took off her socks to start and then kissed Evan quickly before taking the bottle in hand and spinning it herself.

She grudgingly got Kodi, who I don't think any of us were looking forward to kissing, but we hadn't forced her into brushing her teeth like we did the last time we played either.

The turns went around, and the clothes came off and the alcohol continued flowing. How we weren't plastered any of the times we drank together had been an amazing testament to Evan, honestly. She'd taught us all to drink and had diligently watched over us until we'd learned our limits and stuck with them. Evan had taught us to treat drinking as the social facilitator it'd been intended to be instead of as a sport like so many other college students treated it.

We were all completely naked and we paused in our gameplay wondering what we did now that we had nothing left to take off. Each of us came to a decision almost at the same time. We'd all had sex individually or in threes with each other, why couldn't all of us have sex as a group, as well?

I turned and looked to find Kodi and Ben making out together about a foot from Evan and I and Rah stroking Ben while his mouth had been occupied. It looked horribly awkward from the angle I sat at, like Kodi hadn't been looking to top, but I knew Ben wouldn't take to leading into that either. And Rah kind of added into the awkwardness with a poorly placed hand job.

I glanced at Evan who seemed equally as confused by the scene as I'd been, so I got involved kissing trails over each of my friends before they came apart and I pushed them all onto their backs with Kodi on my left, Ben beneath me, and Rah on my right. Taking full advantage of all their nakedness, I kissed each of them before sticking my fingers into the girls and taking Ben into my mouth.

He stood proudly, hung by anyone's standards. All of us knew it and told him several times. He'd been a little hard to maneuver while my hands were occupied. I found it difficult to focus on everything at once, honestly. I should have sat on Ben instead, which would have freed my worry of running my teeth against him, to focus on my fingers and their tasks.

While both Kodi and Rah squirmed with my work, I knew Rah had never gotten over the edge and actually climaxed before. I had no idea why, but ever since she'd told me that she'd never actually orgasmed, I made it my sole purpose of bringing her over the edge once so that she knew what she'd been missing.

I put all my attention on her, then, and she took to kissing me well enough, and it became easy enough to finger her a bit more vigorously in search of her sweet spot.

Rah's cries became more persistent and it became hard

to tell when she went over the edge, but she fought the feeling almost the entire time, too, so it took some patience. Eventually, she made it, and she felt so overwhelmed that she started crying for it.

I couldn't blame her. That first time over the edge for me gave me pause for nearly three whole minutes while I recovered.

Evan started making out with me once I'd stopped with Rah, keeping me from tending to her, but I let Evan pull me eagerly to an empty part of the fort. She laid down letting me lead her in whatever I wanted, and I relished the moment of control over her.

The problem with Evan that'd lingered in the group, especially between her and Ben, had been that she had a small vagina, or so she thought.

Rah, Kodi, and I had been watching a show called *Strange Sex* one day and came across this woman that had Vaginismus which caused her Kegels to clench to the point that she couldn't have sex with her husband which had been the reason she'd sought help.

I always believed that Evan's reasons for keeping objects out of her vagina were mainly because she'd repeatedly been raped as a child and that she'd never found peace with it and never went exploring herself, either. It'd gotten so bad for Evan that even inserting one of my fingers felt painful to her.

I had to try, though.

She laid pale and tentative beneath me, and I did my best to ease her into it. She cringed, and I stopped. I tried moving again and she squirmed under me. I felt certain there wouldn't be much for me to do for her if she kept cringing each time I moved, so I pulled my hand away and she sat up grimacing.

"Sorry," she told me sighing.

"Don't be," I dismissed not upset with her in the least. If anything, I had all my other best friends to play with in that moment.

I took to rolling around the fort with each of them for a moment before my alcohol and the time caught up with me, and I felt exhausted and ready for bed.

Evan had already scrambled out of the fort and taken Addie out for her nightly ritual before they climbed into her twin bed for sleep.

Kodi followed shortly after me and wandered into her bed, and I started brushing my teeth before Evan's head poked in around the doorway of my bathroom.

"Rah and Ben are having sex!" she whispered excitedly, and though I'd seen them having sex before, I moved back into the living room to peek through the hanging sheets to see Rah lying on her back with her knees tucked up and Ben on top of her thrusting.

After only a moment, enough for the image to be burned in my memory for all eternity and both of them to look over and see us watching them, the green-eyed monster in my mind reared her head in jealousy of them together like that.

I couldn't look at them any longer.

I turned and walked back into my bathroom to finish brushing my teeth and get ready for bed. I walked back into my room to crawl into my bed and found Ben standing in the doorway from the hall donning a pair of navy blue boxers lit only with the deep orange glow of the string lights overhead.

I smiled warmly at him in welcome and he nodded at me before walking in and closing my door behind him.

I left my string lights on so that my room held a familiar

dimness as he discarded his boxers and we crawled into bed together. It hadn't been the first time he and I had slept together in any sense of the word, but I adored him and knew in some way he felt it, too.

He had yet to say it out loud.

I kissed him, and he stayed close to me and traced over a nerve on my arm making me shiver.

"Part of the reason sex is so great is because of the nerves. If you find a good one, one that you can trace from top to bottom and back, you've basically turned someone on enough to start having sex right then." He said it so casually I imagined he'd said something about the weather or a class freshman year.

I nodded but felt that nothing really compared to the demonstration he did on my body to prove to me what he'd been talking about.

He started on my inner thigh at a place he'd found while running each of his fingers over the area and removing one at a time to find the optimum location. Then, he took a single finger and slowly, lightly traced dragged it upward moving over my thigh to my hip over my stomach and to my ribs where he'd lost the trail.

Still, it felt so good that I could have let him continue touching me like that the whole night through.

Instead, he let me roll towards him and attempt to replicate what he'd done for me on his body. I got a little of it, not the same, but it'd been enough that he moved over me to kiss me and I felt his erection growing against my side.

I spread for him as he settled between my legs and positioned himself before easing in. We stayed that way for a while, him thrusting and me digging into his back with my fingertips blissfully.

"I'm getting tired, do you wanna switch?" he asked pausing for a minute.

"Yeah," I agreed, letting him roll over to his back so that I could crawl on top of him.

We continued that way until I came and shuttered as it rolled through me. I sighed and looked to see if he wanted to cum as well, but he shook his head and let me roll off. He'd been busy, I couldn't blame him for his exhaustion.

"If only we'd started having sex way back at the beginning. I wouldn't feel so sad about graduating," I told him thinking about how much more we could have been if that had happened.

"Wait, you mean freshman year? We could have been having sex even then?" he said incredulously.

I quirked an eyebrow at him. *Was he really that oblivious? I hadn't been that subtle, had I?*

"What the heck? I'm so mad at myself, now," he groaned knowing how much fun it would have been and all the instances that we found ourselves hanging out alone together in those early years of our friendship.

"Yeah, I would have definitely had sex with you then," I told him pushing a strand of my hair out of my face.

He thought about it for a while in silence and I felt his breaths on my face while he did.

"You do know that I love you, right?" Ben asked after the lull in conversation, and I'd cuddled up next to him and pulled the cord to the lights so that the room plunged into darkness.

I blinked at him unable to truly see anything but a little shocked all the same.

I thought about it. I did know that, actually.

"Yeah, Ben, and I love you," I smiled into the dark and

kissed his shoulder happily. The butterflies had exploded with the news, and I couldn't help feeling a little excited.

Then it dawned on me that Ben had actually been telling us he loved us all along without actually using the words.

"That's why you tell us 'Be good' when you leave us, huh? It's not just to make us lose The Game," I said thinking through all the times I'd heard him say it and the way he'd said it each of those times. *With serious eye contact.*

Ben sighed having lost The Game but agreed that had been the message he'd been trying to convey to us all along. I'd been too blind to see it. I believed everyone else would still be as clueless if they didn't have a similar moment with him like I'd been experiencing.

"Why don't you just say it outright?" I questioned thinking about how much easier it'd be for all of us.

"Where's the fun in that? No guesses at all and it wouldn't make you lose," he told me, and I had to agree that having hidden meanings and puzzles had definitely been something Ben would totally do.

I smiled still being the only one to have ever heard him say that to any of us and flipped over for sleep. He seemed grateful for the decision to sleep, as well, and crashed soon after we got comfortable.

"I had a weird but amazing dream last night," Evan told us the next day moving onto the green couch under the window groggily. It'd been late morning before we'd all wandered out of our rooms, and even though we'd been up way too late the night before, we all had exams to go to.

"About what?" Kodi asked moving slowly around the kitchen in equal grogginess. We'd removed two of the sheets so that the kitchen and living room were no longer separated.

Evan closed her eyes to collect as many of the details she could from the dream before opening them to begin. "It was weird. Desi, Rah, and I lived in this huge mansion somewhere and it had all these awesome things in it, but we got a knock on the door one day and it was Kodi. She'd apparently gotten pregnant by someone and needed help. So, Desi and I took her in and helped her when the baby came.

"Then, we get another knock one day. It was raining and dark and we opened the door to find Ben there. We knew he'd been in the military and everything, but he told us all about how he'd been discharged after an incident in which his leg was sliced off right below his knee and how he had a wicked scar where they'd reattached it.

"Since he was out and had nowhere else to go, too, we took him in. We had a freakin' mansion, so extra people in the rooms wasn't a big deal to us, and he helped us take care of Kodi's baby, too."

We each exchanged looks as if that did seem a little weird but not totally unthinkable for us.

It honestly sounded perfect to me. A community house with my best friends? Nothing beat that, really.

It made sense where each of us ended up in the dream, too. Ben's dream had been to join the Navy Seals, and he'd have come to us to heal and feel a part of society again. He'd never let Evan have any sort of control or play games with him, either. Everything would always be on his terms even when deciding to move into our fictitious mansion with us.

Kodi would definitely come to us completely lost on how to raise a kid, too. I couldn't help but admire how realistic Evan's dreams seemed after she told them to us.

"I wouldn't put it past any of us if that actually happened," I said thinking aloud.

My friends nodded in agreement thinking about the dream and their place in it, too.

"You wanna buy a mansion with me?" Evan asked from her couch, and I considered her for a minute wondering if she'd actually been serious about it even after all the shit we'd been through that semester.

I, honestly, wanted nothing more than to love all of them for the rest of my life. There'd been no questioning it.

"Yes."

31

COVETED TIME

A few days out from graduation, I'd successfully completed at least three of my exams and had started packing up my space to be ready for when my family came to see me. I'd decided to take a break from my work to watch another of the *Extended Edition Lord of the Rings* movies we'd been marathoning together and propped myself in a ball on our brown couch next to Ben.

I'd snuggled into him, content on cuddling since he'd taken so much time in this visit to be with me.

"Ben, it appears you have a *leech*," Evan sneered as she rounded the corner from the hall into the living room looking pointedly at us.

I glowered at her, but Ben started to shake me off at her words which offended me to my core.

How could he let her get to him like that?

Because he'd moved, I sat up sulking and leaned against my knees as I tucked them up against my chest.

We'd never had an issue with sharing Ben before, so why did she have to be like that? Did she suddenly become jealous of his attention on me and decide to act out because of it?

Heck, I'd asked her permission to be intimate with him several times even after she'd given it to me indefinitely and told us we'd never have to ask her permission to sleep together ever again.

I didn't know what to make of her sudden irritation in Ben and me, but I could say that she'd totally thrown off my groove for the evening that even prevented Ben from coming and sleeping in my room that night or any of the following nights after.

Another Evan lesson: Sharing is only permissible until someone wants it more.

As the days ticked on and more of my things came off the walls and went into boxes, the mood around the apartment changed, as well.

Where we'd had sex as a group only last weekend, now Evan was snarly and more cantankerous than usual to the point that Rah and I could hardly stand being around any longer. We'd take off on walks and drive around town or run off and grab a bite to eat all the time to get away for a minute and cool off before re-entering the fray again.

Why neither of my roommates had started packing seemed ridiculous to me. If they'd gotten their stuff, we'd have had more time to play before I sold my bed and moved up to the mountain house my family would be staying in over graduation weekend.

Instead, they put it off continuously and watched as my belongings slowly dwindled down to the barest minimum to the point where I only had my bed and a few pieces of clothing left to work with. Still, we did nothing like we had freshman year together, and the fun fell away to make room for some unnecessary hostility. I didn't understand why.

Eventually, my family arrived and the day to sell the bed arrived, too, which meant that I wouldn't be staying at the apartment ever again.

"So, Desi, you remember my friend Dionna who met us up at the whitewater park, right? She's been so excited all week to take your bed from you even though I've told her how much sex you've had on it. *Jokingly*, of course," Rah chuckled as she walked a petite brunette into our apartment and down the hall to my room.

"Oh, it's perfect!" Dionna singsonged as she entered my nearly empty room and saw the mattress. "How much do I owe you for it?"

"Forty. That's how much I paid for it," I told her as she counted out her money and handed me the cash. "Do you need help getting it outside?"

"No, no, we got it, I think," she said looking to Rah who nodded confidently at her.

"Yeah, it should be fine," Rah confirmed and went to pick up a side of the mattress to start moving it.

It felt good to be rid of that last little bit of my room, honestly, even though Kodi watched it walk out the door with pursed lips and sadness in her eyes.

I loaded what I needed into my family's rental car and moved up to the mountains on the outskirts of town, and Rah had decided to move up there with me. She'd had to move out of her dorm, anyway, so it only made sense since she'd have a bed at the rental house, too.

I knew where my obligations lay if family came around. I'd do what I could with my friends, but on an occasion like graduation, I'd be doing pretty much all family stuff until they left town.

I assumed Evan and Kodi would be doing the same thing considering their families had also come to town for the occasion, but I knew that neither of them considered their families quite as important as I considered mine and would find tons of ways to get out of it.

I didn't have the luxury, nor did I want it, honestly. My family could be really fun to hang around with, and they proved that to me several times while we were together with margaritas and pizzas and board games and fun.

Evan and Kodi let me know how much they disapproved of my lack of friend time, though.

Come drink with us tonight. Kodi would say.

I can't. We're going to the mountain.

Ditch them! Evan responded.

Sorry. This is it.

Evan: **I can't believe you wouldn't pick us over them.**

I'd get a summons every day from one of them in a text asking me to come back down for the night to drink with them. I couldn't, and they'd angrily text me about how much they hated what I'd been doing or who I'd become or how unfair it seemed that my family took all my attention from them moments before graduating and possibly never seeing each other again, but I couldn't do much for it by then. They had to survive without me for those few days, and I hardly thought we'd stop being friends after graduation just because we hadn't hung out together before walking across the stage. Certainly, they were important to me, but when your whole family flies across the country to see you, they take a bit more precedence.

Was I the irrational one here?

It reminded me a bit of how Evan had acted before I'd left for my year in Spain.

She, Ben and I had decided on a trip to Central America the summer before our junior year as a last little hoorah before our year apart. Things had mostly been great while we were there, too, aside from Evan getting sick from dehydration since she only ever drank pop and alcoholic beverages and nothing in between.

"Do you wanna have a threesome together?" she'd asked as we sat around with our deck of cards playing who knows what and drinking heavily despite her nausea. *"I don't know how well I'll be able to participate, but I want to have one with you."*

Ben and I had looked to each other confirming that that sexual scenario had been one from both of our wildest dreams.

"Yeah," Ben had said.

"Definitely," I'd agreed.

We'd moved from the living room of the condo we were staying in to one of the bedrooms. We'd gotten one of the highest floors of the building that looked way off into the ocean though there'd been nothing much to see in the dark. The rainy season meant that the different pressures in the air from the heat of the jungle and the coolness of the mountains created a rolling lightning cloud where bolts of light crashed out on the water nearly every other minute.

We'd opened the curtains wide so that we could enjoy the magnificence of it as we stripped and crawled onto the expansive mattress. The three of us kissed and caressed and learned what we could from one another as Ben had never done anything like that with either of us before.

That had been the night that Ben and I had learned of Evan's vaginal ailments. He'd been disappointed in not being able to fit in her without hurting her, but he'd fully enjoyed me, and the pair of us moved from the bed to the shower to the balcony loving the feeling of the air on our bare skin as lightning crashed over the water and we'd intertwined ourselves on the patio furniture out there.

As we'd packed to leave for our flights back home, Evan went through her stages of loss and grieving then, too. She'd begged me to only go for a semester and come back for the spring. She'd spat angrily at me for being so selfish and inconsiderate for leaving my friends for so long, and I'd told her she could just study abroad with me.

Apparently, that was an unacceptable option for her as she dismissed it entirely.

She'd cried for me as we parted ways in the airport after making it through Customs on the border and I had to catch my flight. That'd made me cry, too, and we'd sat bawling like babies in the terminal while we said our goodbyes.

"You'll be able to text me and Skype me any time," I told her as we hugged one last time.

"I know, it's just not the same. Who's gonna stop me from all the stupid bad ideas I have? Kodi will never be able to do what you can," she admitted, and the last call for boarding sounded for my plane.

"I have faith in you. You'll figure it out," I called rushing towards the gate and hopping on my flight home. We'd waved to each other before I'd walked down the jet bridge and out of sight.

EPILOGUE

MAYDAY

$\mathcal{D}$ad parked his big, red F-150 outside of our building in Mountaineer Village.

We'd dropped Rah and my brother off outside of Mocha's Coffee Shop assuring that we wouldn't be long in getting things cleaned up before we'd be back to get them. We had plans to visit the Black Canyon and Montrose before we were set to leave town tomorrow.

Mom, Dad, and my stepmom, Tammie, all agreed to come help me clean the apartment for inspection if only to have photographic evidence that I'd left the place clean and any damage done henceforth would be at the fault of Evan and Kodi.

Mom became more incapable of keeping her own opinions of Evan a secret, and it showed as soon as I'd unlocked my apartment door and stepped inside.

Though sparse on furniture now, the apartment, like all other moments I'd walked through the front door, looked like a small tornado had ripped through it.

Evidence of macaroni and cheese lay crusted over the whole kitchen that Rah and I had cleaned before moving up to the mountain house with my visiting family. The pots and pans, like every other time they'd been used, sat on the stove and counters with food dried and cooked to their surfaces with no consideration of soaking them to get the food to come off easily when they'd actually need to be washed. Dishes, and I'm not sure how they managed to use *all* of them, were piled up and over the sink and onto the counters around it taking over what available space may have remained had they actually taken the time to put the dirty dishes into the dishwasher to be cleaned.

Addie fur still lined the baseboards throughout each room of the apartment except for mine where she knew she wasn't allowed. Spilled remnants of Code Red, Voltage, Game Fuel, and whatever alcohol they'd been mixing them with set dried to the hardwood in whatever sticky spots some unfortunate socked or shoed foot happened to step in them.

Two days.

It took *two days* in my absence for the mess to overrun them, and even though it hadn't been mine (like every other time Rah and I had cleaned because we couldn't stand the mess any longer), I'd been set to clean it all over again.

"Oh, my Lord," Tammie breathed, stepping in behind me as nothing could have prepared her for the scene awaiting us there.

"I know," Mom told her while turning to face me. "So, where should we start?"

Ben, who'd been sleeping on the old, sunken, brown leather couch we'd inherited with the apartment, cracked his eyes upon our arrival.

I smiled sympathetically at him for the disturbance.

"Hey. Sorry. You can go into Kodi's room if you'd like a quieter space," I said moving into our bare living room.

Ben didn't say anything but shot me a half-hearted glare of disapproval before rolling to face the cushions and continue with whatever kind of rest he'd anticipated getting while we were there.

Turning to reassess my situation, I gazed tiredly at the mess. I knew Delphinium would be coming to pick up all the extra furniture and miscellany I'd collected in my four years in Colorado that I wouldn't be able to carry home on the plane with me. I also knew that in the two days since I'd 'lived' in the apartment, Evan, Kodi, and Ben had trashed the place, especially the kitchen.

"If you wouldn't mind starting on the kitchen and the dishes, I'd appreciate it," I sighed trying not give away my growing frustration towards my roommates. "I'm going to get my stuff together and out of my room."

I turned down the hall and noticed Evan's door cracked and Evan asleep curled in her sleeping bag on the floor of her empty room. Her parents must have taken Addie and her furniture home with them after graduation.

Thankfully, Evan had always been a heavy sleeper, so I snuck up to her door, closed it gently, and continued with what I'd been doing. With any luck, she'd remain asleep until well after we'd left.

Shortly after piling my own belongings into a corner and vacuuming, I heard the knock on the door signaling Delphinium's arrival.

It always seemed funny to me how you could go ages without talking to or seeing someone, and while things in life may be different, they're also strikingly similar, and the base of your friendship remains intact like a breath of fresh air.

I couldn't claim a friendship like that with Delphinium, anymore.

It'd been months since I'd actually seen her in passing, and ages since we'd actually spoken face to face. Her happy relationship to her fiancé Todd wore on her body like an oversized winter coat.

I'd heard of 'love weight,' but Delphinium held a love that barely fit into her already too-tight clothes.

Beyond that, she looked the same.

Her long blonde locks were pulled back into a ponytail at the back of her head. Her crooked teeth stuck out covered in saliva as she chomped loudly at the piece of blue gum in her mouth. She didn't have any makeup on, but her eyes still shone and the too-large rhinestone stud in the right corner of her broad, flat nose took even further attention away from the fact that she still didn't have any eyebrows to make her forehead a touch less pronounced.

As it'd been every other time I'd encountered it, Delphinium's aura held firmly at a high-stress, high-drama frequency, but it seemed unusually high today to the point that I could only assume that the favor I'd asked in her meeting me caused most of it as she couldn't wait to leave.

"Hey, where's the stuff you want me to take?" she asked hurriedly.

"Hey, Delphinium. It's down the hall. We can help you get it into the car," I said through a fake smile though genuinely glad she agreed to take the stuff off of my hands in the first place.

She seemed slightly disappointed when she saw the pile but resigned to taking it if only because she said she would. There were plastic drawers and boxes, toiletry items, blankets, bins, and containers that held things I'd never used in my four years at college. She tried to tell us not to pack a few of the things she didn't need, but we packed it all anyway, leaving it up to her to throw the stuff away that she wouldn't use. It couldn't remain in the apartment as evidence for Evan and Kodi to use against me as collateral damage.

Once everything packed neat enough to the point where we could close the trunk of her red Jeep, I hugged her briefly in parting knowing that would be the last time I'd ever have contact with Delphinium again.

Though we hadn't been on good terms for a couple years, I let some iota of nostalgia wash over me while watching Delphinium pull away and headed back inside to finish cleaning.

I vacuumed the spot on my floor that had been under my pile of things Delphinium had taken before taking pictures of every angle within my room and bathroom.

"How's everything going out here?" I asked as I walked into the kitchen.

"Well, the stove is finally done," Dad said as he moved onto the counters.

"One load of dishes is done, but there're definitely enough left to fill another load and then some," Tammie twanged in her pseudo-Indiana/Kansas accent. "Do you need us to do anything in here?"

She reached the bathroom door in the hall that Evan and Kodi shared, and before I could stop her, she opened it and stopped dead in her tracks.

"Oh, my Lord! They actually live in this?" she asked, disbelief heavy in her voice. "Francesca, Fred, you gotta come see this."

Having lived with them, even if just for a few months, that bathroom had been something I'd only touched once and that'd been to clean the black mold from the toilet after we'd first moved in. As I knew them all too well already, that would be the last room they'd get cleaned out and sanitized. I also knew it'd be a half-assed job at best because Evan would make Kodi do pretty much all of it, and Kodi didn't clean unless forced to do so.

"That's just wrong," Mom cringed stepping up to look at the piles of boxes covered in dust and full of unused items that were only in there because that had been the usual place where things like hair products and lotions were stored.

"You don't have to clean that," I assured them as I stepped up to flip off the lights and close the door. "Rah and I found black mold all over the undersides of the toilet seat, lid, and bowl once. That's the last time I've ever been in there, and I'm leaving that as the only thing Evan and Kodi will have to clean themselves."

We moved to start cleaning again but paused as the door opened revealing Kodi.

She wore her black winter coat, fatigue pants, a blue beanie, and a blue Nike hoodie; an outfit she'd worn so often that I had to wonder if it actually ever got washed. She took one sweeping look of us cleaning, shot me a look of mixed disappointment and concern, before removing her shoes and rushing down the hall.

I glanced at Ben who shot me another half-hearted glare from his place on the couch before Evan came barreling down the hall appearing disheveled but alert and trying to pet her bed head down to a manageable state. Kodi came right on her heels but lingered against the wall in the hallway to watch.

"Desi, can I talk to you for a minute?" she all but demanded gesturing to the rooms at the end of the hall with a tilt of her head.

I sighed, resigned. It'd always been best not to argue with her.

"Uh, I don't think so," Mom interjected before I could even take a step or say anything.

Taken aback, Evan's face flashed quickly through emotions and that had been the tamest one of them to worry about. Panic sat higher on the list, even.

Not used to being countered, Evan flipped like a top.

"Fine! Desi, I don't care about them, but your mom can't be here anymore!" she growled at me while sweeping her arm in the general direction of my dad and Tammie who were still cleaning (possibly in hopes that it would get us out of there faster).

"No," Mom and I told her together as there would be no world in which I'd kick my mom out of our apartment or any place I'd been living.

"If she doesn't leave I'm calling the police!" Evan threatened trying and failing to keep her control over me as we severed each of the strings that bound us right then.

"Go ahead," Mom countered as Evan stormed past Kodi and down the hall to her bedroom.

By that point, my blood boiled in my veins and I couldn't speak or think coherently. All the pent-up energy and emotions, all the wrongs brought upon me by Evan that I'd bottled up for years, came flooding out.

How dare she think she can do that to the one person I love most?! She's ruining everything for her own pettiness and need to be in charge!

My life started imploding.

Evan came storming out a few minutes later exclaiming the cops would be coming in ten minutes, and I couldn't take it.

The dam broke.

I exploded.

"HOW THE FUCK COULD YOU FUCKING DO THIS?" I screamed, doing everything I could to hold my tears of frustration back as I would not give her the satisfaction of seeing me cry. "YOU COULDN'T HAVE JUST FUCKING LEFT US TO FINISH CLEANING *OUR* FUCKING HOUSE, YOU FUCKING BITCH? I HOPE YOU'RE FUCKING HAPPY!"

I watched her green-blue gaze turn to steel and her body tense with the cold slap of my words. Never had I blown up like that on anyone before and here I'd thrown my words like daggers into the very person I'd considered spending the rest of my life with only days before.

"I need to call my dad," she whispered before grabbing her coat and shoes and slamming the door behind her with Kodi like a shadow following on her heels.

I shook with rage and pent-up emotion from months of holding my tongue; from continuing to hold myself back, even then.

I walked through the hall dazed from my outburst as the heat died from my face and mortification, for not only being unable to hold myself back but also for throwing the F-bomb out in front of all three of my parents. *Great!*

Good girl till the end.

I stood in my room half wanting to cry and fully being unable to do so. My chest rose and fell like a dog fending the other predators off from my latest kill, teeth bared and adrenaline ready. The tremors unceasing as I paced the floor of a space I felt detached from in that moment.

Just like that, it all died, and I could have collapsed in that instant. Fallen to the floor and screamed my heartbreak to the sky, to anyone still listening to my torment. I suddenly knew what shock after trauma felt like.

Ben approached my door with caution. He had no need

to fear me as I wouldn't have blown up at him even if I'd had the energy to do so after blowing up on Evan.

I admired the familiarity in him. His constant gray shirt-of-choice, blue jeans, white tube socks with the gray toes and heels, and his mushed mousy brown hair from his night on our inherited sunken leather sofa.

He said nothing. He honestly didn't need to as his presence had been enough to show me his support, but I needed more. I'd always need more from Ben.

"Can I have a hug?" I asked pathetically with a slight pleading edge to my tone.

"Why?"

I thought it'd been obvious but leave it to Ben to put me in my place.

"Please?"

He sighed, but conceded, and as with every other point of contact we'd had, I came to him.

After patting me on the back, twice, he dropped his arms and left me to return to his couch-post and watch the door.

No sooner had I followed him out to the living room than a knock sounded on the door followed by Kodi opening the door from outside letting herself, Evan, and a police officer into our nearly clean apartment.

The officer stood at a little over six feet tall, had dirty blond hair cropped short to his head in a similar fashion to every other 'institutionalized' military-type personnel, and a serious, trying-to-be-friendly expression lay across his features naturally only because of the clear practice in him keeping it there for so long.

He didn't look very old, maybe early 30s. I hoped my impression of him meant he'd be fair to us. *Hopefully.*

"Hi, I'm Officer Bernard. Which one of you is the third roommate?" he asked of everyone in the room. *A Bernard?*

"I am," I said planting a smile firmly in place and stepping up glancing at Evan who started at the mention of the officer's name and was now looking owlishly between our other two friends.

"What is your name, Miss?" he asked pulling me back.

"Desi."

He mulled that around for a quick second before speaking again.

"If it's alright with you, Miss Desi, I'm going to speak with your roommates first."

I agreed to that wondering if going in any other order would change his perception of me, but he followed Evan and Kodi back down the hall into Evan's room wishing to speak with her first as she'd been the one to make the call. Kodi had been asked to wait in her own room until they were finished.

I felt aimless as I stood in the middle of our empty living room waiting for them to finish speaking. I glanced at Ben who'd taken to messing with his phone and watching me from the corner of his eye. He likely wouldn't say anything until the officer left.

What felt like ages probably only lasted about five minutes before the officer opened the door and walked into Kodi's room after knocking.

Evan shot me a glare that held less of the normal malice she would have put behind any other threat. It stung, but I still felt way too angry not to hold my head up smugly to let her know she'd made the greatest mistake of her life in making me an enemy.

She closed her door to a crack and got back on the phone with her dad.

I walked down the hall and into my room as the door to Kodi's opened revealing Officer Bernard and a glimpse of

Kodi sobbing concerned, inconsolable tears standing alone in the middle of her nearly empty room behind him.

She watched me with tears and distress written all over her features as I stood looking coldly as I dared while a policeman stood between us. It only made her cry harder.

"May I come in?" he asked gaining my attention.

"Please," I replied putting a mask of false-charm over my own features.

If he could do it, so could I.

"So, here's the deal," he began joining me in the middle of my small room that I could never really gauge the confinement of until someone taller than me stood within its too-white walls and low, beamed ceiling. "Tell me what happened from your side of things and I'll tell you how they're doing and what we might do to solve this. Deal?"

Never having dealt with an officer before, it seemed reasonable enough to me, so I recalled the last hour or so of my life spent in our apartment from the moment we walked in and I closed Evan's door as not to disturb more of her slumber than necessary, all the way up to Kodi waking her up and the subsequent blow up among the roommates and my mom. He listened to me intently and only spoke after I'd gotten to the point when he'd walked in.

"Well, they seem concerned that they're losing this friendship and that seems to have caused them to act out. Since your name is on the lease, there's nothing I can legally do to remove your mom from this residence as she is your guest. My suggestion to you is to finish this up as quickly as possible and head out as to not cause any further altercations, but I will need to run your ID before you leave if that's alright with you."

I agreed, and we walked out into the kitchen so that I

could grab my ID and he could tell Mom exactly what he'd told me about finishing up.

"How close is this?" he asked my diligently cleaning parents.

"Finished, now," Tammie assured as she threw a rag away once she'd finished wiping out the sink.

"Good. I'm just going to need some ID from you and I'll be on my way."

Evan, while still on the phone, brushed past us and outside where I watched her pace in agitation outside our window. Kodi went out close behind and they both got into Evan's old, black Tacoma and left.

Officer Bernard frowned, slightly ticked that they'd gone like that before he'd been finished. "I didn't get Miss Adams' ID," he muttered loud enough that we could still hear him.

Remembering that I'd seen it sitting out by the front door while I'd been cleaning the floors, I walked over to check if it still sat in the last place I'd seen it.

"It's right here if you need it," I said hesitant to touch it and even more uncertain as I picked it up by the bare edge with my nails, afraid to contaminate it.

He frowned at it and then me before accepting it and running it through his card reader before handing it back. I replaced it as gingerly, and he tipped his proverbial hat to me and the room before walking himself out.

"We need to talk to your housing manager before we leave," Mom said as soon as the door clicked shut. "We need to get you out from under this lease before we go home."

I didn't argue with her as I, frankly, didn't know what to do anymore, so we all slipped on our shoes, told Dad and Tammie we'd meet them, Rah, and my brother at Mocha's, and walked out and down the sidewalk to the apartment complex office, throwing a "Bye, Ben," at the couch before the door shut behind me.

A young woman that I was unfamiliar with sat at her desk and offered us the seats across from her. She'd just started the position as our old complex manager had left a month back and I had never had a reason to come down to the office and chat.

She was average built, her medium brown hair she'd straightened cut in a medium length and tucked behind her ears. She wore a pink and gray striped sweater that fit a bit too snugly but sat high enough that it hadn't been revealing in the least. Her eyes were brown and held a people-pleasing look to them that'd shown through her face as someone that had worked in customer service for a long time and oddly enjoyed it.

"What can I do for you?" she asked in an almost shrill tone that came close to mousy in comparison to her predecessor.

"What do we need to do to get her out of her lease?" Mom asked though it came out in a 'frantic parent' kind of way that didn't sit well with me.

"May I ask what's happened that you need that to happen?" she inquired, false concern all over her body.

We told her about the police incident and she listened as real concern replaced the false emotion she'd started with.

"I'm sorry to hear that happened," she intoned in attempts to convey that she felt even sorrier for what she had to tell us next. "There's nothing I can do to get you out of your lease. Legally, the other parties on the lease are the only ones that can sign you off of it. I can get the paperwork started for you, but beyond that, you'll need their permission to complete it."

She looked apathetic enough that neither of us could

say anything to counter her but having blown up at Evan and then needing to ask a favor of her sat low on the list of things I'd planned on doing that day. We didn't have much of a choice, though, so we had the complex manager start the paperwork and left to get lunch.

Rah's gonna have a helluva time with this one.

I sent a group text to the both of them: **We spoke with the housing manager and to prevent anything like this from happening again, especially since I won't be in the state, would you sign me off the lease?**

Why should I? Evan texted back immediately.

Of course, she can't be easy.

After a few more minutes, Kodi responded: **Okay.**

After a moment more, Evan texted back again. **Fine, but you better be there by 9am sharp or it's not happening. And make sure your mom doesn't come with.**

I sighed with visible relief and disbelief thankful that Kodi had been on my side.

Deal.

As for my mom, I wouldn't have brought her with me in the first place. Basing future encounters on the last time the two were in the same room together had been enough to convince me that there needed to be full states between them for the rest of my life, but I knew I still had to play by 'The Evan Show' and I had to maintain my starring role for a little while longer. Her rules or it'd be no deal.

Dad drove me down from the mountain house to meet my soon-to-be ex-roommates the next morning.

To be sure that they weren't sleeping, we swung by the apartment first where I found Ben in the same spot on the couch lounging and scrolling through his phone in the same way I'd left him the day before. They'd been drinking again as the dishes miraculously made it back into the sink to be cleaned, and the floor looked as if I hadn't spent precious minutes of my life mopping it less than 24 hours ago.

"Hey," I greeted with a hurried smile before running to the back to check both Evan and Kodi's rooms, finding them empty, then running out with a "Bye, Ben," thrown over my shoulder as the door closed in my wake.

Knowing I was closing in on the determined time, I ran the sidewalk instead of hopping into Dad's truck for the 20 yards it'd take us to drive there.

I flew in to see Kodi and Evan sitting in the same two seats Mom and I had occupied the day before, both looking a little startled by my sudden appearance but going right back to being hurt and furious as soon as they realized I'd been the one rushing in.

"Perfect timing," our complex manager smiled as Kodi finished signing the release form. She slid it to me at the edge of the desk where I took a moment to look at the document that would seal my fate with my constant companions for the past four years I'd been a student at Western.

Evan had signed it first which left me the last blank line on all three pieces of paper to scrawl my name with a date to finish at the end.

"Alright, you're all set!" She told us happily, taking the forms that I offered to her. Her mood seemed more for my benefit as the negative energy surrounding Evan and Kodi started choking out any of the other energies Michelle had been attempting to foster in her office until they'd come along.

"Do you need anything else from me?" I asked trying to get away from my ex-roommates as quickly as possible.

"No, you're all set!"

"Sweet! See ya," I shot over my shoulder as I walked out

of the office and quickly hopped into the red truck where Dad waited for me.

I analyzed those final words knowing full well that I'd never see either of them again, let alone speak to them, but it didn't matter as they were consciously removed from my life in every possible way.

"It's all set?" Dad asked as he pulled out of the complex to meet Tammie, Rah, and Mom in the Walmart parking lot across the street.

"It's done," I clipped out, implying that I wasn't in the mood to talk about it though I still felt relieved to be rid of them after what they'd done.

After saying proper goodbyes to my family, Rah and I hit the road to the Springs. We didn't talk much about it only because I didn't know what to think, but she let me have control of the music, so I buried most of my thoughts in car karaoke with her as we'd done during every other road trip we'd embarked upon.

"It's All Coming Back to Me" by Celine Dion shuffled on her phone and played through the car speakers dramatically causing me to heave a heavy sigh.

I couldn't look at Rah as I swiped at the first of the tears raining down my face. Though I hated them now, the loss of my best friends, heartbreak for the love lost between us, and loneliness from the prospects of a world without them seeped in around me.

What friends did I have left?

The fact that I'd be stepping into the world as an adult with a larger list of enemies than friends didn't do much to help, either, and the sobs rolled through me.

It didn't matter that I'd found freedom from my own personal monster. I knew demons came in all shapes and sized, and I never saw Evan coming until I'd been trying to figure out how to break free from her.

The goal, of course, had been a noble one. I wanted her to be better. I wanted her to stop wanting to murder people and shed her wickedness like excess skin. I wanted her to see a light that only I could provide her, and to be fair, I did do all of that in some way.

For a steep price, I'd defeated my demon.

I'd cut that final string.

I'd won The Game.

None of that mattered at all, though.

I wept for the friends I'd lost all the same.

ACKNOWLEDGMENTS

Thank you to my editor friends, including Michelle Rascon, who helped me navigate this entire publishing process once the novel had actually been written. They say getting thoughts to paper is the hard part, but I'd be absolutely lost without any of you.

Also thanks to Delissa for connecting me to all of my editor friends in the first place. I hope you find all of your happily ever afters in this great wide world of ours.

And special thanks to Eric. You make an amazing first reader and I'm proud to be able to share this story with you!

ABOUT THE AUTHOR

Lexi Mohney is an author from Traverse City, Michigan and is currently living in Ann Arbor, MI. Lexi has two beautiful yorkies, a love of art, and a passion for helping others overcome their circumstances. Having spent months on a cross-country road trip that began at the end of summer 2017 to complete Carnal Knowledge, Lexi also enjoys traveling out of country living in beautiful places such as Italy and Japan. She hopes to see every country of the world someday.